KAREN CLARKE writes her novels in Buckinghamshire, where she lives with her husband and three grown-up children. Having previously published twelve romantic comedies, Karen switched to the dark side, co-writing psychological thriller *The Secret Sister* with fellow author Amanda Brittany.

Your Life For Mine is Karen's first solo psychological suspense novel and she's currently working on her second.

When she's not writing, Karen reads a lot, loves walking, photography, going to the cinema, baking and eating cake (not all at the same time).

Your Life For Mine

KAREN CLARKE

ONE PLACE. MANY STORIES

HQ
An imprint of HarperCollins*Publishers* Ltd
1 London Bridge Street
London SE1 9GF
www.harpercollins.co.uk

HarperCollins *Publishers*
1st Floor, Watermarque Building, Ringsend Road
Dublin 4, Ireland

2

First published in Great Britain by
HQ, an imprint of HarperCollins*Publishers* Ltd 2020

ISBN: 9780008400392

MIX
Paper from
responsible sources
FSC° C007454

This book is produced from independently certified FSC™ paper
to ensure responsible forest management.

For more information visit: www.harpercollins.co.uk/green

Printed and bound in Great Britain by
CPI Group (UK) Ltd, Melksham, SN12 6TR

For Tim, with love.

Prologue

After all the planning, I suppose it's natural to be looking forward to what's coming with a mix of apprehension and pleasure. Mostly pleasure, to be honest. The planning has been so meticulous, I haven't left room for anything to go wrong. I've been careful and patient – more than I'd ever have believed possible.

Knowing you're in London today, swanning about without a care in the world, simply brought home the fact that now – finally – is the perfect time to execute my plan to create maximum suffering. It's been a long wait, but that means the reward will be sweeter.

Time to get started.

Chapter 1

The text came as I was getting off the train. I'd kept the volume at maximum since missing a call from my daughter's school a few days ago, and the vibration made me jump.

I fumbled my phone from my bag, ignoring the thrust of commuters keen to reach home after a hard day's work or, in my case, a hard day's wandering around London.

It was probably Vic, checking I was on my way home. He was throwing a surprise party for my birthday, and to celebrate us being together for six months, and although it wasn't a surprise (Vic knew better than that) he wanted to make it special.

Moving down the platform of Oxford railway station as the train pulled away, I pictured him in the kitchen with a checklist: food delivered, house tidied, cake baked – he'd been practising – my loved ones gathered and primed, eager to see my reaction. I'd been practising a look of joyful astonishment I hoped I could carry off.

I opened my messages, a smile hovering. I didn't recognise the number.

Enjoy your birthday, Beth. It'll be your last.

My brain froze. I read it again, heart beating unevenly. *Who is this?* I typed back, fingers slipping across the screen before hitting send. The response came swiftly.

You'll find out.

My heart rate accelerated as I tapped out a reply, not stopping to consider whether it was a good idea. *If this is a joke, it's not funny.*

No joke.

I glanced around, as if whoever had sent the message might be grinning with sinister intent on the platform, but the stretch of concrete was empty, sunshine glinting off the tracks. I'd been boiling on the train, but now cold fingers touched my spine, sending ripples of gooseflesh over my skin.

Who are you?

No reply.

With a plunge of dread, my mind barrelled back to a message I'd found on my car windscreen just after Christmas, *A LIFE FOR A LIFE* printed in big, black capitals on a sheet of plain white paper. I'd thrown it away, assuming someone had got the wrong car, or it was a religious thing, like the leaflets sometimes thrust at me in the street, offering salvation through Christ – but the words had still made me shiver and look around, just as I was doing now.

Another message buzzed in.

Bye, bye, Beth.

I dropped my phone as though bitten. Whoever it was had my name and number, yet no one I knew would do this, even as a joke.

My brain swooped around the possibilities.

'Everything OK?'

I spun round to see the station assistant watching me curiously.

'Fine.' I tried to smile but my face felt stiff as I bent to retrieve my phone.

'Have a nice evening,' she said, giving me a funny look.

'You too.' I stumbled a little as I hurried through the exit towards the car park. She probably thought I'd been drinking.

In my car, I switched on the engine to get the air-conditioning flowing and looked at my phone again. Nothing.

4

I tried to breathe through the tightness in my chest. I'd spent too many years feeling like this in the past. I didn't want to be pushed back to that place.

You know I can report you?

No response.

Perhaps one of my art -therapy clients was playing a prank. They knew my name and could have got hold of my number. It didn't make much sense, but neither did anything else.

Except . . . *A LIFE FOR A LIFE.* With a twist of fear, it struck me afresh that only someone who knew me well would know the impact those words would have.

I jumped when a text from Vic came through.

Are you on your way back?

I let out my breath. *Five minutes. X*

Love you. X

You too. X

I still couldn't say it back, even in writing. I'd been with my daughter's father Matt for seven years, had loved him deeply. My feelings hadn't died the minute he left, but Vic understood. It was one of the things I liked about him. He was a grown-up, who grasped that love was complex. He'd been patient, allowing my feelings to flourish at their own pace.

I manoeuvred out of the car park on autopilot, breathing from my diaphragm the way I'd been taught by a counsellor, but my skin and muscles were stiff with tension as I drove the short journey home.

When I turned into the street where I'd lived for the last six years, my shoulders relaxed a little. Home was a Victorian terrace on a quiet, leafy street overlooking the park near Hayley's school – a house we'd only been able to afford because Matt's grandfather died and left him enough money for the deposit. We would have to sell it soon. He needed a new place, where Hayley could go and stay, and Vic wanted us to buy somewhere together.

I switched off the engine, trying to picture the scene behind the olive-green front door; everyone hiding, waiting for a cue from Vic to leap out and shout 'Surprise!'. Hayley would love it. She'd been to several parties lately, running out with extravagant party bags, eager for her own birthday in October. *Five.* I had a nearly-five-year-old daughter I'd willingly die for. A daughter I'd fight to live for.

Enjoy your birthday, Beth. It'll be your last.

My breath caught when I detected a movement at the landing window, as if someone had been watching me and dipped out of sight. I stared for a moment, but the glass was opaque with the sun's reflection and I couldn't make anything out.

Getting out of the car, I tried to smooth the wrinkles from my flower-patterned, summery dress with a shaky hand. No point checking my face or refreshing my lipstick. If I looked too polished my guests might guess I was in on the 'secret' – if they hadn't already.

The air was thick with humidity, but I suppressed a shiver as I slipped my key in the lock and pushed the front door open, inhaling the smell of home; a mix of clean laundry, Vic's classy aftershave, and a heady waft of freshly-baked sponge cake. He'd neatened the hallway, lining up our shoes, putting Hayley's scooter out of harm's way and straightening our coats on the hooks along the wall.

He didn't live here full-time but came round most days, slotting easily into our lives – more easily than I could ever have imagined – but at times, it still felt wrong that Matt wasn't there, waiting with his guitar to burst into song the second I stepped through the door, his boots left wherever he'd kicked them off, something simmering in the kitchen as he experimented with new ingredients.

Placing my keys on the console table, I was hotly aware of my phone in my bag like a hand grenade. I waited for my breathing to settle. The silence in the house felt manufactured and somehow sinister. A sound, quickly smothered behind the living room door, conjured an image of strangers waiting to pounce. Swamped in sudden dizziness, I shot out a hand to steady myself, overcome by a suffocating certainty.

Somebody in this house wanted me dead.

Chapter 2

'There you are!' Vic emerged from the living room and closed the door, his smile of welcome fading to concern. 'Hey, what's wrong?'

'Oh, nothing.' My voice sounded strained, as though I'd been shouting. 'I felt a bit faint, that's all.'

I wanted to tell him the truth. After Matt, I hadn't wanted a relationship with areas 'not discussed', but Vic had gone to a lot of trouble to make today special and I didn't want to spoil it.

He glanced at the door behind him before coming over, probably wondering how much time he could spare. He looked typically stylish in well-fitting chinos with an open-necked shirt and his favourite loafers; his intelligent, olive-skinned face framed by a close-cut beard. It was flecked with grey and matched his short, black hair. My brother had declared Vic out of my league when they met, because of his polished accent, and the fact he'd been to Oxford University and worked as an eye doctor. Although Jamie had a habit of putting me down, I'd secretly agreed with him. 'Are you sure you're OK?' he said.

'Honestly, I'm fine,' I lied, hanging my bag over the post at the foot of the stairs. I tried to smile and make it true, but my mouth wouldn't make the right shape.

'Beth, you don't look good.' He cradled my face in his palms, his brow creased in an unfamiliar frown as he scanned my face. He was so close I could see gold-specks in his brown eyes, reminding me of the way he'd studied me when I pitched up in his consulting room six months ago, referred by my doctor to determine the cause of my headaches and blurred vision.

'Have you been under any more pressure than usual?' he'd asked, after a battery of tests had failed to reveal a physical cause. 'You'd be surprised how often stress can manifest itself in the sort of symptoms you've been having.'

Undone by his genuine interest, I'd burst into tears and blurted out my life story, ending with my marriage break-up the year before when I'd told my husband he'd be better off with someone else. 'I think, deep down, I didn't expect him to agree with me, and definitely not to move out,' I'd said, between sobs. 'He loves his daughter so much I knew he'd miss her badly. He must have been looking for a way out for a while and I gave him one.'

'Why do you think he'd been looking for a way out?' Vic had gently tugged a tissue from a box on his desk and handed it to me.

'Because I couldn't let go of the past.' I'd scrubbed at my face with the tissue, aware I looked a state. 'I'd been fine for a long time, but after Hayley was born it all came back. I kept going over what had happened and wondering about different outcomes, feeling guilty all over again. It drove Matt mad, he just wanted me to be happy, especially as we had a daughter to think of now, but it wasn't that simple for me.' I shook my head. 'I realised later that hormones had probably played a part, but I was a mess. I started seeing a counsellor again, but Matt thought she was keeping me stuck in the past, going over and over it all, so I stopped, but then I resented him, so we were both on edge, not being natural with each other and treading on eggshells. I knew the atmosphere couldn't be good for Hayley, so I suggested he move out, and he said he agreed and . . .' a fresh bout of weeping had broken out. 'He went and didn't come back, except to see Hayley.'

'And the headaches and vision problems started around that time?'

'Not really, that's why I didn't make a connection,' I said. 'I sort of went into overdrive once he left, trying to make everything as settled for Hayley as possible, so her life wasn't too disrupted, especially as she missed her dad. It was hard for him too, not being able to see her every day, but he went to stay in France for a couple of months – his parents live there – and it was actually easier, but he's been back a while now and although we're civil with each other . . . I don't know, it's not how I'd imagined things turning out, I suppose. We didn't have a big wedding, just family and friends, but I thought we'd be married forever and give Hayley the sort of upbringing he'd had – he has a lovely, big family – and like I had before . . . before everything changed.'

Vic had been calm and accepting, as if it was normal for patients to break down and empty their hearts, crying until their eyes were swollen shut. Maybe it was, I'd thought afterwards, mortified by my emotional outpouring. He'd had the sort of aura that invited confidences, and it was easy to imagine patients opening up to him.

Even so, I'd been surprised when he called a week later, asking whether I'd like to meet for a coffee. Not for dinner, or a drink, which I probably wouldn't have said yes to, being far from ready to start dating. It wasn't even on my radar, but somehow coffee had turned into dinner and a drink, and maybe because he knew the worst and hadn't judged me, I'd been able to relax in his company in a way I wouldn't have believed possible.

It was no coincidence that my headaches retreated around the same time, and even though levels of civility had dipped when Matt found out about us, they hadn't returned, and nor had the blurry vision. Being with Vic had made me realise that Matt had been part of the problem. He'd wanted me to change, but Vic accepted me the way I was.

I reached up now and covered his hands with mine. 'Honestly,' I said, managing to produce a smile. 'I just got a bit overheated on the train.'

'There's nothing else?' As his gaze probed mine, my resolve weakened.

'It's just . . . I had a couple of weird texts.'

He frowned. 'Weird?'

'I'm probably making too much of it, but . . .' I pulled away, annoyed with myself. It was too late to take it back. 'It felt like someone knew what had happened, you know. When I was a child.'

His gaze didn't waver but his posture stiffened. 'What did they say?'

'They were kind of . . . threatening.' Without warning, my mind rolled back to surging waves, burning lungs and thrashing arms. Cold seeping into my bones.

'Look, if you're worried, you should talk to Rosa.'

'Is she here?'

He nodded. 'She switched shifts, specially.'

'Jamie won't like it.'

'She's a police officer. Surely he'd expect you to talk to her.'

He didn't know my brother as well as I did. 'She'll want to know what it's about.'

Vic's eyebrows rose. 'You think Jamie hasn't told her the story?'

'I'm sure he has.' As I dug in my bag for my phone to show him the texts, there was a rush of air behind us.

'Mummy, what are you *doing?* I'm waiting and waiting and you didn't come and I want to have cake and you've got to blow out your candles.'

'I'm here, sweetheart.' Dropping my bag, I fell to my knees to catch my daughter, burying my face in her silky hair as my arms closed around her. 'I was just talking to Vic,' I said, marvelling anew, as she wriggled free, that this soft bundle of energy was mine, dressed in her favourite sparkly princess dress, her bare feet

11

dusty from playing in the garden. 'You were very quiet.' Smiling, I brushed a sweep of fair hair from her heart-shaped face, my heart lifting at the sight of the bright blue eyes she'd inherited from Matt – like fragments of summer sky. 'Were you hiding?'

When she nodded solemnly, my heart swelled further at the obvious effort she was making not to give away the surprise. 'It's because of your birthday, Mummy.' She tilted her head. 'I've been helping.'

'She certainly has.' Vic's voice was gentle as he briefly rested his palm on the top of her head. 'She's been such a good girl.'

He was so natural with Hayley – despite the fact that he didn't want children of his own – but sometimes, when he spoke like that, I felt a pang that it wasn't Matt, which added another layer of guilt to my already towering pile. While Hayley didn't love Vic in the same, heartfelt way she did her father, she liked him a lot, and we were hoping to broach the subject of us all living together soon.

'Come *on!*' Growing impatient, she tugged my hand and I rose, throwing Vic an apologetic smile.

His shrug conveyed all the things he couldn't say in front of her – that we'd talk about the texts later, that he had my back . . . that he loved me.

Why couldn't Matt have been like that?

Banishing the thought, I let Hayley pull me towards the living room as Vic spoke in a stagey voice intended for our guests.

'I was telling Mummy she doesn't have time for a shower after her shopping trip.'

'No, you don't, Mummy, that's silly.'

'Well, I hope I don't smell bad.'

I also hoped no one would think to ask what I'd bought. Instead of shopping – not my favourite pursuit – I'd spent most of my day wandering around the Tate, and taking photos of buildings for an art-therapy project.

Vic thrust open the door with a theatrical 'Ta-da!' and the tension in the room gave way to a chorus of 'Surprise!' and 'Happy birthday!' and a shout of 'About time!' from my brother. In the end, it wasn't too hard to look surprised, though I exaggerated for Hayley's sake, scooping her up and swinging her round as everyone laughed and applauded.

'I can't believe you didn't *say* anything!'

'It was a secret,' she said, flushed with pleasure, before breaking away and darting across to a small heap of presents on a side table as people gathered round me, laughing and wishing me well. For the next few minutes, I let myself be swept along on a tide of goodwill, happy that Vic had managed to pull this off – with my help.

'None of my clients,' I'd said, when he asked who I'd want to be there. 'No extended family either.' Mum and Dad had big families scattered around the country. 'And definitely not Grandpa Buckley. He's stopped wearing his false teeth and Mum says he's started telling racist jokes.'

In the end, we'd settled on my immediate family – Vic only had one older sister, who lived in Canada – a couple of friends and colleagues, Lewis and Jude from across the road with their son Rory, who was Hayley's age, and Pam from next door. She'd been a big support after Matt left and sometimes looked after Hayley, who adored her, partly because she had a chocolate-brown Labradoodle called Baxter. My daughter craved a puppy more than anything else.

Pam was there in a flower-print dress, her short white hair neatly brushed, smiling a little self-consciously. I managed a wave before Mum grabbed me in a crushing embrace.

'I thought you'd got lost,' she said, as I breathed in a waft of the Gucci perfume Dad bought her every Christmas. 'Happy birthday, sweetheart. I bought you that jacket you said you liked, but if it doesn't fit, I've got the receipt.'

'Thanks, Mum.'

'Everything OK?' Her voice dipped into anxiety, always attuned to my mood.

'Fine,' I said automatically, stretching my smile as she scoured my face with her pale blue, searchlight eyes. 'Just hot, that's all.' I wondered whether she'd still be this overprotective when I was forty, fifty – *if I lived that long*. The thought made my heart trip.

'You do look a bit feverish.' Mum was gripping my upper arms. 'Maybe you're coming down with something.'

'I don't think so.' I subtly moved out of her grasp. 'This is such a lovely surprise,' I said, gesturing at the room, which seemed much smaller now it was filled with people. The dove-grey walls – which I'd repainted after Matt moved out – felt as if they were closing in and panic briefly stirred. 'I can't believe Vic has gone to all this trouble.' I looked around for him but he'd vanished, no doubt to check on the food or to fetch more drinks.

'He's a good man; he's thought of everything.' Mum's face relaxed into a smile. 'Make sure you hang on to him,' she said, playfully. She'd been distraught when Matt left, but, once she'd accepted I wasn't heading back into therapy, had cautiously retreated and welcomed Vic into the family with open arms.

'Happy Birthday, Lizbet.' Dad materialised, holding a mug of coffee. He rarely touched alcohol, preferring to keep a clear head. 'If you're thirty-three now, that means I must be . . .' He slung his free arm around my shoulder and pretended to do a sum in his head. 'Getting old.'

'Sixty-four's not old.' I forced a grin, used to him treating me like a child, calling me by his own diminutive of Elizabeth. He'd never forgiven himself for his part in what had happened; it sometimes seemed he'd been stuck in the past ever since, trying to make up for it. 'Thanks for coming,' I said, knowing nothing would have kept him away, even if it meant leaving his beloved furniture repair shop earlier than usual.

'You don't have to thank us for wanting to spend time with you.' Mum slid her arm around Dad's waist and smiled up at me. I looked at them, seeing myself in Dad's hazel eyes, straight nose and the arch of his brows, and in Mum's curves and the way she held herself tall, despite being a petite five foot two. I was a few inches taller, my hair a more reddish-brown, but there was no doubting we were mother and daughter.

As usual, feeling the weight of their gaze, of their hopes and expectations, I was compelled to brighten my smile, to dance my shoulders to the music springing from a speaker on the dresser – Pharrell Williams's 'Happy' – and accept the badly wrapped present Hayley was holding out. She danced from foot to foot, hands clasped as I unwrapped the shiny pink paper to reveal a box containing a charm bracelet hung with a silver heart. The heart was inscribed with the words *Love you forever, Mummy*, eliciting fond murmurs when I read them out.

'It's from *me!*' Hayley could barely contain herself, straining to see the words that had hazed in a blur of tears. 'Daddy helped me when we went shopping on Saturday.'

Matt? I tried not to react. 'Thank you, darling, I love it so much.' I bent to hug her but she'd already raced away, so I slipped it on and held it out for Mum and Dad to admire.

'Where's that brother of yours?' Mum said, letting go of my wrist to glance around. 'I told him to get you something nice. I hope he listened to me.'

I caught Dad's eye and he looked away, smile fading. It pained them both that my once close relationship with my brother had eroded to the point where he had to be 'reminded' about my birthday. He'd softened since meeting Rosa – she'd been good for him – but I doubted it was to the point where he'd go gift-shopping.

'He's around somewhere. I saw him earlier,' Dad said. 'Probably gone to the loo.'

'Graham,' Mum said, as though he'd said a swear word, lightly tapping his arm.

'Linda,' he replied in a similar tone, and they exchanged affectionate smiles.

Bye, bye, Beth.

As the words floated into my mind, my own smile faded.

I had to talk to Rosa.

Chapter 3

I looked around. I hadn't seen Rosa since the initial hubbub, but spotted her by the food-laden dining table, talking to Pam, who was gesticulating wildly as she spoke. Probably describing something in her garden, which was her passion.

'I'm going to mingle,' I said, perspiration breaking out on my forehead. The windows were open, and so were the French doors that led to the garden, but the air in the room felt solid.

'Don't forget to have a chat with your brother,' Mum called after me.

I was waylaid on the way, first by Marianne, the head of Fernley House where I worked, who also ran creative writing classes there, then my oldest friend Emma, who I'd met at art college. After a recent trip to Cambodia, she was settling into a new job with a charitable organisation in London and wanted to catch up.

'I still can't get over you and Matt breaking up.' Her smoky grey eyes were alive with curiosity as she thrust a glass of wine into my hand. 'What actually happened, Beth? You two were made for each other.'

Emma had introduced me to Matt. It was natural she'd wish we were still together. On her last visit to Oxford before her trip, I told her I'd met someone new, but she'd just broken up with her boyfriend and hadn't been very receptive. 'You should get to know Vic.' I put my glass down, too on edge to drink. 'He's lovely.'

'Let's have a night out.' She cuffed my wrist with her fingers as I made to move away, her gaze probing. 'It's been ages since we've had a proper chat.'

'Too long,' I said lightly, easing out of her grasp.

Her angular face softened. 'I brought you a gift.' She swept her long, dark fringe aside with ring-cluttered fingers. 'Your adorable daughter added it to the pile.'

'Thanks, Em, that's really kind of you. I'll look for it in a bit.' Smiling, I backed away, almost into Rosa, who sounded keen to escape Pam's lively chatter.

'I'll bear that in mind,' she was saying, a faint estuary twang betraying her Essex roots. 'Start with great soil and follow the sun.' She started when she spotted me right behind her. 'Hi, Beth.' A grin broke over her face, crinkling her big, brown eyes.

'Hey,' I said, heart banging. I'd rarely spoken to Rosa alone and was surprised that Jamie wasn't glued to her side, as usual. 'Could I have a quick word?'

'Sure.' I sensed her switch into work mode, tensing slightly beneath her thin white top, which she'd paired with cropped black trousers and flat black shoes, her mouse-brown hair scraped back in its usual ponytail. She could have been in uniform. I remembered Jamie saying she took her job seriously, was keen to become a detective – or maybe it was a sergeant, I couldn't quite remember. 'What is it?'

Just then, Jamie came in from the garden. Catching his glance across the room, my nerves twanged a warning. The last thing my brother needed was a reminder of the past. 'I just wanted to say thank you for—'

'Beth?' Vic was in the doorway. 'Maybe not in front of everyone.'

My smile froze. 'I wasn't going to say anything.'

Rosa's gaze flicked between us. 'What's going on?'

My mouth felt dry. 'Oh, it's nothing really.' I looked over at

Jamie. He'd perched on the arm of the sofa, a glass of something amber in one hand, and was grinning at Hayley asking loudly if he could please fetch her some cake because she was *so hungry*. 'I had a couple of anonymous text messages earlier.'

'Oh?' An interested gleam brightened Rosa's eyes. She tended to blend into the background normally – a useful trait for a police officer – but I suddenly saw how pretty she was with her thick dark lashes, smooth skin and neat features. She had an air of quiet intelligence that would have appealed to Jamie. He liked quiet, clever women who got on with things without making a fuss. 'What sort of messages?'

I quickly looked for Mum and Dad. They were loading paper plates with a selection of food at the table, their backs to me. 'Not in here, if you don't mind.'

'Of course.'

She followed me out of the room, to where Vic was waiting at the foot of the stairs with an air of suppressed tension. 'Sorry,' he said. 'I thought—'

'It's fine,' I cut in, wanting to get it over with. 'It's probably a bad joke and I'm reading too much into it,' I said to Rosa. 'But the message told me to enjoy my birthday because it would be my last.'

'OK,' she said calmly. 'That's not funny.'

'No.' If I'd hoped by telling her, the words would lose some of their power, I was wrong. My hand felt clumsy as I fished my phone from my bag. 'It feels like it might be linked to what happened when I was a child . . .' I stopped, checking her face for a reaction. 'You know about it?'

She nodded, while Vic placed a hand on my shoulder as if to steady me. 'Jamie mentioned it.' She spoke in the sort of neutral voice I imagined must be necessary in her job. 'You nearly drowned on holiday when you were seven.'

Nearly drowned.

It sounded like nothing, the way she said it. As if it wasn't the event that had blighted my life ever since. 'Twice,' I said, my

18

voice as choked as if it was happening again. 'I nearly died twice. Secondary drowning it's called, when a small amount of water enters the lungs.' Vic's hand tightened on my shoulder. 'If Mum hadn't insisted on them keeping me in hospital for observation that night, I would have died.'

'Jamie told me.' Rosa's tone was one of respectful compassion. 'I'm sorry.'

She seemed to be waiting for more and, as if from a distance, I heard myself tell her the worst part, even though she must already know. 'A stranger saved my life,' I said. 'He saved me, but he died. He drowned, saving my life.'

'Beth.' Vic's voice barely penetrated the sound of blood roaring in my ears.

'I lived because of him, but he died and I have to live with that and it's been hard, you know?'

'Beth, it's OK.'

'I don't even know who he was, or if he had a family. He must have had a family, I mean—'

'Beth!' Vic's fingers tightened on my shoulder.

I blinked as though waking from a nightmare. 'Sorry.' I exhaled. 'It's . . . it's got easier, but it never really goes away,' I said. 'The guilt, I mean.'

Rosa's gaze connected with mine. 'And you think . . . what? That this message is connected somehow?'

'Maybe someone who knew what happened back then is trying to scare me.'

'Someone connected to the man who drowned?'

I felt a dropping sensation, hearing it said so simply. 'Yes.'

'OK.' A frown wrinkled her forehead. It sounded far-fetched, but with a jarring sense of clarity, I realised I'd been expecting something like this to happen for a long time. For ages, I'd told myself that if I worked hard enough, kept my daughter safe, improved the lives of my therapy clients, everything would be OK. Even on Hayley's first birthday, the house crammed with mine and Matt's families, I'd thought about the man who saved my life, how he'd never celebrate a grandchild's birthday, guilt creeping out like a shadow to spoil the moment.

Maybe none of it had been enough.

'There was a note, earlier in the year,' Vic said. 'On Beth's car. It said *A LIFE FOR A LIFE*. It's like someone's out for revenge.'

'That's a bit strong.' I tried out a laugh, but the word hit home. *Revenge.*

Rosa's frown deepened. I thought she was going to tell me I'd been watching too many crime dramas – which I'd have to admit was true – but instead, she said, 'If the message came from a burner phone it'll be hard to trace, but I could take a look.'

I hesitated. 'I—'

'Mum*meee!*' It was Hayley, sounding fractious.

Dad poked his head round the living room door. 'What are you lot plotting?'

The sight of his wild salt-and-pepper hair, which Mum had long ago given up trying to tame, tightened the knot in my chest. We must look an odd trio, huddled by the front door. 'We're going to get the cake,' I said, knowing he wouldn't question it. 'I got side-tracked.'

'Madam won't wait much longer.'

'I'm coming.' I flashed Rosa a smile as Dad disappeared. 'Look, thanks for hearing me out, but it's probably nothing . . . I mean, nothing serious.'

'You don't believe that.' Her expression was worryingly sombre. 'I'd like to take a quick look if you don't mind.'

'Fine.' I switched my phone on and went straight to my texts. *Odd.*

'What is it?' Vic said as I scrolled up and down.

'Hang on a second, I can't . . .' I looked again, but the last message I'd had was from Vic's phone. 'I can't find them.'

'*What?*'

I looked again, my senses prickling. 'They're not there.' I lifted my gaze to Rosa's. 'The messages have gone.'

Chapter 4

After taking a look herself, Rosa handed my phone back. 'Let me know if you get any more,' she said with a trace of regret. 'Take a screenshot if you can, so at least you have some proof.' I wished I'd thought of it, though I couldn't see how it would help if the sender was using a disposable phone. I'd seen enough thrillers to imagine broad fingers removing the battery before smashing the screen to smithereens underfoot. 'What about the note you mentioned, on your car?'

'I threw it away,' I admitted. 'It was creepy, but didn't mean much at the time.'

'That was my fault,' Vic said grimly. 'I suggested she get rid of it.'

'Someone could have hacked into your phone,' Rosa said. 'Maybe change your passwords.'

Before I could respond, Mum burst into the hallway and we scattered like cats; Vic and I to the kitchen and Rosa into the downstairs toilet with a murmured, 'Let me know if anything else happens.'

'Beth,' Vic said, reaching for me as I stared unseeingly through the window into the back garden. He'd wound fairy lights around the trunk and branches of the magnolia tree, and along the hedge dividing us from Pam's, but all I could see in my mind's eye was someone hunched over a phone, intent on frightening me.

'We can't talk now,' I said. 'Everyone's wondering what we're doing.' I spun round, plastering on a smile. 'Let's go.'

I wasn't sure how I kept it together after that, but I managed to reassure Hayley that I wasn't being a 'party-popper' by letting her blow out the candles on my lavishly frosted cake, aware of Vic watching me closely.

'Make a wish,' I urged her.

'Don't tell, or it won't come true,' Mum cautioned, winking at me. She used to say the same when Jamie and I were little, but I never did get the pony I wished for every year.

After posing for photos with a knife poised over the cake, time passed in a haze of snatched conversations and unwrapping gifts. There was a pretty utensil pot from Marianne, an expensive bottle of champagne from Lewis and Jude (more for their benefit than mine, I suspected, seeing their eyes light up when I smiled my appreciation) and a beautiful, walnut desk-easel from Emma, who waved away my thanks with an airy hand. To my surprise, Jamie produced a three-tier stand on wheels for my paint supplies, explaining he thought it might come in useful. While I knew my parents, and probably Rosa, had had a hand in his choice, I couldn't help being touched. Vic had bought me a ruby pear-drop necklace that looked expensive. 'It's your birthstone,' he said, fastening it carefully around my neck.

I kissed him, wishing it didn't make me think of blood. 'I love it.'

We all ended up dancing the hokey cokey at Dad's insistence, as though I was seven again. Hayley loved it, and only the sight of her earnest expression as she followed the moves stopped my mind returning over and over to the text messages. *Enjoy your birthday, Beth. It'll be your last.* Whoever had sent it wanted me to be scared, and while I knew I was playing into their hands, I couldn't shake the feeling that something malevolent lurked among the smiling faces and bursts of laughter around me.

Senses heightened, I found myself studying Jamie at one point, noticing his gaze tracking Rosa around the room. I wondered whether they'd had an argument. If their relationship was going through a bad patch, he was bound to blame me. It wouldn't be the first time. 'Apparently, I'm too needy,' he'd said, when his last relationship ended. 'Not surprising, considering the years I spent trying to get my parents' attention.' He'd once said that, after my near-drowning, he might as well not have existed as far as our parents were concerned, but I doubted he'd go to the trouble of buying a phone and sending a threatening message. Apart from anything, Jamie had never been shy about telling me to my face exactly how he felt, and despite our strained relationship, I couldn't imagine he wanted me dead. Unless he'd had enough of playing second fiddle and wanted me out of the way.

Catching Mum's eye, I forced a smile and turned to chat to Pam, who wanted to tell me a friend had a Labrador who'd given birth to a litter of golden puppies. 'In case you've thought any more about getting one for Hayley.'

'Except Hayley won't be the one looking after it.' The headache I'd felt brewing earlier strengthened its grip. 'Sorry, Pam, I'm just—'

'It's fine.' Her already rosy cheeks flushed crimson. 'I could help though, if you do decide to have one,' she said. 'You know I think of you and Hayley as family.'

'I know you do, and thank you.' Mustering a smile, I placed an arm around her narrow shoulders. She was small but strong, from years of running her own cleaning company, and her upper arms were still more toned than mine. 'I promise I'll think about it, but don't say anything to Hayley, will you?'

'I won't.' Her gaze turned wistful, watching Hayley spinning in circles on the rug in front of the fireplace with Rory, giggling as she staggered into Mum. Pam didn't have children of her own, had lived alone since her husband died of a heart attack a couple of years before we moved next door. It was something she

23

rarely talked about, but if anyone deserved to be a grandparent, it was Pam.

As we drifted into the garden, where the sun had turned the lawn patchy and dry, Jude sidled over and nudged my arm. 'You're so lucky,' she said in a stagey whisper, watching Vic top up glasses and offer food.

I felt a stab of dislike because she'd never said that about Matt when we'd all been friends, even though he'd designed her website free of charge when she became a Pilates instructor. 'Thanks,' I said shortly.

Jamie interrupted, saying he had to leave, and Jude wandered away. 'I've got an early start tomorrow,' he said, which was probably true. He was a plumber, often called out at unsociable hours. It was how he'd met Rosa, when a pipe burst in her flat, flooding the kitchen. 'You look exhausted,' I said, noting the bruised-looking crescents beneath his eyes. 'You should take on someone to help.'

'Don't you start.' He spoke with the bite I'd grown accustomed to over the years. It was hard to remember that, for a while after my accident, he'd been as protective as Mum and Dad, looking out for me at school, despite being in the year below. Much later, my counsellor suggested that, like Dad, Jamie felt terribly guilty about that day; that if the man who saved me hadn't run into the sea, I'd have drowned while Jamie was waiting at the van to buy ice-creams. But when I asked him about it, he'd looked at me as though I'd grown two heads. 'Of course I don't feel guilty,' he'd said, anger heating his words. 'Christ sake, Beth, let it go.'

While he said his goodbyes to Mum and Dad, Rosa stood back a little. I was grateful she didn't allude to our earlier conversation. Her smile was bland as she nodded briefly in my direction before following Jamie out, her hand reaching for his. It struck me how similar they looked from behind; practically the same height, similar hair colour, though Jamie's was permanently tousled and more dirty-blond than brown, and both with a suggestion of strength in their shoulders – Jamie from regular gym sessions and Rosa from her police training, which required her to pass a fitness test twice a year.

I pleaded a raging headache once they'd gone – which wasn't a lie – and though Emma was disappointed we hadn't had a chance to talk properly, she gamely accepted the offer of a lift to the station with Mum and Dad.

'Call me,' she urged, pressing a kiss to my cheek at the door, her musky perfume catching in my throat. 'I want to know *everything*.'

Something avid in her words made me look at her twice, taking in the sheen of her eyes and vivid splashes of colour along her cheekbones. I hadn't noticed her drinking – which she did a lot when we were at college – but she seemed in the grip of some strong emotion.

'I will,' I promised, resolving to bridge the gap that had sprung up between us lately. 'Thanks again for coming, and for your lovely gift; it was so thoughtful.'

'Listen,' she said. 'Vic seems like a really nice guy. If you're happy with him, I'm happy for you.' She hugged me a little too tightly and hurried out, leaving me with the feeling she'd left a lot unsaid.

'I still don't understand it,' I said, once Hayley was tucked up and sleeping, the calming effect of her bedtime routine worn off. 'I *saw* those messages, so where did they go?'

Vic spat toothpaste in the sink in the ensuite bathroom before coming into the bedroom. 'There are ways if you know what you're doing.' He sat beside me on the bed, patting his face with a towel. 'At least Rosa took you seriously.'

'She probably felt she didn't have much choice.' It came out snappy, my nerves shredded from hours of pretending I was fine. 'Sorry,' I muttered, rubbing the nape of my neck. 'I wish I hadn't told her.'

'You did the right thing.' Throwing the towel aside, Vic knelt on the bed behind me and massaged my shoulders, attempting to release the knots that had gathered there. 'Let's hope it was a one-off and that's the end of it.'

'There won't be any more.' I felt it deep in my bones, without knowing why. 'Not now I've been warned.'

'Should we get you a twenty-four-hour bodyguard, just in case?'

I tensed. 'You do believe me, don't you?'

'Of course I do.' His fingers kept kneading. 'Why would you make it up? I saw how spooked you were.'

I twisted to look at him. He had on the stripy pyjama shorts and white T-shirt he wore whenever he stayed over ('in case Hayley comes in') and a surge of affection washed away my annoyance. 'Listen, thanks again for today,' I said, touching the ruby necklace, which felt hot against my skin. 'I'm sorry if I spoiled everything.'

'You didn't.' He lifted my hand and pressed his lips to my fingers. 'Everyone had a good time and we should carry on doing that, and not let this . . . whatever it is, get between us.'

I fell silent for a moment. 'I left my bag in the hall with my phone in.'

His brow furrowed. 'What?'

'My bag.' I squirmed round to face him. 'It was in the hall. Someone could have taken my phone out and deleted the messages.'

Sighing, Vic pushed away from me and lay down, one arm behind his head. 'Like Rosa said, someone must have hacked your messages remotely.'

'But what if they were deleted here?'

He looked at me sideways. 'Do you still not have a password on your phone?'

I bristled. 'I've never needed one,' I said. 'I always know where it is, I've nothing to hide, and it's easier to access if I need to look something up.'

He lifted his eyebrows. 'Well, I didn't notice anyone sneaking into the hall, did you?'

'No, but I wasn't checking.'

Vic held out his other arm. 'Come here, you.'

I rolled onto my side and rested my head on his chest. The rhythmic bump of his heart almost soothed my racing mind, but I couldn't quite banish the guilty thought that Vic knew exactly where my phone was, and that he hadn't been in the room when I was talking to Mum and Dad.

'Seriously,' he said, making me jump. 'I could sort out some security for you, if it would give you peace of mind. It'll make me feel better too.'

I closed my eyes, shame burning through me. 'Thanks,' I whispered, as he kissed the top of my head. 'I'll think about it.'

Once his breathing had deepened into sleep and darkness pressed into the room, fear wrapped around me, tightening my chest. I couldn't help imagining all the ways I might be about to die. A shove in the back into oncoming traffic, or in front of a train, or a knife driven into my abdomen.

My breathing grew shallow and sweat pooled between my breasts beneath my vest top. I threw off the sheet and turned over, but couldn't switch off my mind, imagining poison being slipped into my food, an injection in my neck, or stomach – insulin, maybe; wasn't that supposed to be undetectable after death? Maybe my demise would be prolonged, intended to make me suffer. Of course there was death by drowning, but I rarely ventured near water these days, so that seemed unlikely.

My mind switched to scenes of torture until I was almost hyperventilating. Every scenario I dredged up felt like it belonged to fiction, too far-fetched and unlikely for real life, but the thought provided no comfort.

Whoever had sent those messages meant every word.

Chapter 5

I had the dream for the first time in ages. Bobbing by the sand on my blue and white inflatable, fingers trailing in the water as I looked through the rippling surface for the starfish Jamie had told me he'd seen. Then, my heart jerking with fear as it dawned on me that the seabed was no longer visible. I was moving too fast, dragged by an invisible current away from the beach. An angry wind had whipped up, sending clouds across the sun, tossing the waves into peaks. Whimpering, I pushed myself up on my hands and knees, gripping the sides of the slippery rubber Lilo, eyes raking the beach for my family, the people there reduced to Lego size. How could I have got so far away so quickly?

Can't swim. Fear flooded my veins as I raised my arm to wave. When I opened my mouth to yell, the inflatable tipped, flipping me into the water.

The shock of the icy plunge snatched my breath as the water greedily sucked me down, filling my mouth, my nose, my lungs, salt water stinging my eyes.

I blinked and choked, limbs thrashing as I was tossed to the surface, fighting for air, hands reaching for the sky. Wordlessly screaming, *Help me, help me,* no breath to push the words out. Water closing over my head, pain blooming in my throat, spreading down and down. I was solid, a statue, sinking, sinking, eyes wide open, nothing but churning water and fire in my—

I shot upright with a choking gasp, one arm groping the air, the feeling of burning lava in my lungs as vivid as if it had happened yesterday.

It took a moment for the images to disperse and my eyes to adjust to the familiar sight of my bedroom. Pale sunlight filtered through the curtains, slanting across the clotted-cream walls, bouncing off the edge of the mirror. I focused on the mattress beneath me, the feel of the cotton sheet I was grasping, the garden-scented air drifting through the open window.

Gradually, my pulse slowed.

Outside, the street was waking up. A dog barked – probably Baxter in the garden next door, let out for his morning snuffle around the hedges – and a burst of classical music, quickly muffled by the slam of a car door. Lewis, across the road, on his way to work as Head of IT for a local pharmaceutical company.

Pushing strands of damp hair from my forehead, I glanced at the digital glow of my ancient bedside clock: 7 a.m.

Vic had already left for the hospital; nothing but a hollow in the pillow beside me to indicate he'd been there. I pictured him moving quietly, not wanting to wake me after my restless night. I wished he'd brought me some coffee and kissed me before he left, like Matt used to do, before he headed downstairs to work on his latest web-design project.

Shaking off the memory, I lay back down, pressing the heels of my hands into my eyes as I relived the dream. It wasn't even a dream; more like recreating what had actually happened, but a heightened version, without the fun bits of that day; eating sand-gritted sandwiches on the stretch of sand at Perran Cove in Cornwall; Dad whacking his thumb with the mallet while putting up the windbreak; exploring the long, winding caves there with Jamie while Dad did a crossword in his newspaper, and Mum read her book, her shoulders turning pink in the sun.

If I thought back – which I tried not to do often – I had to force myself to remember that the beginning of our holiday in nearby Penzance, with its bustling streets and shops and busy harbour, had been idyllic; sun-drenched days, exploring smugglers' tunnels, eating fish and chips, burying each other in sand, and staying up late for a bonfire party on Porthen Beach the night before the accident.

'If only we hadn't gone to Perran Cove,' Mum had sobbed afterwards. Jamie and I had been promised a trip there and pestered from the moment we woke. 'We should have had a lie-in and stayed near the cottage.'

She and Dad blamed themselves, citing the bottle of wine they'd shared the previous night for giving them fuzzy heads, meaning they hadn't noticed more quickly what was happening, and when they did, for not being able to reach me. More importantly, they'd blamed themselves for not teaching me to swim. My fear of water had asserted itself early on. It had been easier not to force me back to the local swimming pool for lessons, but Dad had planned to teach me during that holiday.

'I don't understand why you went in,' he'd wept – the first time I'd ever seen him cry. 'I should have stopped you. What was I thinking?'

I didn't understand it either, except I'd wanted to try out my new inflatable, and maybe there was something about the place that lulled me into a false sense of security – or Jamie's promise that there were starfish in the sea and that the water wasn't deep.

Since having Hayley, I understood more deeply the anguish they must have gone through. Despite being told that the wind had sprung up so quickly there'd been no warning, and that the lifeguard who should have been patrolling the coves had gone for a break, my parents felt they'd failed for not keeping me safe.

'The sight of that man, staggering out of the water with you in his arms will never leave me. We thought you were dead,' Mum cried at the hospital. He wasn't the man who'd saved me. The man who swam out and grabbed me and kept my head above water until help arrived – whose face I couldn't recall – had been washed away the moment I left his arms. Presumably too tired to battle the surging sea, he'd simply vanished. No one knew until the holidaymaker who deposited me at my parents' feet admitted he wasn't the hero of the hour, just the person who'd happened to be out surfing and brought me back to shore. My rescuer's body had washed up along the coast a few days later and wasn't identified for a week.

I knew nothing about it at the time because my parents had done a good job of hiding what really happened. It was bad enough that I could barely look at a bath full of water without crying, never mind go near the sea again, and my drowning nightmares were so debilitating, I had to be medicated in order to sleep for a while. They hadn't wanted the man's death on my mind, on top of everything else, so had dealt with it privately.

I lay in bed for a while with a hand on my belly, drawing in deep breaths, trying to stay in the moment. What would Vic have made of me waking in a sweaty panic? I normally slept well, barely stirring once my head hit the pillow. Matt was the one who'd had to cope with the resurgence of the nightmare in the months after Hayley was born, when I was sleep-deprived and hormones were playing havoc with my emotions.

In the warm light of day, my fears from the night before were embarrassing. Had I really thought that Vic could have deleted the messages? Thank God I hadn't asked him, just to be sure. He'd encountered enough obstacles since meeting me, from Hayley announcing, 'You're not my daddy,' when I introduced them, to being ignored by Matt and threatened with having his legs broken if he hurt me by Grandpa Buckley. He'd be horrified if he even suspected what had gone through my mind.

Already tense, I reached for my phone and switched it on, exhaling when I saw that the only new message I'd had was from Vic. *See you later, Sleeping Beauty. Try to have a good day and DON'T WORRY xx*

Maybe I'd dreamed up the messages. It wasn't lost on me that I was approaching the anniversary of my drowning day (*Why do you have to call it that?* Matt used to say.) In previous years, I'd noticed a subconscious response to the date, a vague feeling of doom, mind bouncing off flashes of memory: the feel of water trailing through my fingers; waking up in hospital and seeing Mum's tear-ravaged face; Jamie, pale with pink-rimmed eyes, bringing me ice-cream *because you didn't get to have one*; and my grandmother with a crumpled handkerchief pressed to her mouth, her normally immaculate hair askew after driving for five hours to check that I was OK.

Then I remembered the pulse of shock I'd felt when I read the texts and knew I hadn't conjured them up. And even if they had nothing to do with what happened that day in Cornwall, someone had wished me dead.

There was a voicemail from Mum. *We had a lovely time yesterday, such a nice thing for Vic to do and wasn't Hayley adorable? Your dad's taken the morning off and we're going to the garden centre. See you soon. Hope your head's not hurting too much! XX*

The subtext was *Please let us know you're OK*, and I automatically obliged.

All good, thanks again for coming. Lovely to see you all. My head's fine and Hayley says hello! I added a few smiley faces for reassurance, then worried it wasn't enough and typed: *Going to do some Pilates before breakfast! X* That would please her as it meant I was 'looking after myself' and 'being normal'.

On impulse, I decided to make it true. It might do me good to stretch away some of the tension that had settled across my back. I had a few minutes before Hayley got up and was sure I could remember some of the moves that Jude had shown me a while back after qualifying as an instructor.

I crossed to the window, squashing an urge to rush around the house, checking for booby traps. Nothing could happen this early in the day while I was at home with my daughter. *Or maybe*

32

it was the perfect time. Annoyed that my train of thought was already derailing, I pulled open the curtains.

A flash of jewel-bright colour caught my eye from the pavement. Recognition tugged as a figure moved out of sight. Obscured by the broad trunk of an oak tree, I couldn't make out who it was. Were they hiding?

I strained to see, heart drumming against my ribs, but the sound of childish laughter floating up the stairs made me whip around. Hayley was a deep sleeper. She rarely ventured out of bed before me, let alone downstairs on her own.

I grabbed my robe off the end of the bed, pulling it on as I darted onto the landing. I paused to check her room where sunshine was poking round the edges of her curtains. Her duvet was a heap in the middle of her bed, the stuffed crocodile she cuddled at night discarded on the floor, next to her dressing gown.

'You are silly!' I heard her say.

A man's voice replied as I flew downstairs, gripping the banister to stop myself falling, fear ripping through me when I saw the front door was ajar.

'Hayley!' I cried, trying to keep the panic from my voice, wondering how I hadn't heard the doorbell. 'I've told you before to come and get me if someone comes to the house.'

I stopped dead in the living room doorway. Hayley turned, eyes bright with laughter. 'It's Daddy,' she said, as though it was the most natural thing in the world.

'Matt!' He was sitting on the sofa, as though he'd never left. 'What are you doing here?'

'Daddy's going to take me to school!' Hayley was in her *Frozen* nightdress, hopping about with excitement. 'I've had my flakes.' She pointed to a pair of empty bowls on the coffee table, and I remembered how Matt had always loved cereal, usually Rice Krispies in a lake of milk.

'You don't normally get your own breakfast.' I tightened the belt on my robe, trying to give the illusion of being in control.

'Daddy helped because I was so hungry and you were sleepy,' she said, pushing her hair off her face. 'Daddy's going to give me a piggy-back because my legs might get tired from walking.'

'School's only five minutes away.'

'But my legs are only little.'

'Well, you'd better go and get dressed and brush your teeth, sweetie.' I kept my tone light. 'I need to have a chat with Daddy.'

When she'd run upstairs, whistling – Dad was teaching her how – I turned to Matt, fighting back memories of all the times he'd sat on the sofa in the home we'd bought together and planned to raise our child in. 'You can't turn up without letting me know,' I said, aware he had every right to, considering it was his house too. 'It's not fair.'

'I miss her,' he said simply. 'Mornings are the hardest.'

I took in his bright blue eyes, and the flop of blond hair and darker stubble that made him look like a rock star. I tried to harden my heart.

'You chose to go,' I reminded him, wrapping my arms around my waist. 'And you can see her whenever you like – just call me first.'

'It's not the same.' He thrust his hair back – the same move-ment that had caught my eye seven years ago, on a night out with Emma at a pub in the city. She'd been in Thailand for weeks, and was on one of her flying visits home. Matt was there with a couple of friends, watching the terrible band that were playing, and when he caught my eye and grinned, as though we were co-conspirators, I'd felt a rollercoaster swoop inside.

Later, after Emma had taken it upon herself to tell him 'my friend fancies you' as though we were teenagers and not going on twenty-six, we'd huddled with drinks at a table by a roaring fire, exchanging stories, and I discovered he was a couple of years older, worked for a web design company in the city centre, but was hoping to leave to go freelance, and played guitar for fun in his spare time.

'Probably as badly as the band just did, but it's a way of blowing off steam,' he'd said. When he smiled, something released inside me, relaxing its hold. After a couple of relationships I couldn't commit to, not wanting to put responsibility for my happiness in someone else's hands, I dared to believe Matt Turner was the reason my life had been saved, because we were destined to be together. We even loved the same music, and although the band's cover of Coldplay's 'Paradise' that night had been awful, the song had become 'ours'.

For the first time since returning to Oxford, I'd dared to look forward to a shared life, a shining future. I should have known it was too good to be true.

'I came to visit you too,' he said now, taking in my bed hair, robe and bare legs, reminding me how much more he'd seen over the years. 'Nice birthday?'

'Lovely, thank you.' I could never get my tone quite right, the easy way we used to chat a distant memory. 'Vic threw a party.'

'Hayley told me.' Only a tightening around his eyes gave away his true feelings. I knew he felt betrayed that I'd met someone else, even though he'd been the one to walk away. 'Did you like your present?'

'I love it.' I held out my arm, self-consciously, to show him I was wearing the bracelet. 'Thank you for helping her choose it.'

'My pleasure.' His voice was dry as his gaze held mine.

I looked away first, scanning the room, wishing I'd tidied up before going to bed. Seeing the surfaces cluttered with plates and glasses, the remains of my cake uncovered in the middle of the table, a fly buzzing over the crumbs, reminded me why I hadn't, and the headache from last night threatened to return.

'What's that?' For the first time, I noticed a colourful box by Matt's feet, which as usual were stuffed into biker-style boots, despite the warm weather outside.

Bending, he picked it up, a frown creasing his forehead. 'Not the sort of thing I'd imagine you ordering.'

I tried to catch a breath as he held it out.

On the side of the box was an image of a girl in a swimming pool, floating in sparkling water on a blue and white inflatable.

So, the wheels are in motion now. I can't tell you how good it feels to finally be doing something after all this time.

I thought you might have spotted me outside the house earlier. Even if you had, it wouldn't have mattered. Easily explained.

Those neighbours across the road – Lewis and Jude, with the annoying kid who's always sucking his thumb – are nosy, at least she is. She had a good poke around upstairs yesterday. I bet you didn't know that. Just like you don't know how this is going to end. Not yet. Like I said, I'm patient.

I can wait a bit longer.

Chapter 6

'Did you see who put it there?' I stared at Matt, recalling the blur of movement I'd seen from the bedroom window; a figure, darting behind the tree.

Matt shook his head. 'It was there when I got here.' He tilted the box to look for an address, but I knew there wouldn't be one. 'It's great that you're doing this, Beth.'

'Doing what?' My voice sounded strange, but Matt didn't seem to notice.

'Making an effort with Hayley at the pool.' Realising I wasn't going to take the box, he quickly put it down again. 'Is it for you, so you can get in the water with her?' His wary smile said he knew it was a risky question.

'I think you know the answer to that.' My legs felt rubbery, but instinct warned me to behave naturally. Matt was no doubt on the lookout for signs of overprotectiveness, that I wasn't doing a good enough job of being a parent. 'I can just about watch while someone's in the pool with her, but can't see myself ever joining in.'

When I'd told Matt about my fear of drowning, he reacted the same way most people did, by offering to teach me to swim, as though it was the physical act of moving my arms and legs through water that was the issue. It wasn't until we went on

37

holiday for the first time, and he tried to get me into the hotel pool, that he understood the full extent of my aversion.

We'd talked about it when Hayley was born, and although he'd have been happy to teach her to swim on his own, I'd made myself go and watch, standing ankle-deep in the toddler pool, my eyes never shifting from her. We'd done that ever since – our Saturday morning ritual. Only now, we took Hayley separately on alternate Saturdays, and when it was my turn, Marianne or Mum came along.

'Here, I got you this.'

Blinking to clear an image of a hooded figure sneaking up to the house with the boxed inflatable, I saw Matt was holding out a brown-paper package. 'What is it?'

'Call it a belated birthday present.'

I let out a shaky breath. 'Matt, you shouldn't have.'

'I know.' He waggled the package so I had no choice but to take it as Hayley reappeared, dressed in her school uniform, her hair flyaway with static.

'Open it, Mummy,' she ordered.

I arranged my face to look pleasantly surprised, but frowned when I pulled out a boxed collection of my favourite Winsor and Newton oil paints.

'I thought they might inspire you,' Matt said.

Pushing aside that he'd been thinking about me at all, I stared at the row of tubes with their familiar griffin logo, ringed with colours that sounded like poetry – Indian Yellow, Scarlet Lake, Mars Violet – and imagined how they would feel as I squeezed out a curl of colour. I cleared my throat around the tears that had built up. 'I don't need inspiring,' I said stiffly. 'I still paint.'

'I don't mean those watercolours for the café and gallery—'

'They sell really well.'

'I know, and they're great, but . . . they're not you, Beth.'

My eyes moved past a series of framed sketches I'd drawn of Hayley as a baby and the hand-made plate with the imprint of her newborn feet, to a large canvas hanging above the fireplace: a swirl of turbulent waves, swelling and tumbling beneath a cloud-less sky, foam patterns gliding across the surface.

'For someone so scared of the sea, you do a brilliant job of painting it,' Matt had said, when I'd shown him the canvases stacked in my studio at my parents' house. 'I was expecting portraits or, I don't know, flowers or abstracts, not this.'

He wasn't the only one puzzled by my obsession with painting the thing that had almost killed me, but committing the images that roamed my mind to canvas was my way of controlling my fear. My favourite was an enormous wave, rearing like a dragon from the seabed against a blackened sky that Mum found terrifying.

'I don't like it,' she'd said when I showed her, a hand flying to her throat. 'I don't like to think of that being in your head.'

It had taken a while to reassure her that painting the ocean was healing for me. It was what had drawn me to becoming an art therapist after I finished my degree. I wasn't interested in being a struggling artist. I wanted to help people and make a living, and these days it was my watercolours that helped pay the bills.

'I haven't used oils for ages,' I said, unable to resist pulling out a tube and cradling it in my palm. 'I gave mine away.'

'I know.'

'Daddy, that's a silly present,' Hayley piped up. 'Vic got Mummy a necklace.'

'Hayley!'

Matt's gaze touched my chest as if wondering where it was and I guessed he was picturing it in my grandmother's jewellery box in the bedroom, nestled alongside my wedding ring, which I'd taken off when people started assuming I was Vic's wife. Not that I slept in our bedroom anymore. I'd moved into the back room after Matt left; the one where he used to play his guitar when he was supposed to be working.

'I'm sure it's a pretty necklace,' he said.

I turned away, trying to stem a flush, wishing I didn't have a reaction to Matt that I couldn't seem to control. 'The paints are nice too,' I said to Hayley, who'd dropped to her knees on the floor and was reaching for the box by Matt's feet.

'What's this, Mummy?'

'Leave it.' I sprang forward so fast I knocked the table and sent a glass to the floor. 'It's not ours.'

'Mu-*uum!*'

'It's nearly time for school.' I picked up the glass, not daring to look at Matt. 'You haven't got your lunch.'

'Can Daddy make it?' She jumped to her feet, the box forgotten, and I was grateful for her butterfly mind.

'Come on then, or we'll be late,' Matt said. 'Don't forget I'm picking you up today and taking you to dance class.' He got to his feet and headed to the kitchen, giving me a quizzical look as he passed.

I smiled, trying not to imagine how Vic would feel to see Matt opening the fridge while Hayley pulled a banana from the fruit bowl, the pair of them chatting while I watched with a curious ache in my heart. No worse than Matt must feel, knowing Vic had made himself at home in the house we'd shared, that we'd decorated together; the house where our daughter was conceived, where family and friends had visited, where Matt set fire to his apron while barbecuing sausages in the garden, lit fireworks on bonfire night, and built a snowman with Hayley a couple of winters ago – the house where Vic stayed more often than he returned to his own place near the hospital where he worked.

Seeing the look on Matt's face, the day he noticed the space on the bookshelf where our wedding photo had been – I'd put it away, mindful that Vic might not want to see our smiling, happy faces beaming out from the steps of the register office – still made me feel terrible. I needed to talk to Matt about putting the house on the market, but today wasn't the day.

'You're going back there then.'

Startled back to the moment, I followed his gaze, to the printout on the worktop. Every cell in my body seemed to freeze. How could I have forgotten my trip next week with Vic? The trip to Perran Cove.

Maybe that was why I'd had the nightmare again.

Taking a deep breath, I moved across to the kettle. 'I know you wanted us to go there, Matt, but it never felt right until now.'

'Vic's idea, I suppose.'

'Actually, yes.' I flicked the tap too hard, splashing water on my robe. 'It seemed like a good time to go, with you and Hayley in France next week.'

I'd known when we split up there'd be no more family get-togethers, but the thought of Matt taking Hayley to visit his parents without me was hard to stomach.

When Vic had suggested we go away too, and cautiously suggested Perran Cove, I'd said yes without really thinking. I wondered now, whether I'd known subconsciously Matt would be hurt that I was taking this step without him.

'It'll be good if I can get to the point of taking Hayley to the seaside without risking a meltdown.' I looked through the window, to see her in the back garden peering through the hedge for Baxter. 'If I can face the sea there, I can probably face it anywhere.'

'Better learn to swim first.'

'Maybe that will come next.'

'Well, I hope it works.' I looked at Matt to see whether he was being sarcastic, but his face was deadly serious. 'I only ever wanted you to not be scared,' he said. 'And to stop feeling bloody guilty all the time.'

'Matt.'

He heard the warning – don't go there – and held up his hands. *Enjoy your birthday, Beth. It'll be your last.*

I thought about telling Matt about the texts. That I hadn't been scared, until yesterday. But if he thought I was in danger he might decide not to bring Hayley back.

'For what it's worth, I think it'll be good for you both.' I thought for a moment he meant Vic and me, but of course he was referring to Hayley. 'Maybe you can take that inflatable with you,' he said.

41

Chapter 7

Once they'd gone, Hayley holding Matt's hand, swinging her lunchbox in the other, I stood for a moment and looked up and down the street, wondering whether whoever had left the box on my doorstep might still be lurking.

'Nice morning.'

Pam's voice made me jump. She was coming out of her front door, dressed smartly for her daily trip into town. 'Lovely party,' she said, eyes crinkled in a smile. 'Is your head better this morning?'

I nodded, distracted. 'You didn't see someone leave a parcel on my doorstep earlier, did you?' Pam wasn't nosy, but had lived on the street long enough to spot something – or someone – unusual.

She shook her head. 'Another birthday gift?' Her neatly drawn eyebrows rose. 'I feel bad that I only gave you flowers from the garden.'

'Don't be silly, I loved them,' I said, though in truth, I found the musky, old-fashioned scent of the roses she favoured a little too strong indoors. 'So, you didn't see anyone?'

'Only Hayley's dad.' Her forehead creased with a pained expression. She thought highly of Matt, and although she'd been careful

42

not to criticise when he left, I knew she disapproved. 'He was here last night too.'

'What?'

'I saw him after everyone had gone.' She pointed to the back of the house, shielding her eyes from the sun. 'He was sitting on the bench in your garden, looking at his phone.'

I felt a kick in my chest. 'Did he say anything?'

'He didn't see me.' Dropping her hand, she said, 'Is he still living in that flat?'

A flush travelled up my cheeks. I knew how it looked, me in our house while Matt lived in rented accommodation a couple of miles away, albeit pleasant enough from what I'd glimpsed when dropping Hayley there once. We'd explained that Daddy had gone to live somewhere else – a fact she'd accepted with enviable ease after lots of reassurance – and I'd thought she should see it, get used to picturing him there. I'd needed to see it too, unable at first to imagine him anywhere without us, dismayed by how little effort he'd made to make it homely – as if he expected his stay to be temporary.

'He is,' I said to Pam, unwilling to mention it was only until we sold the house and he could buy somewhere bigger. We'd become like family to her, and I knew she'd be upset when we moved. 'Going somewhere nice?'

'Just into town.' She patted her crop of white hair and smiled. 'I'm meeting my friend Jenny for a coffee.' She glanced down the road, where a small row of traffic had built up. 'I'd better go or I'll miss my bus,' she said. 'Have a nice day, Beth.'

'You too.'

She hurried off, breaking into a jog as she reached the end of the street, and I backed into the house, breathing quickly, as if I'd been running too. Why hadn't Matt mentioned calling round yesterday? And why had he been loitering in the garden?

In the living room, the sight of the brightly coloured box containing the inflatable filled me with an unnamed dread. I

43

picked it up, hurried it out to the rubbish bin and dropped it in. It was wasteful, but I couldn't have it in the house with everything it represented.

The back of my neck prickled. I wheeled round, certain someone was watching from the street, but there was no one there.

I felt twitchy and on edge as I showered and dressed, jumping at the slightest sound, my imagination flaring again as I ran through possible setups: a figure skulking in the bedroom, waiting to leap out, or someone breaking into my car and hiding in the back, ready to strangle me as I drove.

As I made my way to Fernley House, hands clenched around the steering wheel, my gaze snagged on a black Kia, a couple of cars behind, as shiny as a beetle under the early sunshine. It had been there since I turned out of my road, seamlessly slipping behind a red sports car whose driver was clearly impatient with the traffic, revving loudly as we joined a line of commuters on the ring road. Or was I imagining it, my mind playing tricks, looking for danger where none existed?

'For God's sake,' I muttered, as the traffic started up and the sports car shot past, allowing the Kia to slide up behind me, too close. Was *this* how it was going to end? In some film-style car chase, resulting in me being shoved off a bridge into thundering water below? Except, there was no bridge and I was thankfully nowhere near the river Thames, which flowed through Oxford.

Even so, my heartbeat tripled at the thought, and my palms were slick with sweat as I deliberately slowed the car to just under the speed limit. There was a clear stretch on the other side of the road now. A white van overtook, followed in quick succession by a motorcyclist and a silver SUV, the driver flashing an angry look, but the black car behind stayed put.

I peered into my rear-view mirror, trying to get a clear look at the driver, but the sun was glancing off the windscreen and I couldn't see inside.

I sped up, pressing my foot down. All I had to do was get to

Fernley House. No one could hurt me between here and there without risking their own life too. Someone was trying to frighten me, that was all.

Taking a shaky breath, I flicked on the radio, keeping my eyes fixed on the road. I tried to focus on a discussion about the economy, and when the flat-fronted red-brick exterior of Fernley House came into view, my body deflated as if someone had opened a valve and let all the air out.

I was being ridiculous, I chastised myself, slowing to turn into the small gravelled car park in front of the building. I fully expected the black car to have gone when I flicked a look behind me, and fear leapt when I saw it was still there.

'So what?' I said out loud, my voice defiant. Plenty of people came to Fernley House. Just because I didn't recognise the car didn't mean it had no business being there.

All the same, when it pulled up beside mine, I switched off the engine, grabbed my phone and pressed 99 with clumsy fingers, ready to press the third 9 as I got out. I was hardly breathing as I stood by my open car door, waiting for my follower to emerge.

'Marianne!' It came out as a heartfelt cry of relief that made my colleague's mouth drop open and her eyebrows rocket up to her hairline.

'Who were you expecting?' she said, locking the car with the click of a key-fob. 'You look like you've seen the ghost of a long-dead murderer. Jack the Ripper perhaps, though I doubt you'd recognise him, not having a morbid fascination with true crime, like I do.'

It was such a typical and reassuringly Marianne thing to say, I found myself laughing as I locked my car. 'I didn't realise it was you.' Shaking off the impulse to have a final look around, I walked with her to the entrance, where a cluster of youths were bantering good-naturedly.

Fernley House was an impressive, three-storey Georgian building that had been donated to charity by its owner in the

Seventies, and run as a therapy and trauma centre ever since. Marianne had been there for years, in charge of the small team of psychotherapists, counsellors and occupational therapists. My services formed a small part of the treatments offered. I'd undertaken a work placement there during my therapy training, after leaving college, and was offered a permanent part-time job that left me time to paint, and to collect Hayley from school most days.

'It's Carl's car,' Marianne was saying. 'Mine's in for a service today so he let me borrow it.'

Carl was Marianne's adult son, living back at home after breaking up with his girlfriend of five years.

'I thought he didn't drive.' I recalled her mentioning that Carl had failed his test four times and probably wasn't fit to be on the road.

'He doesn't.' She shook her head. 'He's hoping the car will inspire him to try again.'

Freshly alert to nuances, I detected an underlying tension in her voice. 'Everything OK?' I asked, relieved to focus on something – anything – but my own jangled nerves, but Marianne merely nodded and released her infectious smile. With her frizzy, dyed-red hair, rich, warm voice and eccentric clothes, she was a popular figure at Fernley House, dedicated to helping people rebuild their lives. There was a waiting list for her creative writing classes and she hardly ever took time off, but sometimes I thought she was a bit too close to her job, that she cared too much.

I privately thought it was because she felt more in control here, able to help the people who came through the doors, whereas – she'd openly confessed – she'd struggled for years to parent her twins. At twenty-seven, Carl still bounced back home, looking for handouts every time he lost his job, and his sister Gemma, a single parent, was a convicted shoplifter.

'It's because they've never had a good male role model growing up,' Marianne had said, though she blamed herself too, for not being stricter when they were toddlers. Their father had died not long after they were born and, rather than waste energy – as she'd put it – on meeting someone new, she'd thrown herself into her job so she could provide for them and make herself feel better in the process. Something I understood all too well.

'Hey, what about you?' She swung her gaze towards me, a question in her small, grey-green eyes, her lashes spiky with mascara. 'You seemed distracted last night,' she said. 'Not yourself.'

'I did?' So much for trying to hide how I was feeling. Normally, I'd confide in Marianne. She had a way of drawing people out and was famously level-headed, but something held me back. Maybe it was her reference to Carl, a hint that things were worse than usual at home, or perhaps I didn't want to give voice to my swelling anxiety. 'It was the whole surprise party thing,' I said. 'I had a bad headache too.'

'Probably the hot weather.' Marianne paused in the reception area, hugging the leather satchel she carried everywhere. 'You were right about your parents,' she said unexpectedly. 'They barely took their eyes off you.'

'I know.' I made a despairing face. 'Even when I was at college in London, they'd visit all the time and phone me every day, worry if I didn't reply. It got a bit better after I moved back, but it never completely goes away.' Marianne knew about my near-drowning. 'They're stuck forever with that image of me in hospital when I was seven.'

'Why *did* you move back?'

She'd never asked me that before. 'Apart from it being cheaper?' I shook my head. 'It felt easier, I suppose. I felt I owed it to them to be nearby, so they weren't constantly imagining the worst.' I gave a little laugh. 'I know, it sounds silly.'

'Not at all.' Marianne's smile was genuine this time. 'They seem like lovely people,' she said. 'Even your brother was friendly.'

From past conversations, she'd no doubt expected a glowering Neanderthal, shooting dirty looks and barbed comments in my direction. I suddenly felt bad if that was the picture I'd painted of Jamie. To most people, he was an ordinary, nice-looking, hard-working man with a bit of a chip on his shoulder; the chip being me. 'It's the Rosa effect,' I said, returning her smile. 'I think he's in love this time.'

'Didn't look like that to me.' Marianne nodded to Hal Gordon, the occupational therapist hurrying past, his leather sandals squeaking on the parquet floor. 'He looked furious with her at one point.'

'When she was talking to me, probably. He wouldn't want me trying to influence her opinion of him. Not that I would,' I said quickly. 'I'm happy for him.'

Before Marianne could respond there was a commotion at the entrance as a small group arrived together for their creative writing class, greeting each other like the friends they'd become.

'I'll see you later,' I said, giving Marianne's arm a squeeze, before making my way to the art room. As I entered, breathing in the scent of paint and linseed oil, I recalled with a spark of shock, Mum asking Dad where Jamie was, and seeing him creeping in from the garden with the air of someone hoping not to be noticed. By Rosa?

Or me?

Chapter 8

I currently had a rota of five clients – we preferred the word client to patient – either referred through the NHS, or privately by word of mouth.

At seventeen, Katya was the youngest. She reminded me a little of myself at her age, discovering that art was an escape and a solace as well as an all-consuming passion. I had no doubt that one day, Katya MacDonald would be a name that people would recognise. She had a talent as natural as breathing, yet until she came to Fernley House, she had no idea how good she was.

Abandoned by her mother at the age of eight, after the sudden death of her father, she'd been thrust into the care system and fostered but never adopted. *No one wants children, they want babies.* She'd emerged from school with good grades but no self-belief, her arms and thighs criss-crossed with scars from years of cutting herself.

She hadn't done it since coming to Fernley House, she'd told me shyly. Painting had filled the void she'd felt for the past nine years – that and her growing attachment to me, which had lately begun to be a slight concern. Not enough to raise with anyone, but enough to remind me how vulnerable she was, and how easily she might interpret everyday kindness and attention for something more. It wasn't a crush, despite the gifts I'd occasionally found pushed in my bag – a star-printed scarf identical to one of hers I'd admired, and a miniature portrait she'd painted and put in a cheap, silver frame – more that she saw me as a mother figure, or older sister.

'Hey, Beth,' she said, her voice high and soft, approaching my desk before I'd put down my bag. 'Did you have a nice birthday?'

'Yes, thanks.' I looked at her, surprised. 'How did you know?'

'Oh, I remembered.' Her fingers played with the ends of the gauzy scarf she'd tied round her high, black ponytail, which fell over her shoulder. She was make-up free as usual, dressed in pale denim dungarees and a long-sleeved T-shirt, the glitter of a tiny nose stud her only adornment. 'July 18th?'

I couldn't recall discussing my birthday, but must have mentioned it in passing. It was surprising the direction conversations took during a session.

'You look nice,' she added.

I was wearing my usual work outfit of cargo pants and sneakers, with an unbuttoned shirt over a white vest top, but I knew she felt the need to compliment me. 'Thank you.' I rolled up my sleeves and went to open the windows. The heat in the room felt oppressive.

'Did you take some nice photos?' Katya was studying me with her wide-apart eyes, the irises an ethereal shade of blue that made me think of frozen lakes.

'How did you know I'd been taking photos?'

Her smooth, pale cheeks flushed raspberry pink at my tone. 'You said you were going to take some pictures, for inspiration?' Her voice rose, turning it into a question.

'Sorry, of course I did.' I softened my tone, pulling my mouth into a smile. I *had* mentioned it, when Katya asked what I was doing over the weekend. 'Yes, I took lots. Mostly of buildings.'

'Buildings?' She wrinkled her nose, looking a lot like Hayley did when presented with a plate of vegetables. 'Is it for a new project?'

I knew she wasn't keen on some of my painting exercises,

designed to challenge my clients' perception of themselves and explore their creativity.

'I know you prefer painting people, but it's good to try different forms.'

'Like you do?'

I hesitated, aware of my hypocrisy considering I mostly painted Oxford landscapes these days. Buyers seemed to like my pastel images of the city's medieval buildings and colleges, the Bridge of Sighs and botanic gardens, and I'd discovered I enjoyed painting them. 'You might discover you love it,' I said, dodging the question. 'Buildings are a good way to practise precision.'

'I'm happy to give it a try.' Katya's tone was touchingly eager to please – too eager, perhaps. 'Did you get that for your birthday?' Her gaze slipped to my bracelet, one slender hand reaching out as if to touch it.

'Yes, it's from my daughter.' I'd debated leaving it at home. I never normally wore much jewellery, but now I had on the ruby necklace as well as the bracelet from Hayley.

'It's really pretty.' Seeing sadness cloud Katya's face, I could have kicked myself. The last thing she needed was me thrusting my loving relationship with my daughter in her face. Though she had a good bond with her foster mum, Dee, she could never forget being abandoned by her birth mother. 'I got you something.' Brightening, she dipped her hand into her Aztec-patterned tote bag, and something about the movement and flash of colour made me stiffen.

'Katya, did you come straight here this morning?'

She raised her head, her eyes wary. 'What do you mean?'

I hesitated. Even if Katya had been outside my house earlier, it was unlikely she'd admit it. Anyway, I was certain she didn't have my address. 'Oh . . . I just, I thought you might have gone to Nell's,' I said, referring to the community café down the road, where my paintings hung for sale alongside some of my clients' work. 'I know you love her pastries.'

'No, I didn't go to Nell's.' She lowered her gaze and pulled out a lilac tissue-wrapped gift. 'Happy birthday for yesterday.'

She hadn't answered my question, but I took the gift, trying not to betray my reluctance. It was the third time that morning I'd been handed a package I wasn't expecting. 'You shouldn't have,' I said as I pulled at the silver ribbon around it, wondering whether I needed to set some boundaries.

'It's OK, I wanted to.'

Perspiration beaded my forehead. I glanced at the windows again, where a listless fly was buzzing. The sun pressed against the glass, slanting beams across the wooden floor and up the wall, decorated with rows of artwork.

'Do you like it?' Katya's anxious voice drew my attention to a book nestled in the delicate wrapping. I froze for two, three seconds, staring at the cover.

'Beth?'

I dragged my gaze from an artist's impression of leaping waves, crashing against granite-black rocks. 'What is this?'

'It's a book of famous seascape artists.' Her brows hardened into a line above narrowed eyes, reminding me for a second how her usually mild expression could suddenly switch to rage. 'Don't you like it?'

'No, I mean yes, it's lovely.' I turned the book over to look at the description on the back, but the words jumped and distorted. 'You shouldn't have, Katya. It looks expensive.'

'I thought you'd like it.' Her voice flattened into disappointment. 'You said you used to love painting the sea. I thought it might inspire you.'

Struck by the oddness of our exchange, which was almost identical to the one I'd had earlier with Matt, I said, 'I'm happy doing what I do now,' injecting my voice with an authority I didn't feel. 'But it's a beautiful book.' I let my eyes graze the cover again, a tremor passing through me. 'I'll treasure it.'

I looked up to see her smile, revealing her slightly crooked front teeth. 'I bet your paintings are way better than theirs.'

'I doubt that very much.' Back on firmer ground, I slid the book into my bag while Katya headed to her usual spot by the window. As I reviewed my previous session notes, trying to marshal my thoughts, I could feel the weight of her gaze. I glanced up, but she was facing the window, her expression unreadable.

I managed to push everything out of my mind during my session with Katya, guiltily glad when she became too absorbed in her work to talk. Once she'd left – unusually swiftly – I was kept busy with Tom, an ex-soldier with PTSD who talked non-stop as he pushed great blocks of paint across his canvas, the action of moving his brush seeming to unlock his emotions.

After typing up my notes on both sessions, I went to find Marianne, hoping she'd be free for lunch, but when I nudged open the door to the creative writing room she was deep in discussion with two of her students and gave a discreet shake of her head. She never minded if her sessions ran over, was happy to grab a quick sandwich at her desk, but I liked to get out for some air.

I emerged into bright sunlight, my rumbling stomach reminding me I'd left the house that morning without breakfast. I headed to Nell's, aware of Katya's book in my bag as it bumped against my hip. Nodding to Nell through the café window, I sat at a table outside, trying to keep my mind fixed in the present. Across the road was a church, and a gift shop displaying framed prints in the window. It reminded me I'd had a voicemail from a gallery near Christchurch, which had sold my paintings in the past, about an upcoming exhibition. I pulled out my phone to call them back, relieved to see I hadn't had any new texts.

Tabitha, the gallery owner, sounded delighted to hear from me. When I told her I had several seascapes I'd like her to consider, she suggested I send her some photos.

'We can take about ten,' she said.

I thought of all the canvases stored at my parents' house, which

53

I'd never intended to exhibit or sell. 'I've got plenty,' I told her. 'I'll pick a few of my favourites.'

'Do you have a title? It would be good to start a social media campaign and of course there'll be a press release.'

'Making Waves.' I hadn't known I was going to say it until the words popped out, but it was as good a title as any. Better than 'Drowning', which had been my first thought.

'Great.' I could hear the smile in her voice. 'I can't wait to see them.'

As I ended the call, I was hit with a horrible thought.

Will I still be alive then?

'Carrot and coriander,' Nell said, making me jump as she placed a bowl in front of me, her fragrant soups too good to resist, even during summer. 'You look serious.'

'I do?' I returned her smile, which was also hard to resist. She was small, with a round face and spiky white hair, her short frame clad in an apron with the café's name on the front. Pushing seventy, she showed no signs of slowing down, the café her life as well as her livelihood. Nell was distantly related to Hugo Stanning, who'd donated Fernley House – but without his wealth, she often joked.

'I was thinking about work,' I said.

'You lot do a good job up there.' She nodded in the direction of the house, which was as much a fixture of the landscape in this part of Oxford as the café. 'Helping those poor souls. You never know what people are going through, do you?' She dipped her head to the left, where a middle-aged couple at the next table were chatting quietly over glasses of iced tea. 'They were at each other's throats before you got here,' she said, lowering her voice to a whisper. 'Now, they look like butter wouldn't melt.' She pointed to the soup. 'Eat up, before it goes cold,' she said in her normal voice, distracted by the arrival of a group of teenage girls, loudly deciding what flavour of ice-cream they were going to choose – a recent addition at the café.

'Ew, soup,' I heard one of them say as they passed. 'Gross.'

Nell threw her hands up in mock despair before following them inside. My smile faded as I watched her retreating back. I picked up my spoon and began to eat, but Nell's words rang loudly in my ears.

You never really know what people are going through, do you?

I picked up the freshly baked roll that accompanied the soup, but my stomach had twisted into a knot and there was no way I could eat. I felt suddenly exposed out there on the pavement, in full view of anyone passing – or watching.

The back of my neck went cold. I turned, but apart from a pair of mums with toddlers in pushchairs coming slowly up the street, and an elderly man with a dog on a lead, there was no one there.

But how would I know, if they were hiding?

My eyes skimmed the pavement opposite. Someone was coming out of the gift shop; a man, tall and dark-haired, wearing business clothes. He paused and looked over at me, waited for a car to pass, then crossed the road.

Gripped by sudden panic, I rose, bumping the table so that everything jumped and my spoon clattered to the ground.

'Sorry I'm late, I wanted to get this,' the man said. He wasn't even looking at me. I turned to see a woman, waiting outside the café, her face lit up in a smile. She exclaimed with pleasure when he held out the bag he was carrying and opened it for her to peer inside.

'Oh, it's gorgeous,' she said, pressing a kiss on his cheek. 'Mum will love it.'

Heart thumping, I bent to pick up the fallen spoon, meeting the curious gaze of the middle-aged woman who'd been chatting to her partner. It seemed to say, *What's going on with her?* I gripped the back of the chair, but was too on edge to sit down again.

'Sorry, it was delicious, but I have to go,' I said to Nell, thrusting a ten-pound note across the counter, ignoring her cry of, 'What about your change?' as I hurried out.

I practically jogged back to Fernley House, glancing over my shoulder as if I was being chased. When I reached my car, I threw myself inside and locked the doors, panting like a dog. Catching sight of myself in the mirror was a shock. I looked out of control; wild-eyed, with strands of hair escaping my topknot, my face sweaty and red.

Making myself breathe deeply, I pushed air out of my lungs – *in, out, in, out* – until my heart had stopped racing and my cheeks had cooled down. I had to think clearly, and stop looking for connections that didn't exist. I couldn't – *mustn't* – let myself fall apart. That was exactly what someone wanted me to do.

What I should be doing, was trying to find out who.

Chapter 9

Normally, after work, I'd go home and work on a painting until it was time to pick Hayley up from school, but I found myself driving to my parents' house, overtaken by the urge to do something besides cower in my car feeling powerless.

They lived in Headington in the same bay-fronted, red-brick semi I'd grown up in, away from the spires, books and bicycles people associated with Oxford, but close to another famous landmark: the huge fibreglass shark that looked to be diving through the roof of a house opposite the football ground. There'd been talk of us moving after my accident, and making a new start, but Mum wanted to stay close to her parents, and Dad thought the upheaval might be too much, so it came to nothing in the end. The house hadn't changed much, mine and Jamie's bedrooms trapped in time, the adjoining garage in need of updating.

I entered the kitchen through the side door, which still had a dent in the frame where Jamie once threw a cricket ball that veered off course. 'Only me!'

'Beth, what are you doing here?' Mum got up from the scrubbed pine table that had seen years of dinners and homework, looking delighted but anxious.

'I want to have a look through my canvases,' I said. 'I'm preparing some work for an exhibition at the Whitehaven gallery.'

'Oh, Beth, that's fantastic.' She extricated herself from a swathe of curtain material. She'd been making soft furnishings for friends and neighbours, and supplying a local interiors company since Jamie and I were little. It was rare to see her away from her sewing machine. 'Couldn't it have waited until Saturday?' she said, casually. 'You were coming for lunch anyway.'

She was subtly probing, wanting to know the real reason behind my visit, and a mix of frustration, love and irritation rose in my chest. If I hadn't nearly drowned – if that man hadn't died – how different would our lives have been? It was an age-old question, and one I'd never have the answer to. I couldn't turn back time, as my counsellor had pointed out more than once, and I couldn't change the past. *Everything happens for a reason*, Matt used to say – Emma too – but it never rang true for me. There was no reason I could fathom why a man had to die so I could live. Life was random, beyond my control, and that was what scared me so much. *Survivor's guilt* was my official diagnosis – irrational but real, though naming it hadn't helped much. I sometimes felt as if I was grieving for the relationships I *could* have had with my family, even though reason dictated I was lucky to have them at all.

'That man's family,' I said, surprising us both. 'They must be still furious with me, don't you think?'

'Oh, Beth, not this again.' Her face slack with dismay, Mum sank back onto the bench where she'd been working, clutching at the fabric. 'I thought you'd come to terms with it.'

Sucking in a tiny breath, I fought to keep my composure. 'I have, it's just . . .' My gaze strayed to the old-fashioned wildlife calendar by the fridge, Mum's neat handwriting marking out appointments and reminders. 'It's coming up to the date when it happened,' I said slowly, shifting a couple of crafting magazines as I sat down opposite her. 'It reminds me, that's all.'

'I know it does.' She reached across the table and gave my

fingers a brief, comforting clasp. 'But it was so long ago, love; it's in the past.' Hearing the plea in her voice – *don't rake it up again, please* – I knew I couldn't tell her about the messages and start her worrying again.

Years ago, just after I turned thirteen, I'd been half-listening to a TV drama about a man seeking revenge on the woman who'd killed his mother in a drink-driving accident, when Jamie had said carelessly, 'I bet his family feel like that about you.'

'Whose family?' I'd looked up from my sketchpad where I'd been drawing our black and white cat Bella, trying to get the tail right as she kept swishing it about.

'That bloke who died saving your life.' He'd given me a look of withering disbelief. 'Who did you think I meant?'

His words had felt like blades across my skin. Until that moment, thanks to my parents' efforts to shield me, my fears had been focused solely on being around water, on drowning, on falling asleep and reliving the ordeal in my dreams. My feelings about the man who saved me had reduced to an abstract sense of gratitude that he'd seen I was in trouble from the cliff path and swum out to rescue me. Initially, when I left hospital and asked who he was, demanding to meet him so I could thank him, Mum suggested I write a letter because he lived a long way away. So, I had, accompanying my words with a drawing of him as a cartoon Superman, captioned 'My Hero' surrounded by pink love hearts. *I can never thank you enough for what you did,* I'd written in my best script, with the fountain pen my grandmother had given me for Christmas.

Mum wept when she read it, but I hadn't really understood why. It didn't occur to me to ask his name then, or where exactly he lived, and I'd trusted her when she said she'd send the letter for me. I remembered watching out for the postman for a while after that, in case the man replied, and being vaguely disappointed when he didn't. Dad said he probably didn't want to make a fuss and that I shouldn't worry about it.

Only after Jamie's bombshell – deliberately dropped I understood later – did I confront my parents and learn the truth. That the man, whose name was withheld by the police when his body was found, had drowned.

My parents had wanted to make contact with his family through the police, to offer their condolences and to offer to help in some way, but the message had come back that they wanted no further communication and that was that. The letter I'd written was never posted.

It explained so much about the depth of my parents' devastation and guilt, which I'd thought was about almost losing me, but turned out to be so much more.

'Why didn't you tell me sooner?' I'd raged – horrified they'd kept it from me – that finding out so bluntly, so much later, had reopened a wound that became deeper and more painful than I could have imagined. 'He DIED,' I'd yelled, unable to take it in. 'He *died*, because of *me.*'

Nothing anyone could say could console me. I wanted to know everything: who he was, whether he'd had children, a wife, a mum and dad, brothers and sisters, but no one knew anything, not even his name, and my suggestion we contact the police again had been rebuffed. 'It would cause more harm than good to bring it all up now. Just leave it, Beth, please.'

Jamie, shocked by the ferocity of my anger and guilt, had apologised for telling me, but with the edge of resentment I'd started to recognise – and dread. 'You'd have found out one day, and it would have been the same,' he muttered, the rash of spots around his jaw seeming to pulse with misery. 'I know you'd have tried to find out about him.'

He was right, I would have, and maybe Mum and Dad would have told me eventually anyway, but the timing had been awful, the truth too great a shock, and knowing my brother had told me to hurt me had been hard to bear.

I was taken out of school for a week and put into counselling,

60

having weekly sessions for the rest of the year, and occasionally after that for a couple more years, whenever the guilt threatened to overwhelm me.

'The best thing you can do is embrace life, make the most of the chance you were given and live it to the full, don't waste it,' had been the gentle advice, but even that brought its own pressure. *How* should I live my life to the full, make it count, make it worthwhile? How was I supposed to justify my existence?

'Imagine how awful *our* lives would have been if we'd lost you,' Mum had pleaded, in tears of helplessness. 'Isn't that enough?'

'Our lives are awful now anyway,' Jamie said, but so quietly only I could hear. I knew he'd have preferred me not to exist if it meant our parents would notice him again, and stop being angry with him for telling me the truth. I couldn't find the words to tell him I'd give anything to go back to before, when he used to make me giggle by doing impressions of the teachers at school, and let me draw him in silly poses.

Immersing myself in painting had helped, and so had escaping to London to study at the Royal College of Art. Qualifying as an art therapist had eventually allowed me to feel I was making a difference – that maybe I'd justified my existence after all. With each year that passed I'd let myself off the hook a little more, but it didn't take much for guilt to dig its claws in once again.

'You have to keep looking forward, not back, for Hayley's sake as much as yours.' Mum's voice snapped me back to the moment, to the kitchen filled with sunlight reflecting off an army of photos on the cluttered dresser; Jamie and me, taken before the accident, grinning innocently and gap-toothed at the camera, and several taken in the years afterwards, carefully staged to portray us as a happy family, no visible undercurrents evident to an outsider.

We'd all had counselling for a while, when it became obvious our family dynamic had fractured – when I didn't know the full story – but Jamie had remained silent throughout and Mum and Dad, always a tight unit, had each other to lean on.

I found myself wanting to say something now, about how awful it must have been for Jamie, keeping the man's death a secret all that time, but looking at Mum's face and remembering how hard she'd worked to help us all move on, my courage failed. Talking to Dad was out of the question too. He'd recoil at the mere hint of revisiting the past he'd mostly managed to bury.

'Beth?'

I met Mum's querying gaze and adopted a breezy tone. 'How's Dad?'

Her face softened. 'Busy,' she said, her shoulders dropping. 'He's working on an antique table at an old rectory near the canal in Marston.'

I smiled. 'He'll be in his element.' Dad's reputation as a furniture restorer took him to some interesting places – interesting to him, at least. If he wasn't on site, he'd be in his repair shop a few streets away with his small team of employees.

'It's down to that BBC programme *The Repair Shop*,' Mum said. 'People are turning up with things for fixing, instead of throwing them out.'

'That's good, isn't it?'

'It's good for your dad – you know he'll never retire.' Mum rose and crossed to the fridge. She was wearing a coral-coloured knee-length dress she'd made herself and she'd varnished her toenails to match. 'So, this exhibition,' she said, clearly keen to move on. 'Are you painting something new?'

'I have some here that I want to use.'

'Why don't you pop out to the studio and have a look while I make us something to eat?'

'Not for me, thanks,' I said, rising. 'I'll need to get back soon for Hayley.'

She turned. 'I expect she's looking forward to seeing her other grandparents.'

The hint of animosity in her voice wasn't to do with Matt's parents. She liked them. It was about them going to France without me, and she was far from happy about my upcoming trip to Cornwall with Vic. I nearly hadn't told her and Dad, but knew they'd find out somehow and then it would be worse.

'I'm sure she'll have a lovely time,' I said, firmly. 'It's only for a few days, Mum. Dan and Gayle haven't seen her for ages.'

Mum looked at me, a jug of freshly squeezed orange juice in one hand. 'And are *you* looking forward to going away?'

I felt sick suddenly. 'I'm sure it won't be that bad.'

Relenting, Mum switched to her soothing tone. 'Of course it won't. I think you're really brave to even try it.' She opened her mouth then closed it again.

'What?'

'Oh . . . nothing.' She didn't meet my eyes as she placed the jug carefully on the worktop. 'It's just a shame you're not going with Matt.'

'Mum.' It came out as a groan.

She held up her hands. 'I'm sorry, Vic's lovely, and I'm sure you'll have a good time, but Matt must feel awful that you're doing this without him when he tried so hard.'

I gave her a look that I hoped said everything I didn't have the energy to repeat. Not when we'd been through it already.

'OK, I get it.' She turned to take a glass out of the cupboard. 'New man, new experiences, but don't you think Hayley would prefer her dad to be there and—'

'*Mum*, for God's sake.'

She swung round, eyes wide. 'Oh, Beth, I'm sorry. I know it's a decision you won't have made lightly, and it's none of my business. I'm sorry, forget I said anything.'

'You know, he came over this morning.' I folded my arms, then dropped them. I looked like an angry teenager. 'He still thinks he can drop in whenever he likes.'

'*Weeeell*, it's still his home, and Hayley's his daughter,' Mum pointed out, as if I didn't know. 'You can't really blame him, Beth. He misses her. And you.'

'He wanted me to change, be someone different.'

'He wanted you to be happy, Beth. To stop feeling as if you didn't deserve what you had.'

I ignored the scratch of her words, heard too many times over the past few years. 'Anyway, it's not for much longer.'

'What do you mean?'

'You know we'll have to sell the house.'

Mum's features froze. 'But you both love that place. I remember when you first saw it, you fell in love with it. You said it would be your forever home. You couldn't wait to get out of that poky basement flat.'

'It wasn't that bad.' Matt and I had been happy for the year we'd been holed up in his bachelor pad, despite the hefty bills and leaky gutter outside the bedroom window. 'Anyway, I can't stay,' I said. 'Vic and I need a place that's our own.'

A variety of emotions chased over her face. 'But . . . it's Hayley's home too.'

'It's just a house, Mum, and it's full of memories. Of Matt,' I clarified. 'And he won't want me living there with Vic.'

'Does he know you and Vic are going to buy a house together?' Her voice sharpened. 'Have you told him?'

'Not yet,' I admitted. 'But remember, Mum, he was the one who moved out.'

'I do remember.' She was gripping the edge of the worktop with both hands. 'But I also remember you told him to go, Beth. You said he deserved someone better.'

I nodded, feeling the prickle of tears. 'Yes, and he agreed.'

'In the heat of the moment, maybe. *He* hasn't found anyone else, has he?'

'Oh, Mum.' A wave of tiredness crashed over me. 'I'm not having this conversation again. Matt will always be in Hayley's life and that's fine, but I'm with Vic now.'

She rallied, straightening her back and tilting her chin. 'And he's a lovely man, who thinks the world of you,' she said. 'I think he proved that yesterday.'

The word *yesterday* brought me back with a jolt to the messages. 'Mum, I . . .'

Her expression refocused. 'What is it?'

'Do you have the key for the studio?'

She studied me for a moment. 'It's where it always is.'

'Thanks.' I twisted my mouth into a smile as I reached for my bag and took my phone out. 'I need to take some photos.'

'Beth,' she said, as I headed to the boot room where the key hung on its usual hook by the back door.

'Yes?' I glanced back, drawn by the appeal in her voice.

'I'm here if you need to talk.'

'I know.' I made myself hold her gaze. 'Everything's fine, I promise.'

Chapter 10

The studio was really a glorified shed tucked away at the bottom of the garden, which Dad had transformed so I could paint in there, transferring garden tools, old bikes and pieces of furniture into the garage, proclaiming the car would be fine out on the drive.

I turned the key in the padlocked door and stepped through it, breathing in years' worth of turps and old paint trapped in the sun-warmed walls. I hadn't been inside for ages. Cobwebs draped across the windows on either side and the skylight – installed to maximise brightness – was coated in dead leaves, but it was still a peaceful space that transported me back to early mornings, swaddled in an old shirt of Dad's, when I'd set up my easel and squeeze buttery blobs of paint onto my palette, adding a drop of linseed oil and swirling the colours together, before choosing my favourite brush to load with pigment.

Sweeping the first stroke of colour on a virgin canvas was still my favourite part; a new painting held so many possibilities. The world retreated and my heart would lift as the colours smudged together and became a restful sea under a cloudless sky, or an eddy of stormy waves, a hint of blue in leaden clouds, or a rocky shore dotted with ocean-tossed yachts. It was always a shock to come back to reality, like waking from a dream. Often, hours would have passed, drinks and sandwiches left by Mum untouched on the old wooden sewing box inside the door. *Losing myself in art is how I find myself.* I'd read that somewhere and it struck a chord.

My twenty or so paintings were still stacked against the wall, each one protected by bubble wrap. It struck me now what a waste it was, keeping them hidden away. I had no illusions they were masterpieces, but flicking through them, I could see they had something – a rawness or innocence – that might appeal to an audience. They *meant* something, and if I could see it, maybe others would too. They told a story.

'Yeah, the story of a disturbed mind,' I imagined Jamie saying. He'd professed not to understand art, but I knew it was more about me being given my own space to work in; being 'spoilt'. *We have to tiptoe around Princess Beth and her delicate feelings in case she gets upset,* I'd heard him say to a friend who came round to play football in the garden, only for them to be told off by Dad because I was 'working'.

I liked to think I'd have been more understanding in his shoes, but he was a teenage boy whose life had been pushed off course because of me. I couldn't blame him for being upset.

Momentarily lost in the moment, I worked through the paintings, moving the bubble wrap aside to snap a photo of each on my phone.

Some of the pictures had formed part of my portfolio for art college, and I recalled the burst of pride I'd felt when my tutor remarked that my 'Monster' seascape reminded him of a famous painting, 'The Wave', by a Japanese artist called Katsushika Hokusai. 'It's good to have a specialty,' he'd said with a rare gleam of approval. 'You've got talent, Beth.'

I carefully replaced the paintings, my mind pleasantly blank. Straightening, I ran a finger through the layer of dust coating the surface of the old chest, still cluttered with brushes and jars, where I'd stored my paints, pencils and palettes.

Something struck a jarring note. I ran my finger along the

window ledge and stared at the ashy smudge on my skin. No one ever ventured in here but me. Mum had occasionally run a cloth over the surfaces, but I'd preferred to do it myself, protective of my painting space. The shed was kept locked, as far as I knew.

I looked at my fingertips, breathing faster. They were clean, apart from the one I'd trailed though the dust, but wouldn't my paintings have been dusty too, having not been touched for so long? Crouching, I ran my hands over the bubble-wrapped edges of each one. They came away clean.

Ears thrumming with my heartbeat, I looked around more closely, immediately spotting what I hadn't seen before: the faint trace of a footprint on the dusty concrete floor.

Someone had been in here.

For a moment, it felt as if all the light had been sucked away, but when I looked through the skylight, the sun was a hard, round ball in the sky.

I looked down again, checking the trail of prints I'd left, and knew the footprint wasn't mine. There had to be a simple explanation, so why did I feel so spooked? It was too big to be Mum's, too small to be Dad's, and I couldn't think who else would have been in here. *Jamie?* I picked up my phone and took a photo. Maybe Rosa, or one of her colleagues, would be able to identify the markings and maybe the size.

Suddenly the studio didn't feel like a haven. I quickly locked up and made my way back to the house, reassured by the familiar whir of Mum's sewing machine.

'Find what you wanted?' she said, not looking up as I came into the kitchen.

I moistened my lips. 'I did.' I looked at the clock on the wall. 'I'd better make a move.'

'OK.' She pushed a lock of hair off her forehead. 'See you Saturday.'

A drop of perspiration snaked down my back. 'Has anyone been down there recently?'

'The studio?' She glanced up with a frown. 'No, why?' Without waiting for a reply, she added, 'It could probably do with a clean, but I know you don't like anyone going in there. Does it look bad?'

'A bit dusty, but it's fine.'

'What then?'

'I thought some things had been moved, that's all.'

'Oh, no.' She stood up and hurried to the boot room. 'Ben next door had his shed broken into a couple of weeks ago.' She locked the back door and rattled the handle to make sure it was secure. 'They took his petrol mower and leaf blower while he was out shopping. It wasn't even a proper break-in because they'd found the key hidden under one of his gnomes, so he can't even claim on the house insurance.'

'That's awful.'

She looked worried now, one hand at her throat. 'Was anything missing down there?'

'No, no, nothing like that.' I felt both relieved and ridiculous. Perhaps the footprint I'd seen belonged to the same person. Whoever it was had somehow got in, looked at the paintings and decided they weren't worth stealing. 'I was probably imagining it anyway. I haven't been in there for so long,' I said. 'But maybe don't leave the key where burglars can see it.'

'That's what Rosa said when she heard what happened next door.' Mum's anxious expression gave way to a smile. She liked Rosa. I knew she was hoping Jamie would ask her to marry him. 'I should have listened,' she added. 'Put it in the bits and bobs drawer, to be on the safe side.'

I did as I was told, making a play of hiding the key among the jumble of cables, string, pens, old receipts and paperclips that had accumulated, so that Mum laughed and said, 'Good luck to anyone trying to find it in there.'

As I drove away, I made myself think of her smiling face, instead of checking my rear-view mirror to see whether I was being followed.

*　*　*

Halfway home, I remembered Matt was picking Hayley up and taking her to dance class and decided to take a detour to Rosa's to show her the photo of the footprint. If it belonged to the same person who'd stolen from Mum's neighbour it might be helpful. If it didn't . . . at least it would be on record. I didn't want to be one of those victims who doesn't go to the police until it's too late, or assume people will peg me as paranoid, even if I am.

Victim. A word I hated. *You were a child, a victim of circumstance, you can't hold yourself responsible,* my counsellor had said.

The man who'd saved me had been the true victim, the innocent one, and his family were victims too. Had one of them found me and wanted me to pay for his death? Would knowing I'd suffered a surfeit of guilt, that I'd tried, in my own way, to make amends be enough?

Bye, bye, Beth.

Feeling my chest tighten, I inhaled and exhaled deeply, until I arrived at Rosa's rather industrial-looking apartment block in Folly Bridge, not far from St Aldates police station. Jamie had moved in about a month after they met, which we'd thought was too soon as he'd not long been out of a relationship, but it was clear pretty quickly this time was different. He'd met someone who seemed to understand him and didn't judge. In her line of work, Rosa had to be open-minded and she'd brought out the best in my brother. He'd become surprisingly domesticated, taking over cooking duties, and we'd been round for dinner a couple of times.

As I got out of the car, glancing around with hawk-like intensity, as if someone might be approaching with a concealed weapon, my phone began to ring. I fumbled to answer it.

'God, you scared me,' I said to Vic, relieved to hear his voice. 'I'm really jumpy today.'

'I'm not surprised,' he said, rather grimly. 'I was calling to see how you are.'

'I keep thinking someone's going to leap out and get me,' I admitted, leaning against the car. The hot metal burned through my shirt, but I didn't care. It was good to feel something other than anxious. 'I've just been over to Mum's.'

I told him about my morning, omitting the part about Katya's gift, picturing him in his leather chair in his consulting room, or standing at the window looking out at the car park.

'It's probably best to carry on as normal, and the exhibition's a good distraction,' he said. 'You can't let whoever sent that message get into your head.'

He didn't mention security again, and I understood why. In the golden light of a warm July day, with normal life going on, the idea that someone might *actually* mean me harm was too surreal.

'I'll cook dinner this evening.' Vic's voice was warm in my ear, melting some of my tension. 'You can put your feet up and relax, do some painting if you like. I can entertain Hayley, or Baxter next door will, if Pam doesn't mind.'

I smiled, remembering what Pam had said about her friend's Labrador having puppies. Maybe we should get a dog for protection, though something fierce would be a better idea. As my imagination cut loose, I pictured a snarling Alsatian grabbing a black-clad arm as it reached for me in the night.

'What is it?' Vic said. I realised I'd made a sound. 'You're thinking about it, aren't you?'

'How can I not?' My voice was too high. A passer-by shot me a look, reminding me of the woman sitting outside Nell's café. I looked more closely, checking it wasn't her. 'Someone told me I'm not going to live to see another birthday,' I said, lowering my tone. 'How am I supposed to react?'

'I wish I'd seen the message.' Vic's voice held a hint of frustration.

'Why?' I tensed. 'In case I misinterpreted it?'

'No, of course not, but . . . do you remember when we drove past that cottage for sale last month, and you said we should make an appointment to view it because it was perfect?'

'Of course I do.' I'd been drawn by the wisteria-tangled trellis

71

and brass knocker on the front door. 'I know what you're going to say.'

'You were convinced when you looked online that it had three bedrooms, and had recently been updated—'

'But when we got there, it had two bedrooms and badly needed updating. I know, but this is completely different.'

'I'm just saying, you saw what you wanted to see.'

'Are you saying I wanted to see a message from someone threatening to end my life?'

'No, but I know how guilty you still feel about what happened to that man, and maybe the message tapped into something but didn't mean someone really wants you to die.'

I took my phone from my ear and stared in disbelief. 'I can't believe you're saying that, Vic.'

'Look, I'm sorry.' He gave a heavy sigh. I guessed he was pinching the bridge of his nose, which he tended to do when tired or overworked. 'I suppose I don't want to believe it, so I'm looking for reasons why it might not have meant what you think.'

'*Enjoy your birthday; it'll be your last* doesn't leave room for doubt.' I felt an irrational flare of anger. 'What would your interpretation be?'

'And you're sure that was the exact wording?'

'Why are you doubting me now?'

'I'm not.' His voice was firm. 'I just wish I knew what to do.'

I huffed out a breath. 'You're not the only one.'

'And you haven't had any more?'

'I'd have said if I had, but . . .' I was going to tell him about the footprint in my studio but stopped myself, worried I sounded obsessed. Plus, I didn't know if it was related in any way. 'I can't help going over it. I keep checking my phone,' I said instead. *So much for being an open book.*

'That's understandable, but you've spoken to Rosa and unless – God forbid – anything else happens, I don't know what else we can do, apart from be vigilant.'

72

'So, I'm destined to be constantly on edge until I'm killed sometime during the next year, date unknown?'

'Beth—'

'No, Vic, that's exactly how it's going to be.' I clamped a hand to my forehead, feeling dampness there. 'I'm always going to be looking over my shoulder.'

'Listen, Beth, we're going away soon—'

'Yes, to the place that still gives me nightmares,' I cut in.

'We can always cancel it.'

'No, no.' I subsided. 'I don't want to cancel it.'

'I'll be with you twenty-four seven.' Vic's tone was reassuring. 'In the meantime, let's get you a personal alarm,' he said. 'They make a hell of a racket if anyone you don't like the look of comes near you.'

'And then what?'

'Call the police.'

'Whoever it is doesn't intend to be caught.' My voice snagged. 'This is something they've planned.'

'You don't know that.'

I didn't know anything for sure. 'I need to find out who sent that message, Vic.' Silence swelled down the line. 'Vic?'

'How do you intend to do that?'

'I don't know yet.' I glanced up at the apartments, hoping Rosa was in. 'I've got to go,' I said abruptly. 'I'll see you later.'

It's funny, knowing how spooked you are. I mean, I knew you would be, but it feels better than I thought it would. And why shouldn't I enjoy it? At the end of the day, you're alive, he isn't, and that's not right.

Yes, there's your broken marriage, but it didn't take you long to move on, did it? A few kind words, a shoulder to cry on and wham, you're all loved up again. Poor Hayley. It's obvious she'd rather be with her dad and she will be, sooner than you think.

I saw you, checking your rear-view mirror this morning on your way to Fernley House, thinking you were being followed. It made me smile, because you wouldn't suspect me, not in a million years. And you won't.

Not until it's time.

Chapter 11

Rosa answered the intercom, sounding slightly out of breath. There was a buzz to let me in and I pushed the door open, as if it was normal to turn up unannounced on a Monday afternoon.

The apartment was on the second floor, down a corridor that smelled of vanilla, filled with natural light from a floor-length window at the end. It was a lot more attractive than the block of flats I'd lived in with Emma in London, where the bare lightbulb on the staircase always fizzled out before we reached our door, leaving us squealing and fumbling with the lock, certain someone was lurking in the shadows.

'This is a surprise.' Rosa greeted me with a querying smile as she opened the door, wearing a silky bathrobe with a flower motif, her hair wrapped in a towel. I'd obviously disturbed her having a bath or shower.

'I'm sorry to turn up like this.' I looked past her at the open-plan living space, guiltily hoping Jamie wasn't around.

'He's out on a job,' she said, as though reading my mind, gesturing for me to come in. I caught a drift of coconut-scented shampoo as I stepped past her. Tendrils of hair had escaped her towel and were clinging to her neck, which was pink, as if she'd been soaking in hot water. 'I'm on duty later, so was making the most of having the place to myself.' Her smile as she closed the door grew unexpectedly mischievous. 'Jamie tends to make his presence felt.' She indicated the sound system in the corner, surrounded by vinyls of his favourite bands, and a guitar that Matt had taught him to play propped against a speaker. He'd liked Matt, almost against his better judgement, but it had made family gatherings easier as he was less likely to prod at me when Matt was there.

'Jamie's always loved his music,' I said, edging further inside, trying to shed my nervousness. I'd never been there on my own with Rosa and I knew Jamie wouldn't like it. He'd worry I might say something to put her off, though I never would. 'Doesn't it disturb your neighbours? When I shared a flat, years ago, we could hear the man upstairs taking a pee.'

'Was that with your ex?' she asked, padding barefoot to the island that separated the kitchen from the living room.

'No, a girlfriend,' I said. 'We were at art college together; it was all we could afford. Not like this.' I looked at the painting I'd given them when Jamie moved in, hanging above the big sofa, the sulphur yellow sky in the picture complementing the touches of colour in the cushions and curtains. 'It's lovely,' I said, eyes drifting over the beechwood coffee table and stripy rug, across to the dining table by the window. 'I've never seen it in daylight.'

Rosa's laugh was surprisingly mellow as she ran cold water into a tumbler. 'You're always welcome to call round,' she said, filling another glass and bringing them over. 'You don't have to wait for an invitation to dinner.'

My cheeks tingled with colour as I took a glass and gulped a mouthful of water. I wanted to tell her I *did* have to wait. Because that's how it was with Jamie. Our relationship precluded spontaneous get-togethers; they had to be carefully orchestrated, by him. But I guessed she already knew that and was being polite. 'Same to you,' I said. 'I mean, you're always welcome at ours.'

'Thank you.' She looked at me over the rim of her glass, as

though checking I was being serious, and I wondered what she really made of us all; imagined her telling her family that the Abbots were a strange bunch.

There was a cheerful cluster of photos of her family on a desk tucked into an alcove: a smiling older couple who were clearly proud of their daughter judging by their expressions, and an older brother, who looked a lot like Rosa. He and his wife lived in Scotland with their baby twins, and I remembered Rosa telling Mum that her parents had moved up there last year to help out.

Above the desk was a framed commendation certificate for her courage and integrity when responding to a woman threatening to jump off a roof. Not for the first time, I felt a bit shallow for thinking what I did made much of an impact compared to her line of work.

'I'm assuming this has something to do with yesterday,' she said, after taking a small sip of her drink. She crossed to the sofa and sat down, signalling for me to do the same. She was more assured on her own territory, and I had an image of how she must be at work.

'I haven't had any more messages, but someone has been in my studio at Mum and Dad's.' I felt a lurch of embarrassment, knowing she must have seen what was, in effect, a converted shed in their garden. 'I took a picture.' I dipped my hand into my bag, but as I opened the photo gallery, I had a horrible sense of déjà vu and wondered whether the picture would still be there.

It was.

'It's not very clear,' I said, showing her the screen. 'I thought you might be able to find out more about it, the size, what brand, that kind of thing.' As she reached over and took the phone, I had the impression that I was being a bit pathetic and she was privately reframing the scene to replay to Jamie later, but her brow crinkled as she enlarged the image with her fingers and studied it closely. 'There was a robbery next door last week, so it could be the same person.' My mouth felt dry. I picked up my glass and took a couple of sips. 'Mum said you told her off for leaving the keys by the back door.'

She looked up and smiled. 'I wouldn't say told off. But it's surprising how complacent people are about home security.'

'There was no sign of a forced entry.' I winced at the formal wording. 'Someone must have seen the key and swiped it, which wouldn't have been hard considering the back door is always open at this time of year.'

'It's what we call opportunistic crime.' Rosa sounded more official by the second. 'People make themselves easy targets.'

'It doesn't mean they deserve to be robbed.'

Surprise flickered over her face. 'Of course it doesn't.' She touched my phone screen a couple of times. 'I've sent myself a copy of the picture. I'll see what I can do.'

'Oh, right. Thanks.' I felt chastised as I took my phone back. 'Sorry, I didn't mean—'

'Beth, it's fine.' Her eyes were gentle. 'I can see this isn't easy for you.'

I was suddenly close to tears. 'There was a . . . a package too this morning, left on my doorstep. A Lilo.'

'Lilo?'

'An inflatable, like the one I . . . the one I . . .' My breathing came faster.

'The one you had on the sea that day?'

I nodded.

'And you don't know who left it there?'

'No.'

'Do any of your neighbours have CCTV?'

I thought for a second. 'Maybe Lewis and Jude across the road, but it's just for home security. I don't think it covers our side of the road.'

'Are you asking me to launch an official investigation, Beth?'

My breath caught. 'Maybe not official, no, at least not yet.' I pressed my lips together, knowing there was no going back. 'What

78

I told you yesterday, about the man who drowned . . .' I stopped, cleared my throat.

Rosa shifted slightly, her robe falling open to reveal her long, sculpted legs, pale as skimmed milk. She clearly wasn't a sun-worshipper. 'Go on.'

'I've tried to find out about him, on and off over the years,' I said, reducing the frantic hours I'd spent scouring newspaper archives online to a single sentence. 'Never had any luck.'

'Jamie said you wanted to hire a private investigator to trace his family.'

Shit. I couldn't believe he'd told her that. 'It was a long time ago, when I was going through a bad patch.' I shifted out of the glare of sunlight falling across the sofa. 'I thought if I could find them and . . . I don't know, apologise, or something. Tell them how grateful I was, that his sacrifice hadn't been wasted . . .' My words petered out.

'But you didn't?' she prompted softly.

'I was told that even if I did discover who he was, it might make things worse.' I remembered the feeling of powerlessness. 'It could give his family a focus for any anger they might feel.'

'And you think this is what's happening now?'

I looked at her, grateful she understood. 'Maybe.'

'And you'd like me to find out?'

'You probably have resources you can use.'

Rosa nodded briefly. 'A national database. His death will have been recorded somewhere and of course there'll be a coroner's report.'

A shiver fluttered across my chest, hearing her say it so baldly.

'I know death records are available to the public, but without a name to go on I had no chance.' I hesitated, feeling as if I was standing on a precipice. 'And you think you could find his relatives?'

She regarded me for a moment then placed her glass of water on the floorboards. 'What are you planning to do with the infor-mation, if I do find something?'

79

For a moment, I could only hear the blood swooshing in my ears. 'Just talk.' My voice sounded small. 'Say sorry, I don't know. Ask, why? Why are they doing this now?' I held up my phone. 'Ask what they're hoping to achieve, tell them they can't punish me any more than I've punished myself—'

'Except, they can.' Rosa's voice cut me off.

'Sorry?'

'If, as you claim, your life's been threatened, that shows intent to do harm.'

My mind reared away. 'Or to scare me.' I dropped my phone in my bag. 'They want me to *think* they mean harm, but really it's a reminder that . . .' I looked around unseeingly, '. . . that life is precious and can be taken away at any minute, but I know that already, Rosa, I don't need reminding. I'm reminded at work every day, hearing people's stories, the terrible things they've been through. I know how precious life is, I have a daughter for God's sake.' I stood up, too agitated to sit still. 'What would happen to Hayley, if something happens to me?' I stared at Rosa, not giving her time to reply. 'She needs me – I'm her mum. I can't stand by and let something happen to me. I want to be in her life, even if someone thinks I don't deserve it.' I covered my face with my hands, my shoulders shaking, jumping when gentle fingers landed on my arm.

'It's going to be OK, Beth.'

I lowered my hands and looked at Rosa in front of me, solid and sure in spite of her towel and robe. 'Murder's rare in real life, if that's what's worrying you,' she said. 'It's incredibly hard to kill someone in cold blood. It's usually a crime of passion, committed in the heat of the moment, often fuelled by alcohol or drugs, or by someone who's mentally ill, or a psychopath.' She gave my arm a comforting rub. 'Believe me, Beth, those are rarer than you think, despite what you see on TV. Cases like that make the news precisely because that's what they are. Big news – not stuff that happens every day.'

Her words were comforting. For a moment, I wanted to lean in and hug her, but her hand fell away and she took a step back, as if remembering we didn't know each other very well.

I wiped tears from under my eyes. 'I can see why Jamie wants to hang on to you,' I said with a watery smile. 'He's a lucky man.' A look crossed her face, like the sun going in. 'Is everything OK?' I said, carefully. 'Between you and Jamie, I mean?'

'Fine.' Her expression grew guarded as she turned, touching the towel around her head as if she'd forgotten it was there. 'I should take this off and dry my hair,' she said, a smile darting over her lips. 'It'll look terrible, otherwise.'

'I don't want to pry, but—'

'Your brother.' She paused, fixing her gaze on the window. The sun had shifted, illuminating her face. She looked older suddenly, her eyes radiating sadness.

'Rosa, what is it?'

'Oh, nothing, really.' Her fingers smoothed the edge of her robe. 'He thinks I spend too much time at work, that's all, and he's probably right.'

Oh, Jamie. 'But he knows how much you love your job. He's proud of you.'

'I know.' She looked down, addressing her words to the floor. 'About what we've just discussed,' she said, 'I'd rather he didn't know, if you don't mind.'

'Rosa, I'm so sorry.' Shame washed through me. I hadn't thought what an awkward position I was putting her in. 'The last thing I want is to get between you and Jamie. He's so sensitive about the past.'

When her eyebrows popped up in mock surprise, I nearly laughed with relief that she could see the understatement. 'Exactly!' I smiled. 'So, forget I said anything. I'll figure it out myself.'

'No, no. I want to help,' she said firmly. 'If it gives you answers, or peace of mind, or stops something awful happening, it'll be good for everyone, including Jamie.'

So, they *were* having problems. 'I won't say anything, I promise.'

We looked at each other solemnly, then I checked the time. Matt would be on his way to pick Hayley up from her dance class. 'I have to go,' I said. 'Could I quickly use your bathroom?'

'Of course.' Her professional persona back in place, she inclined her head towards the door. 'You know where it is.'

I used the toilet, absently admiring the small, minimalist room – as tidy as the rest of the apartment – then stared at myself in the mirrored cabinet over the sink as I washed my hands. At least there was no outward sign of my inner turmoil. I didn't want Hayley or Matt picking up that anything was wrong.

I smoothed my hair behind my ears, then straightened the towel on the rail, feeling a pang of remorse when I noticed Rosa's clothes in a heap by the laundry basket and remembered she'd been trying to relax before going to work.

There wasn't much sign of Jamie, apart from a bottle of shampoo on the side of the bath that I recognised as his favourite brand. He was fussy about personal grooming, and spent a fortune on toiletries.

On my way to say goodbye to Rosa, I paused and glanced inside the main bedroom, where Rosa's police uniform was hanging neatly on the wardrobe door, the pillows on the bed plump and inviting. Next door was the room Jamie used as a study, slightly ajar. I pushed it wider and went in, knocking over a pair of his work boots just inside, blinking through the gloom.

The room was at the back of the house, and the curtains were pulled across the window, but there was no mistaking the mess. Jamie's surfboard was propped against one wall, next to a blown-up image of him riding a wave that I could hardly bear to look at. If my way of coping with what had happened in the past was to stay away from the sea, my brother's had been to embrace it, learning to surf and sail on holidays in Cornwall with friends, as if trying to prove a point, though I'd never quite worked out what it was.

On the desk that housed his laptop and printer, sheets of A4 paper spilled onto the floor. He did his own accounts, despite being able to afford to pay someone to do them for him, but I knew it was his way of staying in control.

About to close the door, I noticed a balled-up sheet of copier paper on the floor beside the shredder, as if Jamie had thrown it there. It was covered in printed words – or rather, one word. Moving closer, I saw the word LIFE typed over and over in different fonts and sizes, covering the entire page.

A LIFE FOR A LIFE.

'Beth?'

Heart racing, I backed out of the room, bashing my elbow on the doorframe.

'You forgot your bag,' said Rosa, dangling it from her fingers. 'You're brave going in there.' She gave a small grimace. 'I'm not allowed.'

'Not allowed?'

'Let's just say, I don't mind.' Her tone was wry. 'He's very untidy.'

'He always was – you should have seen the state of his bedroom when he was a teenager.' I felt disloyal, talking about him like that, but couldn't stop spouting words. 'It looks like he's been doing a lot of printing.'

Rosa nodded. 'He's designing some flyers to post through doors,' she said. 'He's keen to find more business.'

I nodded, trying to smile as I took my bag. 'Thanks,' I said. 'And I'm sorry again for dropping in like this.'

'No problem.' She followed me to the door, leaning past to help with the latch. 'I'll keep you posted.'

I hurried downstairs and out onto the pavement, blinking in the brightness as I dashed to my car. As I fumbled with my seatbelt and started the engine, all I could think was, what if the threat to my life had nothing to do with the man who'd drowned at all?

What if it was closer to home?

Chapter 12

'Do you know where Jamie is? He's not answering his phone.'

'Actually, he's here,' Dad said cheerfully. He wasn't as attuned to my tone as Mum was. 'I just got back from a job and he was here, tinkering with my old bike in the garage.'

'Your bike?' I said, momentarily distracted.

'He's thinking of taking up cycling.'

'Right, I'm on my way over.'

'Beth, what—?'

I rang off, too wound up to explain, and called Matt. 'Could you drop Hayley at Pam's?' I said, hoping my voice sounded even. 'I'm going to be a bit late back.'

'Sure.' He paused. 'Everything OK?'

'Why shouldn't it be?'

'No reason; you've never asked me before, that's all.'

'Well, I'm asking now.'

I ended the call and drove back to my parents', not really thinking about what I was going to say to Jamie, only that I needed to look him in the face. Surely then I'd know if . . . *if what?* If he really did hate me enough to wish me dead?

Pulling up outside the house, I could see him in the garage, crouched by Dad's old mountain bike, one hand on the saddle as he examined the front wheel. For a second, I was overtaken by a powerful memory of Dad teaching us to cycle in the lane at the side of the house, one hand on the back of each bike as we wobbled precariously, shrieking with fright and excitement. Pushing the image away, I got out of the car and strode through the gate, fuelled by something hot and dangerous. 'Can I have a word?'

Jamie's head whipped up, surprise flashing over his face. Dad mustn't have mentioned I was coming. He'd have scarpered if he'd known.

My brother straightened with a wary glance, and wiped his oil-grimed hands on his work overalls. 'What's up?'

'Have a guess, Jamie.'

His light brown eyes narrowed. He wasn't used to me challenging him. I let him get away with his barbs and putdowns because I felt responsible and knew they helped him feel better in some small way. 'I don't know what you're talking about.'

'You want me dead?'

'*What?*'

His incredulous laugh set off a spark of fury and everything I'd kept inside since my birthday bubbled over. 'Why now? After all this time, Jamie, why now?' When he didn't respond, I ploughed on. 'You have a good life, you have Rosa. Why do you still want to punish me?' I shot forward and gave him a shove. 'Do you really hate me that much?'

'Beth, stop it.' Dad was there, pulling me back as I lunged at Jamie again, batting at his forearms, which he'd raised to defend himself. 'What are you doing?'

'What on earth's going on?' Mum appeared, her face stretched with shock. 'What's happened?'

I broke from Dad's clutch. 'Just tell the truth, Jamie.'

'About what?' Dad looked between us, pale beneath his summer tan.

Jamie's lips had compressed into an angry line. 'Apparently, Beth thinks I want her dead.'

Mum's wide-eyed gaze swung from me to Jamie. 'Do you?' Seeming to realise it was the wrong thing to say, she slapped her hand to her mouth. 'Jamie, I—'

'Don't bother apologising.' He curled his lip. 'You'll take her side as always.'

'Come on now.' Dad patted the air between us. 'There are no sides. We're a family, a team, and we shouldn't be fighting.'

'You must be joking.' Jamie's voice shook a little. 'A team of three, maybe.'

'Oh, Jamie, we've never made you feel like that.' Mum sounded on the verge of tears, her fingers laced under her chin. 'I don't understand what just happened.'

Seeing my parents' stricken faces, my anger burned out as fast as it had ignited, leaving shame in its wake. Despite the atmosphere whenever we got together, we hadn't come close to a confrontation for years. 'I shouldn't have come,' I said. 'I'm sorry.'

'What's this about?' Mum's lips wobbled. 'What's going on, Beth?'

'Yes, what's going on, Beth?' Jamie's voice was as hard as the look he gave me. 'What is it you think I've done?'

Unconsciously, Mum and Dad had moved closer to me, one on either side, as though I needed protecting. Catching Jamie's look of contempt, I could see that in spite of the front he put on most of the time, his resentment of me was as strong as ever.

'Forget it,' I said. 'It's not like you're going to tell the truth, is it?'

'The truth about what?' Dad looked bewildered. He was wearing the baggy shorts and sun-faded T-shirt he changed into after work, ready to sit in the garden with a glass of beer, and now I'd turned up and ruined his evening. 'What is it you think he's done, Beth?'

'Don't worry about it.' My tone was falsely bright. 'Obviously my mistake.'

'Something must have happened.' Mum's eyes pleaded with me to deny it.

I couldn't bear to look at her expression. 'Just a prank, I expect,' I said, in the same bracing tone. 'I'll get to the bottom of it, don't worry.'

I cast Jamie one last look as I left, trying to read his face, but his features looked cast in stone. I was no nearer knowing the truth than I had been when I arrived.

As soon as I entered the house, I heard running water. My heart jerked. It was a noise that still brought back the sound of the sea that day at Perran Cove.

Shaking off thoughts of my showdown with Jamie, I swiftly checked the kitchen, then took the stairs two at a time, wondering whether I'd left the shower running that morning. It wasn't like me, but my mind had been otherwise occupied. I stopped on the landing. The sound was coming from the main bathroom. Maybe Vic had come over early and was taking a bath. I hadn't noticed his car outside, but the parking restrictions meant he often had to leave it round the corner.

'Vic?' I nudged the door, already knowing there was no one inside. If he'd fancied an early bath, even if he wasn't busy all day with patients, he'd have gone to his house, five minutes from the hospital.

'Hello?' Hating the timid sound of my voice – *had I really yelled at Jamie, less than ten minutes ago?* – I shoved the door so hard it bounced off the wall and I had to throw out a hand to stop it slamming in my face. The room was empty, Hayley's nightdress draped over the little pink footstool she used to clean her teeth at the sink. My gaze moved to the bath. The taps were running slowly, water spilling smoothly over the side, like an infinity pool.

'Shit!' I pitched forward, feet slipping through half an inch of water on the black and white tiles. I caught sight of my frantic reflection in the water, and for a terrifying second, imagined someone looming behind me, pressing my head under the water and holding me there until I stopped moving. With a gasp of fright, I plunged my hand in and yanked the plug out, looking away as the water glugged and swirled down the drain.

I sank to my knees, arm dangling over the bath, willing my brain to stop screaming and start thinking rationally. The taps must have been left running, and I hadn't noticed. Perhaps Vic had started to run a bath before leaving for work, after a hot and sticky night, and changed his mind. *Highly unlikely.* Hayley would have noticed when she came in to clean her teeth while I was talking to Matt downstairs. Unless she'd turned the tap on. But surely I'd have heard water running at the time?

My mind shied away from the alternative – that someone had been in the house while I was out. Had done it purposely, to scare me. It would explain why water wasn't gushing through the ceiling downstairs as it would have been if the tap had been running all day. *Jamie?* It wasn't as if he had an employer who could vouch for his whereabouts.

Recalling the hard look he'd given me in the garage at our parents' house, I dropped my forehead onto my arm, wetness seeping through the knees of my trousers. This couldn't be happening. The front door had been locked so . . .

My head whipped up. The bathroom window was open. I hadn't checked before leaving the house. It must have been ajar all night and it was just about feasible that somebody could have climbed up the drainpipe outside and levered themselves through. There was no sign anything had been disturbed, but that didn't mean anything.

Springing into action, I grabbed some towels and threw them down to soak up the worst of the water, then kicked off my soggy sneakers and ran round the house, scanning each room. As far as I could tell, everything was as it should be.

Breathless, I sank on the bottom stair and pushed my hands through my hair, tugging the roots. It was a warning; it had to be.

'Mummy!'

I nearly screamed when Hayley hurled herself at me and threw

88

her arms around my neck. I'd left the front door wide open and the smell of her, mingled with sunshine and ice-cream dispelled my fear.

'Hey, you.' I hugged her tightly, looking up at Matt. 'I thought you were dropping her at Pam's.'

He shrugged. 'I wanted to spend some more time with her.'

'Aren't you working?' It was a silly question. Matt was freelance and set his own hours.

'I've just finished a project,' he said. 'I'm having a bit of time off.'

'I did a swan dance. I'll show you later, Mummy.' Hayley let go of me and raced through the house to look for Baxter in Pam's garden.

'She loves those classes.' As Matt hovered on the threshold, watching Hayley go with a nostalgic look, I had a flashback to him in the delivery room while I was in labour. He'd broken the speed limit on the way to the hospital, after my waters broke on the way to the airport to visit his parents in France. Once there, he grew calm, talking me through my rapid contractions, gripping my hand throughout.

He'd joked during my pregnancy that he'd like our baby to arrive walking, talking and potty-trained, but from the moment he held Hayley in his arms, it was obvious he was besotted. 'You were in my heart before you were born and will be there as long as it's beating,' he'd sung softly, his love immediately expanding to include our daughter.

When we'd talked about trying for a baby as soon as we were married, I'd worried about what sort of mother I'd be, scared I wasn't up to the task. I cried with happiness and relief when I held her to my breast, marvelling at her shell-like fingernails and delicate nose while we tried to work out who she most resembled; my chin, Matt's hair and eyes – definitely her father's daughter, but mine too.

We'd rained down promises: the sort all parents probably make, about keeping her safe, protecting her always and giving her siblings to play with.

Now, it felt as if we were failing her. *I'd* failed her, pushing Matt away as my feelings of survivor's guilt gradually resurfaced – what right did *I* have to be a parent when a man was dead because of me? I'd doubled my efforts when I returned to work, trying to make a difference, while throwing myself into being the perfect mother at home, until there was no energy left for my marriage.

'Are you OK?' Matt was studying my hot face. 'Why are you sitting on the stairs, looking as if the world is about to collapse?' *Because it is.* 'And why are your knees wet?'

Avoiding his stare, I said, 'What have you been doing all this time?'

'It's not that late.' He looked at the watch that once belonged to his grandfather and had an old-fashioned winding mechanism. 'I thought we'd get a milkshake on the way home. Dancing's thirsty work.'

'A milkshake's not a proper drink.' Why was I being such a bitch?

'Come on, Beth. One every now and then won't do her any harm.' He rubbed a hand round his jaw. 'I seem to remember you being partial to a milkshake, once upon a time.'

Another jagged memory, of us with Emma and the boyfriend she was seeing at the time, in McDonald's after watching a gig in London, me five months pregnant, choosing a strawberry milkshake because I'd been craving one since my morning sickness had eased. 'Not for a long time,' I said.

He glanced down. 'I like the barefoot look.'

Maybe he was remembering the time he'd painted my toenails with a look of fierce concentration that had made my heart contract. 'The bathroom's flooded.'

'What?' He glanced past me to the top of the stairs. 'How come?'

'Someone left a tap running and the plug in the bath.' I was being heavy on the sarcasm.

'Bit careless.' Matt's tone was guarded, as though trying not to say the wrong thing, and I suddenly longed for the early days

90

of our relationship when we had no boundaries and could tell each other everything.

'There's no real damage,' I said, in case he was having visions of the ceiling collapsing. 'I should go and dry the floor.'

There was a squeal of laughter from Hayley in the garden and the sound of Pam's voice, followed by a bark of excitement from Baxter.

'Thought any more about getting a dog?' Matt hooked his thumbs in the front pockets of his jeans, seeming reluctant to let me leave. 'She said Pam knows someone with puppies for sale.'

I felt a zip of anger as I pushed to my feet. 'I asked Pam not to say anything to get Hayley's hopes up.'

Matt looked taken aback at my tone. 'I don't know if Pam told her directly, maybe she overheard—'

'Why were you lurking about in the garden last night?' I cut in. 'Pam saw you, looking at your phone.'

He lowered his head. 'I wanted to give you the paint set,' he said quietly. 'It felt odd, not being part of your birthday. I was going to knock, but I could see you were having a good time and didn't want to intrude.'

'You were spying on me?'

'Christ, Beth, no!' He looked at me, annoyance flitting over his face. 'I wasn't *spying* as you so charmingly put it. I thought you wouldn't want me there, with Vic playing man of the house.' He paused to let the jibe settle. 'I considered phoning to say happy birthday but didn't, and then I left, OK?'

I swallowed to ease the tightness in my throat. 'So, you didn't send me a message?'

He looked thrown. 'Should I have done?'

The fight went out of me. 'I don't know,' I said. 'Sorry. I'm a bit all over the place at the moment.'

'Work?' He used to worry about the emotional pressure that came with my job, before he grew to resent it for seeming more important to me than our family.

91

'No, it's not work.'

'Being thirty-three?' Reaching out, he gently flicked my arm. 'You're still two years younger than me.' I tried to smile, but my mouth trembled. 'What is it, Beth?'

'I'm fine.'

Ignoring this blatant lie, he said, 'Is it "the holiday"?' putting quote marks around the words with his voice. 'You know you don't have to go.'

'I do want to go,' I said sharply. 'I have to, for Hayley's sake. I don't want her growing up scared of the sea like me.'

'But to go to the place where it happened . . .' He shook his head. 'Is it what you'd advise a "client"?'

'What's with the quote marks?' I felt my brow furrow. 'And you know we don't advise our clients; that's not what we do. We—'

'Provide a safe space for them to explore their feelings, I know.' His voice was quieter too, and I couldn't work out whether he was making fun of me.

'Someone sent me a text on my birthday, saying it would be my last.' I had an irrational urge to hurt him. 'Was it you?'

'What?'

'That inflatable you brought in, yesterday.'

'What about it?'

'Are you messing with me, Matt?'

For a second, he looked genuinely confused. 'For God's sake, Beth, what are you talking about?' There was a heavy beat of silence before he held out his hand. 'Show me these messages.'

'How do I know you're not acting?' My voice bounced back, too sharp.

'Show me.'

I looked away from the heat in his eyes. 'I can't – they've gone.'

'That's convenient.' His words were hard-edged, and when I glanced up, I was met with a flinty gaze. 'If anyone's sending you messages, Beth, it'll be one of your patients,' he said. 'Have you reported it to someone at Fernley House?'

92

'That *would* be convenient, wouldn't it?' I gave a disbelieving laugh, even though I hadn't completely discounted it being one of my clients. 'Easy to blame someone with mental health problems.'

His shrug was short and angry. 'Isn't that the obvious answer?'

'For you, maybe.'

'Why the hell would I want to hurt you?'

His expression was too hard to look at, so I stared instead at his shadow, stretching long and thin on the path behind him. 'You still have a key for the house.'

'Yes, but I don't just turn up and let myself in.' The words *even though I could if I wanted to* hovered in the air. He could have driven over and left the bath taps running while Hayley was at her dance class. 'I thought you knew me, Beth.'

'I don't know what to think right now.'

'If you're taking this seriously, you should talk to the police,' he said grimly. 'I've got nothing to hide.'

'Maybe I already have.' I checked him for a reaction, but he'd half turned, pushing his hair off his forehead. 'I don't like this, Beth.'

'Me neither.' I curled my hand around the edge of the door, lowering my voice as Hayley clattered into the kitchen. 'I've got to go.'

'Listen, maybe it's just as well I'm taking Hayley away for a few days.' His tone had toughened again. 'You obviously need some space to sort out whatever's going on.' Our eyes collided and I felt a spinning sensation. 'Out of curiosity,' he added. 'Have you accused Vic?'

My grip on the door tightened. 'I didn't accuse you of anything,' I said. 'I'm asking everyone.'

Anger tightened his brow. 'Everyone but Vic,' he said tightly. 'You're blind where he's concerned.'

I stared, cheeks burning. 'What's that supposed to mean?'

'It means, he got his feet under the table pretty fast, didn't he?' Matt had said it before, but the words hit harder this time. 'You do know he took advantage of you when you were vulnerable?'

'Oh, Matt, just stop it.' There was a ridge of unshed tears in my throat. 'You couldn't be more wrong about him.'

Matt took a step back, palms raised. His eyes, once bright and warm, were lit with battle. 'Don't say I didn't warn you.'

He turned and strode away. I wanted desperately to call him back and apologise for crossing a line, beg him to tell me the truth, but he was starting his car and I could only watch as it pulled away – a black Renault he bought after our split, replacing the motorbike he'd ridden for years; a car I'd never sat in with him.

I closed the front door and leaned my forehead against it, swallowing tears and forcing breath through my body.

'Mummy, please, please, *pleeeease* can we get a dog? I promise I'll look after it by myself.' I spun round to see Hayley with her hands clasped under her chin, rocking from foot to foot. 'I want to call it Biff and he can play with Baxter.' Biff was the star of her favourite book, *Dogs Don't Do Ballet*. 'Please, please,' she implored. 'Daddy said if I asked you nicely, you might say yes.'

I tried to smile, pushing aside an image of Matt's angry face, which had superimposed itself over Jamie's furious expression, and my dad's look of dread. *Who else was I going to upset today?* 'Let's think about it after our holidays,' I heard myself say, and as she squealed and hugged my knees, I resolved to have a word with Pam for breaking her promise to not say anything about the puppies. 'Did you leave the bath tap running this morning?'

She tipped her head up and gave an uncertain frown. 'I get my bath after dinner.'

'I know you do, sweetie.'

It wasn't until Hayley was tucking into fish fingers with chopped carrots and cucumber, chatting about her friend Sukie at dance class, that it hit me again like a kick to the stomach that if the threat was real – if whoever had sent the messages really meant to harm me – I might not be around to see my daughter cuddle a puppy.

Chapter 13

'Beth, are you absolutely certain *you* didn't leave the bath taps running?' Vic was in the kitchen, cooking pasta with fresh tomatoes, chilli and herbs. I'd left him to it while I supervised Hayley's bedtime. 'Don't look at me like that,' he added, holding up a wooden spoon as if to ward off an attack.

'Honestly, Vic, don't you think I'd remember something like that?'

'It's just odd, that's all.'

'Not if it's part of someone's plan to freak me out.'

He swivelled to look at me properly. His eyes were pouched with tiredness. I guessed he'd had a disturbed night, thanks to my tossing and turning, and felt a stab of guilt. 'Who has a key to the house?'

My heart skipped a beat. I knew what was coming. 'Pam next door, in case of an emergency,' I said. 'But she'd hardly come in and turn on my bath taps, would she?'

'Doesn't Matt still have a front door key?' He turned back to the pan. His shoulders were relaxed as he stirred, but I knew he didn't like that Matt could potentially come into the house any time he wanted.

'He wouldn't turn up uninvited,' I said, remembering too late he'd done just that, and he'd brought me a birthday gift too. He was probably regretting that now. I tried to remember where I'd left the box of paints. 'Why would he do something so awful?' The question was directed as much to myself as Vic.

He turned down the heat under the pan, moved to the fridge and took out a jar. 'Maybe he's hoping you'll turn to him for support.' He tipped some capers into the pan on the hob, his movements as slick as a chef's, never rushed or clumsy. 'It's obvious he still loves you.'

The words rang between us like a bell, clear and true. I remembered Matt's reaction when I told him I'd met someone new. How – white-faced – he admitted he thought that once I'd had some space, I'd realise we were meant to be together, that it had been hard for him to stay away for so long.

'And he's trying to win me back by threatening me, tapping into my worst fears?' I said, shakily. 'Not a brilliant plan.'

'I think he'd like full custody of Hayley.' Vic carefully stirred the pasta. 'Perhaps he's trying to paint you as an unfit mother.'

Though quietly spoken, his words reverberated through me. I hoisted myself onto one of the kitchen stools at the breakfast bar. 'We agreed joint custody, no courts, no disruption, to keep things as settled as possible for Hayley,' I said. 'Nothing's changed.'

'He doesn't like you being with me.' Vic picked up the chopping board and rinsed it at the sink. 'Now he realises we're serious, that things will have to be made official, it might have tipped him over the edge,' he said. 'And it must be hard for him, seeing another man around his daughter, hearing her talk about me.' He threw me a loaded glance over his shoulder. 'Who better to mess with your head than someone who knows you so well?'

Sickness fizzed in my stomach as his words sank in. The thought that the culprit was a stranger was frightening enough, but hearing Vic confirm my theory that it could be someone I knew, a loved one, was truly terrifying. 'I don't know,' I said.

My thoughts pinballed from Jamie, who'd resented me for more than twenty years, to Matt, who'd been there when the inflatable appeared; he'd been in the garden on my birthday too, and this morning had turned up out of the blue. I could hardly bear to believe he was trying to scare me in a warped attempt to win me back, or get custody of Hayley, but it seemed like too much of a coincidence. The text messages . . . they didn't seem like the sort of thing Matt would stoop to, but maybe I didn't know him that well anymore.

I decided not to tell Vic about Matt's visit this morning for now. It would only fuel his suspicions. Hayley hadn't mentioned her dad taking her to school. If she did, I could say he'd got the date wrong. I needed to be sure before I took things any further—

'It might be best to keep contact with Matt to a minimum,' Vic said, making me jump. 'And the sooner we start looking for a place of our own, the better.'

'Hang on, what did you mean, by *make things official*?' I tried desperately to shake off my chaotic thoughts. 'Was that some sort of proposal?'

When he turned, his relief at the change of topic was evident. It must have been hard for him to say those things about Matt. He'd probably thought about it all day, trying to decipher the most likely explanation. 'Maybe not quite yet,' he said, a smile cutting across his face. He looked younger when he smiled, like the version of him I'd seen in old photos from his time at medical school, with friends, and his older sister, Fran, who was a paediatric nurse in Ontario.

I'd spoken to her once, via Skype, when Vic decided we should 'meet', a bit drunk after his Christmas party with colleagues from the hospital. Though she was stunning, a female version of Vic with raven hair and deep brown eyes, I'd found her a bit stiff and cold – though it might have been that the time difference meant she'd just woken after a long shift.

'She couldn't wait to get away from the UK,' Vic had said, when ten minutes of stilted conversation ended abruptly as the screen froze on her face mid-sentence then went black. 'She never got over losing our parents, hated living with our aunt. Once she'd hung around long enough to see me graduate, she left and never looked back.'

He'd rarely spoken about his family until then, and hearing the sadness of loss in his voice, I understood why. Vic was all about looking forward, or living in the present – the same philosophy we tried to foster in our clients at Fernley House – but I knew he felt the lack of family, and I'd questioned why he didn't want children of his own.

'I couldn't bear them to go through what my sister and me went through if anything happened to us,' he'd said.

Now, his smile broadened. 'I was thinking about us getting our own place before I put a ring on it.' He spoke with such a typical mix of playfulness and formality I couldn't help smiling back.

'Not the most romantic way to ask for my hand in marriage.' I repressed a mental image of Matt in the living room at Mum and Dad's, after we'd been out for a meal and they'd gone to bed, when he'd brought me a cup of tea and a biscuit, dropped to his knees in front of me and said, 'I think we should get married.' Worried Vic might guess my train of thought, I added quickly, 'I'd have to get divorced first,' surprised by the pang of pain the word produced.

'That's what I really meant about making things official.' Vic picked up the pan and started spooning food onto plates. 'I think Matt might have guessed where things are heading.'

My smile had slipped. 'Right.'

'You know, you can love, protect and respect someone, but you can never own or possess them, and shouldn't want to,' he said quietly. 'It's something Matt needs to learn.'

Looking at the wooden bowl of salad leaves on the worktop, in various shades of green, shiny with oil and balsamic vinegar, I felt a plunge of despair. I wanted so badly to live in the present, but couldn't escape my past.

Did Matt want to keep me there?

'By the way, I got you a personal alarm,' Vic said. 'I think you should keep it with you until this thing is resolved.'

With a superhuman effort, I resurrected my smile. 'What, you just popped out to Tesco and picked one up in your lunch break?'

His mouth twitched. 'Actually, we keep a few at the hospital, since one of the staff had a stalker who kept turning up when there was no one else around.'

I shuddered as we took our plates and cutlery into the living room. The doors to the garden were open, the room soft with peachy light, the air scented with jasmine. After checking the intercom was working, in case Hayley woke up and needed me, I sat on the sofa beside Vic, trying to soften my muscles and get comfy; to empty my mind, at least until I'd eaten.

Vic picked up the remote and aimed it at the TV. 'Let's hope Rosa can get to the bottom of things, before we go away,' he said. 'Does your brother know?'

My fingers tensed round my fork. I hadn't even mentioned confronting my brother, earlier. 'That Rosa's on the case?'

Vic nodded, shaking a paper napkin across his lap.

'He doesn't.' I thought of the word I'd seen printed over and over on the copier paper in Jamie's study. 'You know what he's like,' I said, tension knotting the back of my neck once more. 'He'll accuse me of raking up the past again. Rosa said she'd rather we didn't tell him.'

'I can't say I blame her.' Vic's voice dipped into disapproval. 'The way he behaves towards you at times makes me wonder whether *he* might have something to do with what's going on.' Jamie hadn't taken to Vic the way he had to Matt, despite Vic's efforts to be friendly. He'd gone as far as telling me I was an idiot to let Matt go.

'You thought it was my husband a few minutes ago.' I was aware that I was being a hypocrite, accusing Vic of jumping to conclusions, when I'd done the same thing myself.

99

Vic gave me a long, focused glance. 'I'm as in the dark as you are,' he said. 'We're just discussing possibilities here.'

'Well, I've spoken to Jamie.' My gaze fell on the paint box on the floor by the armchair where I'd left it that morning. It seemed to pulse with light and colour and I knew I should tell Vic where it had come from. *Would Matt have brought me a gift, if he was trying to scare me?*

'When?' Vic's eyes were still on me, his fork poised over his plate.

'After work,' I said, glossing over the details, aware I was holding things back again without really knowing why. 'He says it's nothing to do with him.'

'Well, he would, wouldn't he?' Vic ate a mouthful of food, chewing purposefully. 'I bet he didn't take it well.'

'He didn't.' I pushed my pasta around, wishing with all my heart that my parents hadn't witnessed the exchange. How was I going to explain myself to them? What had Jamie told them after I left? My phone had rung as I drove home, but seeing Mum's number flash up, I'd ignored it.

Now, as if attuned to my thoughts, my phone vibrated with a text.

'Shall I get it?' Vic tensed, fork halfway to his mouth, but I'd already risen and snatched my phone from my bag. There were a couple of messages from Mum, but it was the latest text that made my heart leap.

'It's Rosa.' I sat down and scanned her message; the first I'd ever received from her. 'Apparently, Jamie told her I'd been to see him.' My mouth dried. 'She hasn't told him I went to see her too.'

He was pretty upset, Beth, she'd written. *I wish you'd told me you suspected him.*

My face burned with shame.

Things have been tricky between us lately. What did that mean? *I'm not going to tell him I'm looking into things for you, because I know he'll be angry and will ask me not to. Just wanted to let you know. Rosa.*

'Maybe she could keep an eye on Matt too.' Vic had put down his plate and shifted closer to read the message. He put his arm around my shoulders. 'Will you ask her?'

I leaned against him. 'I'll think about it,' I said. I hated lying again, but couldn't face involving Rosa any further than I already had; couldn't bear giving voice to my concerns about Matt to anyone else. 'Can you pass me the wine?'

After another restless night, I decided to take matters into my own hands and call Jamie the following morning after dropping Hayley at school. When I'd watched her skip up the playground, holding her best friend Daisy's hand, looking forward to the last day of term before the summer holidays, I got back in the car and phoned him.

'Jamie Abbot,' my brother said, in the smiling tone he used with everyone but me. He must not have registered it was my number, we called each other so rarely.

'Hey, it's Beth.' My voice was brittle.

'Now what do you want?' He'd switched to coldly furious. 'Haven't you done enough damage for one week?'

'Did you tell Mum and Dad what it was about?'

'No, don't worry, sis. I didn't want to burst their little denial bubble. Let's pretend everything's fine in the Abbot family.' His tone was flat. 'I'm assuming you're one of us again, since you broke up with Matt.'

I wasn't; not just because it was easier to have the same surname as Hayley, but because it hadn't crossed my mind to change it back.

'Jamie, I . . .' I closed my eyes briefly. 'Things are a bit weird at the moment.'

'Mum tried calling you when you left.'

'I know,' I said. I'd read her texts before bed.

Whatever you're going through, we can help, love. We're here if you need us. XX

Whatever Jamie's done, you know he didn't mean it. He loves you, we all do. XX

I'd replied, thanking her and apologising for my outburst, knowing it was what she wanted to hear, though I knew she'd still be fretting even as she reassured Dad it was 'nothing' just 'brother and sister stuff' as she'd done so often over the years. 'It's fine, I smoothed it over,' I said, thinking about the power of words, how they had the ability to distort as well as reassure. Did Mum believe me? I doubted it.

'So, what was it all about?' Jamie said. 'Why do you think I want you dead?'

I couldn't tell him about the balled-up paper I'd seen in his study without admitting I'd been to see Rosa when she didn't want him to know. 'Someone sent me some texts on my birthday, and . . . there was some other stuff too.'

'So, go to the police.' His tone grew challenging. 'Isn't that what any normal person would do if they've had a death threat, rather than accuse their own brother?'

Interesting that he didn't suggest talking to Rosa when he mentioned the police. Could he be calling my bluff?

'Rosa mentioned you were making some flyers to promote the business,' I said to divert him.

'When?'

Shit. 'At my party the other evening.'

'What's that got to do with anything?'

'I'm just showing an interest, that's all.'

'Beth, you can't accuse me of threatening you one minute, then be all friendly the next. That's not normal.' I couldn't think of a response and wished I hadn't called. 'Anyway, how did she know about that?' he said, sharply. 'She must have been in my office.'

I remembered what Rosa had told me. 'Isn't she allowed in there?'

'It's private.' He pushed out a sigh. 'Not that it's any of your business.'

Despite it being the longest conversation I'd had with my brother in ages, I wanted it to end. We never talked properly, not in a friendly way, about anything that really mattered. 'Does this flyer have the word *life* in it?' It wasn't subtle, but it was too late to take it back. 'As in, *A LIFE FOR A LIFE?*'

I had no idea what I expected him to say. *Oh yes, like on the note I left on your car, months ago, because . . . why?*

'What are you on about?' He was wary now. 'I can't remember. I didn't get very far with it.'

I wished I could see his face, but then again, I hadn't been able to read him yesterday. It struck me that he'd got better at hiding his feelings.

'Look, I've got to go, I'm on my way to a job,' he said. 'We can't all afford to go to work when we feel like it.'

'Jay, that's not fair,' I began, but he'd gone.

I looked at my phone through a blur of tears. He'd seemed different after meeting Rosa. There was a glimpse of the man he'd become; a man I could see getting married and becoming a father one day. Was this the real him, still simmering under the surface, desperate to punish his sister for ruining his childhood?

How bad *were* things between him and Rosa?

I took out a tissue and blew my nose. All the other mothers at the school gates had gone, some to coffee mornings I wasn't invited to, because everyone knew I worked at Fernley House.

I drove there on autopilot, uncaring whether anyone might be following me. If Jamie had sent the texts and left the message on my car, I doubted he'd risk tailing me now in his van, especially during work hours.

Something struck me. His girlfriend was a police officer, so how did he think he'd get away with any of it? Unless he didn't care. If their relationship was under strain – if he thought Rosa was planning to leave him like all the others – perhaps he'd had enough. *Deal with the cause not the problem.* I knew on some level Jamie thought I was the cause of his problems, and as horrible as it was, and as terrible as I felt for suspecting him, it wasn't much of a stretch to think he might want to be rid of me altogether.

103

Chapter 14

Vic had given me the personal alarm, which I'd attached to my keyring. He'd warned me not to set it off by accident as it was the loudest on the market, with an ear-piercing siren that could be heard for miles.

'Sounds perfect,' I'd said, comforted by its solid feel and huge activation button. 'What if I can't get it out of my bag in time?'

'You could always wear it on a cord around your neck.'

'Someone could strangle me with it.'

'You've definitely watched too much *CSI*.'

I'd decided to keep it either in my hand, or where I could easily grab it, and felt less afraid as I got out of the car at Fernley House and caught up with Marianne, who was heading inside.

'You look better than you did yesterday,' she greeted me.

'Bit of a back-handed compliment, but thanks.' I wasn't sure what she was seeing, but I didn't feel any better, especially after my conversation with Jamie. 'You OK?' Once more, her smile lacked its usual dazzle.

'Oh, it's Carl,' she said with a shrug. 'It's hard, having him home, if I'm honest. He's so lazy around the house, and he's talking about going back to college and doing a course, which he'll expect me to pay for.'

'I thought he worked for that insurance company in Bicester.'

'Not anymore.' Her mouth turned down. It was so unusual for her to look miserable, I felt a prickle of alarm. 'He was late too many times, kept missing his train now he's not living down the road, so they've let him go.'

'Oh, Marianne, I'm sorry.' I linked my arm through hers and gave it a squeeze. 'I'm sure things will improve.'

'Ironic, isn't it, that we do so much to help people here, but when it comes to our own families, it's bloody hard.'

'I can't argue with that.' I thought of Jamie as we entered the house. 'Marianne, what do you know about Katya?'

She stopped, flashing me a puzzled look. 'Kozlov?' she said, and I remembered there was a Katya in her creative writing class.

'My Katya,' I said. 'MacDonald.'

'You've seen her records.' Marianne swung her satchel across her body, where the strap dissected her substantial bosom. Her smock-like top was creased, and there was a tea stain on the front. I wondered whether things were even worse on the home front than she was letting on. 'You must know the story,' she added.

'I do, but you had a couple of sessions with her when she was referred,' I said. 'Before she came to me.'

'I don't know any more than you, love.' She frowned. 'Problems?'

I hesitated. 'No, no. Just curious.'

Marianne nodded and looked at her man-sized watch. Aware my first client would be arriving any second, I said, 'See you later for lunch?'

'Sorry, Beth.' Marianne shook her head. 'I'm not good company today.'

'Look, why don't you talk to Carl and—'

'It's not just that,' she cut in. 'It's coming up to the anniversary of Mick's death. Twenty-seven years, but it doesn't get any easier.'

I felt ashamed for forgetting, too wrapped up in my own approaching 'anniversary'. At least I was alive – for now – unlike Marianne's poor dead lover. 'Let me know if you want to talk about it.'

'Thanks.' She looked as if she could burst into tears for a moment, then someone called her and she bravely refreshed her smile. 'No peace for the wicked.'

Watching her stride away, her cropped trousers straining around her hips, I felt a burst of admiration. Mostly, Marianne got on with life and enjoyed it, despite being dealt a rough hand when it came to the father of her children.

Maybe if I'd known my life was going to end when I turned thirty-three, I'd have made more of an effort to appreciate it, instead of worrying that every minute I was alive was a minute someone was suffering because of me.

'You're not going to die,' I muttered, making my way to the art room, clutching the alarm on my bunch of keys as if my life really did depend on it. 'At least, not today.'

I finished my session on a high, after a breakthrough with my last client Claire, a slender woman in her sixties, who always dressed smartly, her shirt tucked into her knee-length skirt. Claire had lost her daughter to breast cancer two years ago and had struggled since to find any meaning in life, despite having a husband and two sons. On her first day at Fernley House, three months ago, she'd shown no enthusiasm for painting, despite asking to be referred by her GP. She'd studied art when she was younger, she told me, her eyes dull with grief, but gave it up when she married and became a mother, taking a job as a school secretary to fit around the children.

Halfway through that first morning, she walked out of the art room. I didn't think I'd see her again, but she returned the following week and every Tuesday since, gradually opening up as she painted beautiful landscapes, mostly of Snowdonia where she'd holidayed as a child, sketching scenes from memory before adding splashes of colour.

Today, she'd told me with a spark of excitement that a friend had asked her to create a piece of art for her new home and she'd accepted.

'I used to feel so guilty for doing something I enjoyed when my Chloe's not here anymore, but I don't think she'd want me to be unhappy for the rest of my life,' she said, tears not far from the surface. 'She used to tell me I was wasted being a secretary, that I should do things I loved, especially once she and the boys had grown up and left home.'

'She was right, you should,' I told her, and although there were a few tears, she quickly dabbed them away and chatted easily while washing her brushes, about her plans to return to Snowdonia with her husband for their fortieth wedding anniversary.

'We're only here once, aren't we?' she said, blinking at me over her half-moon glasses. 'Chloe's time was cut short, but I still have Ted and my boys and I want to be here for them.'

I sat for a while after she'd gone, her words like an echo in the air.

We're only here once.

I'd spent half of my life feeling guilty for being alive, secretly waiting to be found out. Now that I had been, part of me wanted to confront it. But how, when I didn't know for sure who my enemy was?

Frustrated, I decided to go home and begin painting. It was the only way I knew of losing myself for an hour and calming the confusion in my head.

First, I hurried to Nell's to buy a loaf of bread, surprised when she looked up and beckoned me to the front of the queue.

'Someone was asking about your picture today. Asked if it was of anywhere in particular.' Her eyebrows rose, creating a gridwork of lines on her deeply tanned forehead. 'Seemed really interested, but didn't buy it in the end.'

'What did you say?'

Nell gestured for her son Kenny to take over serving. 'I said it was just the sea, not anywhere in particular as far as I knew. That's true, isn't it?'

'Yes, it's true.' I turned to look at the picture in question, adorning the opposite wall with several others – one of them a self-portrait by Katya, her wide eyes dominating her face.

'He seemed to think it might be somewhere in Cornwall,' Nell said, removing her disposable gloves. 'Heron Cove, or somewhere.'

For a moment, I felt suspended in time, as though the world had stopped turning. 'Perran Cove?'

'That's the one.'

The air felt too shallow to inhale.

'Beth, are you all right?'

'This man,' I said faintly. 'What did he look like?'

'Not sure.' Nell's face puckered. 'It's hard to tell when they all have beards these days.'

'He had a beard?'

She raised her eyes, thinking. 'Yes, he did, sort of darkish.'

'What was his accent?'

'Couldn't really tell.' She pursed her lips. 'Local, maybe?'

'It wasn't him who asked about the painting, Mum, it was the other one.'

We turned to look at Kenny, who was scooping vanilla ice-cream into a cone, his mop of grey hair squashed under a hat with *Nell's* on the upturned peak. 'She's getting mixed up,' he said to me with a grin, seeming not to notice I was rooted to the floor. 'Her eyesight's not what it was.'

'There's nothing wrong with my eyesight,' Nell huffed.

'You were serving someone else.' Kenny's voice was mild, used to placating his mother. 'It was the bloke with the scruffy blond hair. I thought it was odd he was wearing a leather jacket when it's so warm outside.'

'Maybe he had a motorbike.'

'He didn't have a helmet.'

'Well, he wasn't the one who asked about the painting,' Nell insisted. 'You were distracted by that woman you fancy and weren't paying attention.'

Kenny rolled his eyes. 'Sorry,' he said to the girl waiting impatiently for her ice-cream. 'Let me start again.'

Nell looked at me, eyes sharp as pins. 'Is there a problem?' she said. 'Do you know this man?'

'No, I don't think so.' I loosened my grip on the edge of the counter. 'Did he say anything else?'

'Just to tell you he'd been asking, if you came in.'

Perran Cove. It wasn't a name someone would pluck from thin air, and the painting wasn't even of a cove. It was a stretch of golden sand, dotted with tourists, the tide a long way out. It had to be someone with knowledge of that day.

'He was with a woman, I think,' Kenny piped up, taking payment for the ice-cream he'd handed over. 'She was standing with him, anyway.'

'Are you sure they were together?' Nell narrowed her gaze at him. 'If it's who you're thinking of, she was standing behind him.'

'Well, they left together.' Kenny shook his head and gave an exasperated laugh. 'Honestly, Mum, you'd be terrible trying to identify a criminal in a line-up.'

'Eyewitnesses often make mistakes.' A youngish man in board shorts and a neon-green vest stepped up to the counter. 'Memory's unreliable, and visual perception varies, depending who you talk to. I'm studying criminology,' he said with a grin.

I turned to Nell. 'You're certain he wasn't a regular?'

'I've never seen any of them in here before.'

'I vaguely recognised the man in the leather jacket,' Kenny ventured. 'Wouldn't swear to it though.'

I left without the loaf, hardly aware of anything but the buzzing in my head as I returned to Fernley House.

A man. Could he have been asking about the painting on behalf of the woman Kenny had mentioned? Maybe I'd got it all wrong and there were two people out to destroy me, working as a pair. Should I call Rosa? But say what?

Oh, a man was in my local café today, asking about one of my paintings. He thought it looked like the spot in Cornwall where I nearly drowned.

Hardly damning evidence. *Coincidence?* I'd read somewhere that there are no coincidences, just synchronicities – two events that come together for a purpose. The purpose in this case being to warn me my time would soon be up. Or make me think it was. But to what end? It was still hard to imagine Matt on some twisted campaign to bring us back together, but . . . *messy blond hair, leather jacket.* Both could apply to Matt – or Jamie. Matt's wardrobe didn't vary much between seasons, and the studded biker jacket Jamie had bought with his first wage was usually in his van, if he wasn't wearing it.

By the time I reached my car, I was sweating, my clothes clinging unpleasantly to my skin. I threw myself in the driver's seat and locked the doors. Scanning the area for signs of anyone watching, my gaze snagged on something.

There was a leaflet trapped beneath my wipers.

Chapter 15

I scrambled out of the car, the attack alarm digging into my palm, and tugged the square of shiny paper free. There was an image on the front of a girl in glittering water, googles pushed into her hair, giving a jolly thumbs-up to the camera. *Learning to Swim Saves Lives!* a cheery line of text informed me. Below that, *Drowning Prevention Week* was stamped over a cartoon lifebuoy. Across the bottom was the number of the leisure centre where Hayley went swimming every week, opening hours and session times listed beside it, with an invitation to book a course of private lessons for adults.

Success guaranteed, or your money back.

A cold feeling reached through my limbs to my heart.

There was nothing homemade about this message. I'd probably seen the flyers at the leisure centre without really taking them in, but it didn't matter. The meaning was as clear as the first time I'd found a note on my windscreen.

A LIFE FOR A LIFE.

I swung around, looking at the other cars. Maybe it was an advertising gimmick, but as far as I could see, mine was the only car to have been targeted.

With a frustrated cry, I threw the paper on the ground. As

I bent to pick it up again, I saw a movement in my peripheral vision and swivelled round. A figure was peering round one of the pillars into the car park – a pale face, curtained by long dark hair. *Katya?*

Realising she'd been spotted she shrank back. 'Katya, wait!' I slammed my car door shut and ran, colliding with someone walking up to the house.

'Beth?' It was a red-faced Marianne, hair frizzing around her face. I registered her startled expression, her words a fading hum as I hurried past.

By the time I reached the pavement, Katya had got to the end of the street and was glancing over her shoulder, her hair as shiny as a crow's wing beneath the sun's glare.

I waved, but she didn't slow down. I started running again, catching my breath when she darted across the main road to a blast of horns. *'Katya!'*

She didn't look back. As her tiny figure was swallowed by a crowd, I juddered to a halt, heaving air into my lungs. Had Katya left the leaflet on my car? Why had she run away? What was she even doing here?

I jogged back to the car, my breathing fast and shallow, every nerve end prickling. I should call Katya's foster mother Dee and ask if everything was fine, but when I called the number I stored in my phone for emergencies, it went to voicemail.

Unsure what to say without alarming Dee, I hung up. Worried she would wonder why I hadn't left a message, I called back. 'Hi, Dee. It's Beth Turner from Fernley House.' My voice was full of fake energy. 'I thought Katya had left her phone behind, but just realised it's not hers. So sorry to bother you. Bye!'

I dipped my forehead to my fingertips, pressing hard. I shouldn't have called. Dee was bound to question Katya. Unlike most young people, Katya wasn't permanently attached to her phone, but it would be unusual for her to forget it.

Hot and tearful, my eyes skimmed my surroundings for anyone

112

lurking as I tried to figure out why Katya had taken off like that. Seeing no one, I started the car and swung away from Fernley House.

I couldn't face going home, so drove to Oakdale, the private hospital where Vic worked for half the week; a large, brick and glass structure softened by clever landscaping, designed so the building didn't intrude on the expensive houses in the surrounding neighbourhood.

I parked haphazardly, grateful there was a space right by the entrance. One of the perks of a private hospital was an abundance of amenities sadly denied the NHS – something I stopped teasing Vic about when I realised it made him defensive. Dividing his time between Oakfield and the John Radcliffe Hospital made him uncomfortable with the disparity, but he'd argued there was a place for private practice that wasn't about him earning more money, but easing the burden on the NHS by treating patients who could afford it.

I entered the plush, air-conditioned, hotel-like lobby, ignoring the smooth-featured woman on reception as I hurried past and down a well-lit corridor, lined with botanical prints. I paused to check I had the right room before knocking. *Vic Berenson, Consultant Ophthalmologist* was engraved on a nameplate fixed to the door. I couldn't hear voices inside, so knocked and let myself in, thankful to see he wasn't with a patient, but sitting behind his mahogany desk, looking bronzed and healthy as he stared at his computer screen, long fingers tapping the keyboard. For a moment, I was thrown back to the first time I stepped inside this room, with no idea the man I was about to see would change my life.

Back then, he'd risen to greet me with a smile and an outstretched hand, before guiding me into a comfy leather chair and offering me refreshments.

'I'm Vic Berenson,' he'd said, smoothing his tie as he sat down, regarding me with intense dark eyes that seemed to see into my soul. 'Tell me how I can help.'

This time, he stood with a startled expression and said, 'Beth!'

I had the feeling I'd interrupted something private and was struck by how different he seemed at work; not a stranger exactly, but someone quite separate from me with his own thoughts and routines, doing and saying things I'd never be privy to.

Had I ever felt that way about Matt? But Matt had mostly worked from home, his career not as critical as Vic's, not as dependent on discretion.

Disorientated, I took a step back. 'Sorry, I shouldn't have just turned up.'

But Vic was coming towards me and took my hands in his, eyes searching my face, which I knew was flushed and damp.

'Has something happened?' he said. 'You look hot.'

'Thanks,' I deadpanned.

His mouth tilted. 'Not that kind of hot, although . . .' He looked down, hand tightening around mine. 'You've got your alarm,' he said, noticing I was gripping my keys. 'You won't need that in here.' He drew me to him, his arms closing around me. I rested my head against his chest, aware my hairline was sweaty. Vic smelt citrussy and fresh, as if he'd just stepped out of the shower. I breathed him in, my muscles slowly unclenching. I reached up to kiss to his jaw just he turned his head and our lips met, I melted against him, remembering our first kiss, outside this very building.

After our first coffee date, Vic told me he had a patient to see and I'd walked back to the hospital with him, stopping on the way so he could show me the house he'd shared with a Finnish eye surgeon called Lilja, before she took up a teaching post at a hospital in Helsinki.

I'd felt intimidated by Lilja, who Vic had been engaged to for four years, imagining her as not just beautiful, but frighteningly accomplished – she played the violin and spoke four languages, he told me – but the first time I went to his house for dinner, he revealed she had a terrible temper. She once threw a lamp through

114

the window and a neighbour called the police. He stayed with her because it seemed easier than leaving. He'd confessed he felt relieved when she was offered the teaching post and told him she was going alone; a fresh start for them both.

I'd looked her up online that evening. She *was* beautiful, but I wasn't intimidated anymore. Vic had kissed me that day in a way that suggested he was the sort of man who knew what he wanted and had found it. There was none of the flirty banter I'd had with Matt, which went on for several dates, but I liked that Vic was serious. I'd felt the possibility of reinvention, of being with someone I hadn't annoyed a thousand times.

On our fifth date, he told me he loved me. *When you know, you know.*

'Tell me what happened,' he said now, picking up my hair and letting it fall through his fingers. He looked at me intently, as if committing my face to memory. 'You haven't just turned up here to kiss my face off.'

I wished I had. 'Something silly.' I moved out of his arms, away from the strength of his gaze. 'I found this on my car,' I said, rummaging the crumpled leaflet out of my bag and handing it to him.

He read it, face darkening when the significance dawned on him. 'Only your car?'

I nodded, and told him about my conversation with Nell at the café. 'It's escalating, Vic.' A choke of fear rushed up my throat. 'Something's building, I can feel it.'

He tipped his head back and stared at the ceiling, a pulse ticking in his neck.

Dropping onto the chair I'd last sat in eight months ago, I stared blankly at the state-of-the art equipment Vic used for examining eyes.

'Right, I'm packing up here,' he said, springing into action. 'I'll grab some stuff from my place and stay at yours for the rest of the week.' He crossed to his desk and pressed a concealed buzzer.

115

Seconds later a young man with bouncy black hair came in, eyes darting between us as if looking for evidence of intimacy.

'Niran, I won't be in for the rest of the week,' Vic said. 'Can you refer my patients to either Susan Davies, or Hugh Nevin at the John Radcliffe?' It wasn't an order, but his tone had a ring of authority that brooked no argument.

Niran glanced at me. I could only imagine what he must be thinking. Vic was committed to his work. It had to be serious if he was taking unscheduled time off, especially when he'd already booked some holiday time for next week. 'Of course, Mr Berenson,' he said evenly. 'What shall I say?'

'Family emergency.' Vic's gaze flicked to me and I read the message in his eyes. *Don't you dare feel guilty about this.*

I summoned a smile, determined to be grateful that he didn't want me to go through whatever was happening – or about to happen – on my own. That he wanted to protect me. As much as I wanted to believe I was a capable, independent woman, who didn't need saving – *again* – by a man, or anyone else, in that moment I didn't feel it. I wanted backup and Vic was happy to give it. I wasn't strong enough to turn him down. I needed him.

You're the kind of woman who needs a man to save you. Repeating old patterns. You don't even realise it, do you, despite all the counselling and therapy training. Sad, really. I mean, it's nice that you're trying to make a difference, but teaching people to paint their feelings doesn't cut it, Beth. You know it too, deep down. I can tell.

It's funny, because you look so strong on the surface and I don't think you realise that. It's how you talk, how upright you are, walking about with your game face on, pretending you're in control – as long as the past stays where it is.

But we both know what can happen beneath the surface, don't we, Beth?

People can drown.

Chapter 16

Vic insisted on driving Hayley to school the next day, and got out of the car to wait at the gates while I took her inside.

There was comfort in knowing he was there; another set of eyes to look out for me. If I was being watched, they'd know I'd told Vic about the flyer on my car. Why else would he be driving us to school, instead of going to work?

'Is Vic going to be my new daddy?' Hayley said, as we walked up the playground.

Startled out of the tenuous sense of security I'd felt since Vic and I left the hospital the day before, I gently squeezed her fingers, which were tightly wrapped around mine. 'Of course not, sweetie. Vic is a very good friend, but you already have a daddy.' An old question rose unbidden, like silt from the seabed. *Had the man who drowned been someone's daddy?*

'Daisy has two daddies.' Hayley swung my arm, more relaxed. 'One is called Steps, I think.'

I hid a smile. 'If Vic and I got married, he would be your stepdad,' I said. 'But you wouldn't have to call him Daddy.'

'Can I still call his name Vic?'

'Of course you can.' Pausing, I crouched to face her, wishing we didn't need to have this kind of conversation. I'd never expected this when I married Matt. It hadn't even crossed my mind that, one day, we wouldn't be together. Several of the other mums were divorced, single or remarried, navigating new relationships, but I knew how confusing and unsettling it must be for a child, however carefully handled. My parents could have split under the pressure of what happened to us, but they hadn't. Part of me wished it was the same for Matt and me.

'You don't need to worry about any of that,' I said to Hayley, sweeping back stray strands of hair that refused to stay in her ponytail. 'Are you looking forward to going on holiday with Daddy, and seeing Gran and Grampy Turner?'

I knew she was, but wanted to see her smile and clap her hands. She obliged, her whole face lighting up. 'I wish you were coming with us, Mummy.'

I held her, blinking back tears, determined not to think of them having a good time without me – so good, she wouldn't want to come home. 'We'll go on holiday soon,' I said. 'Maybe to the seaside. Won't that be fun?'

'Yay!' Pulling away, Hayley clapped her hands again. 'I'm going to make a great big sandcastle.'

'Yes, you are.' I smiled as Daisy ran over, and when their teacher came to usher them inside, I had to resist the urge to call Hayley back for one more hug.

She'll be safer in France with Matt, even if he's the one threatening me. Walking back to where Vic was talking to Daisy's mum, who was visibly braless under her T-shirt dress, another thought rose. If something happened to me, it would be terrible for Hayley, but she would hopefully recover one day. If something happened to her, I never would. Another horrible thought followed. What if the plan was to destroy me, by hurting my daughter?

I couldn't let that happen, but how could I stop it when I had no idea who I was up against, or when they were going to strike?

* * *

'What are you going to do today?' Vic said, once we were back at the house. It was my day off and I normally worked on a painting. 'Shall we go out? Get away for a few hours, do something normal? It's a shame to be cooped up indoors.'

I looked through the kitchen window at the garden, which was a lot less unkempt than it used to be, thanks to Vic discovering a love of gardening. I'd done my best after Matt and I moved in, planting wildflower seeds in the borders, which never sprouted. I was generally too busy to bother, and Matt's efforts had only extended to mowing the grass in the summer months. Despite a wealth of advice from Pam, whose garden was a riot of colour and life, ours had been woefully neglected until I met Vic.

'Maybe we can have lunch out there,' I said, a scrunched-up feeling in my stomach at the thought of food. 'I just can't concentrate at the moment on doing normal things.'

He rested his hands on the worktop and lowered his head. 'I hate whoever's doing this to you,' he said. 'It's so cowardly, apart from anything.'

The depth of anger in his voice struck an answering chord. 'I know.' I curled my hands into fists. 'I wish they'd just confront me, so we could . . . I don't know. Talk it out or something.'

'How am I supposed to keep you safe?' He raised his head, eyes meeting mine. 'I can't be with you twenty-four hours a day for the whole of the next year.'

'You won't have to be.' I felt the pump of blood around my body. 'Between you, me and Rosa, we'll get to the bottom of this.'

'And if it's Matt?'

My throat tightened. However unlikely, I couldn't push the possibility away, especially since Vic had watered the seeds of my anxiety. 'If it is, I'll cope, I promise.'

'You shouldn't be making promises to me.' He sounded anguished as he ran a palm over his hair. 'I feel so bloody helpless, Beth.'

I moved forward and touched his arm. 'Let's not think about it today.'

He covered my fingers with his and after a few seconds, nodded. 'It's a deal.'

There was a moment's silence. I looked around at the mess left over from breakfast. Matt used to love to plunge his hands into a soapy sink full of water, even though we had a dishwasher, singing in a silly baritone as he washed up. Vic had no problem with loading the dishwasher, but I'd never heard him sing.

'I think I'll tidy up in here, then start a new canvas,' I said. 'I've got some oil paints I'd like to try.' At least that wasn't a lie, though I knew I should be binning Matt's gift, not planning to use it.

'You go on up, I've got this.' As Vic gave my fingers a final squeeze I let go of my breath, wondering whether there'd be a time when my feelings weren't threaded with guilt about something. 'I'll bring you some coffee, and then get on with my paperwork,' he added, making an obvious effort to lighten the atmosphere. 'I might even have a look at some property websites, see what's out there.'

'Good idea.' I wished I could see into the future and know for certain we'd be buying a home together soon.

As if he was thinking it too, Vic gave a wry smile. 'I suppose we have to try and stay positive,' he said. 'Go and do some painting and forget everything else for now.'

I climbed the stairs to the comforting sounds of clattering dishes in the kitchen. Vic had turned on the old transistor radio I'd had in my bedroom growing up, and the sound of a string quartet filled the house. *Very Vic.* I allowed a smile. Just for this morning, I would follow his advice and put everything out of my head but painting.

I'd set up the easel Emma had bought for my birthday, facing the window to make the most of the light, the paint stand from Jamie still in its box by the door. The room was a spare bedroom really, painted in creamy, calming neutrals, a cushion-cluttered day bed along the wall where I'd sometimes lie and do breathing exercises.

Glancing through the uncurtained window, I saw Baxter lying in a patch of shade next door, panting gently, and smiled to see Pam reading a magazine on her sun lounger in shorts and a sleeveless top, a cold drink on the grass beside her. She'd told me once she'd loved sunshine holidays when she was younger. She and her husband had thought about buying a guest house in their favourite seaside resort in Cornwall – or was it Devon? It saddened me to think she'd spent so many years alone, mourning her dead husband, when she had so much love to give. Though Marianne still missed Mick, especially coming up to the anniversary of his death, she was at least open to meeting someone new these days.

Turning back to the room, I decided to send Tabitha the photos I'd taken of the paintings for the gallery exhibition and ask for her feedback. Returning downstairs to get my phone, remembering I'd left the oil paints in the living room, a kernel of hope unfurled. If I could make it through to my next birthday – assuming someone was messing with my head and didn't really intend me to die – I was going to approach life differently. If one thing had come out of the last few days, other than a permanent headache, it was the will to carry on living. Not with the ghosts of the past dragging me down, but fully, in the present, making the most of each moment the way I should have been for the past twenty-six years. *Twenty-six years.* Something about the number tugged at my memory and floated out of reach.

'Just getting my phone to call the gallery,' I called from the hall to Vic.

'Coffee's on the way,' he replied. There was a crash and a muffled swear word. I stifled a laugh. He was wrestling with the old coffee machine Emma had bought me and Matt as a wedding gift, knowing I loved real coffee. I didn't mind instant these days, but appreciated Vic making the effort. I tried not to feel guilty all over again that he was acting as my bodyguard, instead of seeing his patients.

Taking my phone from by bag on the hall table, I was surprised to see I'd had a text from Emma, as if thinking about her had conjured it up.

Can we meet somewhere for a drink tomorrow evening? I need to talk to you. I can come over your way x

My heart flipped. I remembered the look on her face as she left my party with Mum and Dad, and the sense I'd had that she wanted to tell me something. But going out for a couple of hours meant leaving Hayley. Vic was booked to give a talk at Oxford University tomorrow evening, and after my last conversation with Matt, I couldn't ask him over – apart from anything, Vic wouldn't be impressed. Mum and Dad would love to babysit, but I couldn't face them either after my outburst with Jamie.

The obvious answer was Pam. She'd be over the moon and could bring Baxter with her. Not just for Hayley – his bark would scare anyone who came to the door. Not that Pam would answer the door to anyone, even Matt, without calling me first.

Feeling apprehensive, I typed: *7.30 p.m. The White Hart, St Andrew's Road? X*

It was a traditional old pub in Headington, easy to get to.

See you there x

So sparse. I thought of all we'd shared over more than a decade of friendship, how close we'd been before our lives took us down different paths – hers to far-flung countries, mine back to the city I was born in.

Emma knew everything about my past and what my family had been through. It would be good to talk to her properly. Maybe it would help bring us back together.

Slipping my phone in my pocket, I recovered my paint box from the living room and ran a hand over the wooden lid. I could clearly picture Matt choosing it, knowing I wouldn't be able to resist. I shook off an image of him mooching around my

123

favourite art-supplies shop. He'd probably ordered it off Amazon in an attempt to throw me off the scent.

Throw me off the scent. I shook my head, an ache passing through me at how my thoughts kept angling towards suspicion.

Tucking the box under my arm, I stood for a moment, looking around the room. I was rarely alone in it at this time of day. I'd either be at work, or painting upstairs, barely aware of my surroundings. Washed with sunlight, tidied and cleaned by Vic since the party, cushions plumped and straightened, surfaces shiny, Hayley's toys tidied into the wicker chest beneath the window, it looked like a stage set; a room dressed and ready for the players to step in and bring it to life. It lacked the lived-in feel it used to have, when Hayley's toys would be scattered around, the cushions awry, surfaces littered – *happy chaos* Matt called it.

Now, standing there, the melancholy sound of a piano concerto drifting from the kitchen, it felt as if something was missing. Something I'd never get back.

I gave myself a mental shake. I was being maudlin. The music, the text from Emma, Vic being here instead of at work, not to mention the fact that someone wanted me dead . . . my world had been rocked. Of course I felt off-kilter. It had nothing to do with the room and everything to do with my state of mind.

My gaze crept over my seascape above the fireplace once more, something niggling. I moved closer, swearing under my breath when I knocked my shin on the coffee table.

My eyes were drawn to the corner of the painting, where the water seemed to swirl, aquamarine tinged with white. Something didn't belong there, almost invisible unless you were looking closely. A shape, carefully etched in silver, as though scored with a metal tip. A crudely drawn arm, pushing through the surface of the water as though calling for help. Someone drowning.

The air rushed out of my lungs.

Chapter 17

'I can't believe all this has been going on and you haven't said a word.' Emma stared in wide-eyed disbelief after I'd blurted everything out.

I started the minute we sat down, drinks in front of us, when Emma shrugged off her denim jacket with a casual, 'So, how are you, Beth?'

'I suppose I was trying to take it all in, and didn't want to believe it was happening.' It was an echo of what Vic had said a couple of days ago, though it seemed longer than that – as though I'd been under siege for months. 'Do you really think I'm in danger?'

'Yes, I do.' She came to sit beside me on the leather banquette and took my hand. The old pub was busy with a rowdy birthday party that had spilled out into the leafy garden at the back of the building. No one was taking any notice of us, tucked in a corner booth, but I couldn't help scanning faces every now and then, looking for something out of place.

Like in my painting.

Vic had rushed into the living room, alerted by my shout.

'I've never looked at it this closely before,' he'd said, peering to where I was pointing, the outline of the arm barely visible unless it caught the light. 'It's the sort of thing someone could have done ages ago and you've only just noticed.'

I'd jerked away from him. 'But, why?'

'I don't know.' He attempted to hug me, but I shrugged him off. 'Some sort of joke?'

'How is that funny?'

'Sorry,' he'd said, concern shadowing his face. 'That was a stupid thing to say. I just . . .' He shook his head, at a loss. 'I don't know what to think.'

We'd gone back and forth for a while, trying to come up with an explanation that wasn't linked to everything else that had happened. Failing to come up with anything, Vic said something about fingerprints and suggested calling Rosa, but my energy had drained like a battery going flat. I'd retreated to my painting room to sit in front of my easel, the unopened box of oil paints in my lap. Vic brought up coffee and a sandwich, tiptoeing in as though I was an invalid, and gave my shoulder a supportive squeeze, but when he'd gone, I curled up on the day bed and closed my eyes against a drumming headache.

'And you can't think who might be behind it?' Emma's body was tipped towards me, giving me her full attention, just like she used to do. Looking at her was like going back in time. She was the only female I knew these days who didn't have children and wasn't in a relationship, and despite faint lines around her eyes, she could have passed for the eighteen-year-old I'd met on the first day of my art course. She'd offered me a cigarette, which I'd refused, confessing – as she lit hers with a flashy, gold lighter – that she was only there because she didn't know what she wanted to do. Her life was 'fucked', she said, and the only thing she was any good at was drawing. Very good, as it turned out, but she'd never intended to do anything more than coast through our time at college, more interested in partying and meeting boys than working, sweeping me along with her.

She was all hard angles, sweary, but quick to laugh – a wicked sound that turned heads – and never serious for long. At first, I couldn't understand why she'd singled me out, suggested a flat-share, and when I asked, she shrugged and said, 'Sometimes, you just click and you don't know why.' Later, when she told me how she'd found out at fifteen she was adopted, after her aunt let it slip at a drunken barbecue, and it had messed her up, I thought maybe she'd sensed the damaged part of me, and was drawn to it without realising.

We were opposites in so many ways, but good for each other too. She could always drag me from a bout of guilt, insisting a party was the cure. 'Get drunk and you won't care.' She'd laugh, pulling me out of bed and helping me dress. 'Alcohol's good for guilt. Why else do you think you were saved?' And although I never drank a lot, or took drugs, I always felt better, brighter, funnier around her, the effect lasting for days, sometimes weeks. And I was good at talking her down when she wept and raged about the family who'd kept her in the dark. She'd loved her adop-tive parents – a wealthy, middle-class couple who thought they couldn't have children, then had two in quick succession a year after adopting Emma. 'I just wish I'd known from the start,' she'd cried, her face swollen with tears. 'I'll never forgive them, ever.'

I'd taught her how to breathe to calm the storm inside her, and how to do yoga, though she could never master the poses and we'd end up helpless with laughter.

I missed her a lot when I started my therapy training and she went travelling with another friend. She'd return for a few months before taking off again, a pattern that lasted several years. It was on one of her visits home I'd met Matt, and two years later she flew back from Australia to be at our wedding.

'What does Matt think?' she said now. 'You have told him all this, haven't you?'

I shifted, uncomfortable under the weight of her question. 'I might have asked him if he sent the messages,' I admitted. 'Vic thinks he wants sole custody of Hayley.'

Shock stripped Emma's face of expression. 'You *are* joking?'

Miserably, I shook my head.

'But he knows you better than anyone.' Her voice had risen. 'He'd *never* do something like this, Beth.'

'He's . . . different lately.'

'Yes, because now you're with someone else and he wishes he'd never left.'

'Bit late for that,' I said. 'Have you been talking to him?'

'He's my friend too.' Recovering a little, she shook her head. 'But no. I just think you should have worked harder to stay together.'

'Says the woman who's never had a long-term relationship.' I could have bit my tongue the minute I said it. 'Sorry.'

She held up her hands. 'No, you're right,' she said evenly. 'But I can't believe you think Matt's behind all this, that he was the one asking about your painting at the café.'

I suddenly felt foolish, no longer sure of anything. 'Well, obviously I don't want to believe the man I married, the father of my daughter, would try to gaslight me.'

Emma gave an incredulous laugh. 'Of course he wouldn't.'

Half-annoyed she was so defensive of him, I said, 'What about Jamie then?'

'Jamie?' Emma looked thrown by the question, her dark eyebrows drawing together. 'You know, at your party, I was a bit disappointed he'd hooked up with that cop.'

'What?' It was my turn to look at her in disbelief. 'You don't still have a crush on my brother?'

She waved a hand in front of her face, embarrassed. 'Look, he was an idiot when he was younger, and I wouldn't have gone there anyway after the way he treated you, but . . . he *was* hot.'

'Ew!' I laughed, for what felt like the first time in ages. 'I'd completely forgotten you secretly fancied him,' I said. 'I remember now, when you first came round to ours and couldn't stop looking at him, and you said, "That's *him*? That's *Jamie*?" as if you'd expected him to have two heads or something.'

She gave a reluctant smile. 'It was just, when you told me how he was horrible to you most of the time and blamed you whenever things didn't go his way, I thought he'd be more of a creep.'

'He was never that.' Guilt crept in. 'He liked you too, I could tell, but I think you scared him.'

Emma didn't dispute it. Most men were a bit scared of her. 'I had a little chat with him at your party and he's actually matured a lot,' she said. 'I thought he seemed . . .' She paused, seeking the right words. 'He's grown up, I guess.'

'Since meeting Rosa.'

Emma rolled her eyes. 'You're telling me the love of a good woman can actually make a difference?'

I remembered the sadness in Rosa's eyes when I'd asked if she and Jamie were OK. 'A week ago, I'd have said yes.'

'Oh?'

'When I spoke to her, I got the impression things weren't that great between them.' I hesitated, but needed to get it off my chest. 'I worry he might not be treating her well.'

Emma frowned as she pulled her glass of wine across the table. 'I didn't speak to her, but got the impression she can handle herself.' She raised her glass to her lips. 'She's nearly as tall as him, for a start.'

'It's not always physical though is it?'

'You're talking about coercive control?'

'Oh, no, I don't think it's anything like that.' *Did I?* I picked up my wine and drank half in one go. 'I feel bad for flying off the handle with him, especially as Mum and Dad were there,' I said. 'I don't think I've ever said a negative word to Jamie before. I worry too much about upsetting him.'

'Maybe you should have,' she said. 'If it helps, I didn't get a bad feeling around him at the party, and you know how good I am at reading people.'

I surprised myself by laughing again. Emma's instincts were

terrible when it came to men, which was probably why she'd never had a lasting relationship.

'I just need to call Pam and check Hayley's OK.' I picked my phone off the table where I'd laid it next to my car keys.

'She's absolutely fine,' Pam said, answering right away. 'She wanted to go to bed straight after her bath, so Baxter could curl up on her duvet.'

I briefly thought about objecting. Letting dogs on beds didn't bode well for when we got one of our own, but I remembered how much I'd loved it when Bella used to jump on my bed when I was little, purring loudly and pawing the duvet before settling down, warm and heavy on my legs. Always on my bed, never Jamie's. Another black mark against me.

'I haven't mentioned the puppies,' Pam said. She'd apologised when she came round, saying Hayley had overheard her mention it at my party, and I instantly felt bad for assuming she'd ignored my plea. 'It's fine,' I said. 'I'm sure we'll end up getting one after we've been on holiday.'

'You're still going then?' Emma said, after I ended the call. 'To that place?'

That place. 'If I'm still alive.'

'Don't even joke about it.' Emma gave a worried glower. 'Is that why you're carrying that thing around?' She nodded at the alarm on my keyring. 'I had one for a while, in Thailand, but I lost it.'

'I'm hoping I'll never have to use it, but if I don't know when, or how, or *who* is coming after me, I need some sort of protection.'

'Jesus.' Falling silent, Emma drank some more wine. 'And you think someone must have hacked your phone and deleted those texts?'

'That's what Rosa thinks happened, and Vic agrees.'

Emma's features froze. 'Where is he tonight?'

'He's giving a talk at Oxford University, about developments in the treatment of glaucoma. I know,' I said, when she feigned a brain-dead expression. 'It sounds dull, but he gives really good talks. They're always inviting him.'

He hadn't wanted to go, but when I told him I was meeting Emma, he reluctantly agreed, as long as he could drop me off at the pub and pick me up afterwards.

Emma had that look again, fidgeting forwards on the seat, fiddling with the stem of her glass. Her other hand smoothed the fabric of the halter-neck maxi-dress she was wearing, which revealed her collarbones and bony shoulders. As if seeing her for the first time, I realised she looked amazing.

'What is it?' I said. 'You wanted to tell me something the other night, didn't you?'

'You don't miss much.' Her attempt at a laugh fell flat. 'It's . . . look, about Vic,' she said, unusually reticent. 'How well do you actually know him?'

Of all the things I'd expected her to say, it wasn't that. 'What do you mean?'

She turned her head, looking through the open doors into the garden as if wishing she was out there. The pub was half empty, people wandering outside to make the most of the summer evening, sun glinting off pints of beer and brightly coloured cocktails. A raucous burst of laughter made me jump. 'Emma?'

'I looked him up,' she said, turning to me once more. Her face was determined. She knew I wasn't going to like what she had to say, but was going to say it anyway. 'When you said you were seeing this eye surgeon guy, that you'd gone for a consultation and bam, the next thing you know he's asked you out for coffee, and suddenly he's in love and he's practically moved in—'

'Hang on.' I straightened, indignant. 'Firstly, he hasn't *practically moved in*. I didn't bring him home for a couple of months, because I wanted to be sure it was going somewhere, before I introduced him to Hayley. He stays over sometimes, but he's still got his own house, and anyway, we're looking for somewhere together.'

'You're selling the house?'

'We want our own place, Emma.'

'And you've discussed it with Matt?'

It was obvious from her tone she knew I hadn't. 'I will, once he's back from France and we've been to Cornwall.' Which brought me back to Vic. 'I looked him up too,' I said, in response to her bombshell. 'I mean, that's what people do isn't it, when they meet someone they like?'

'And?'

'And, nothing. As in, nothing sinister, obviously.' I wasn't sure whether to be offended that she was questioning my judgement, or grateful she was looking out for me. 'I wasn't going to bring someone into my life without checking them out,' I went on. 'But I think his job, his years of training, his good reputation, and the fact he's well-liked by his colleagues speaks for itself.'

Emma held my gaze. 'You do know that a large percentage of high achievers – presidents, bankers, doctors – have psychopathic traits, and that psychopaths are convincing liars?'

'For God's sake!' I looked at her, frightened. 'Don't you think I'd have had some inkling by now if Vic was a psychopath?' I picked up my keys and phone, ready to leave. 'You don't know him, Emma. If you did, you'd know how wrong you are.'

Still, she didn't look away. 'I saw him, with a woman.'

I froze. 'What?'

'I was in Oxford, shopping for your birthday present in the art store on Broad Street—'

'How did you know it was him?' I cut in. 'You only met him once before.'

'He's quite memorable-looking,' she said drily. 'And I'd looked him up, remember. Plus, it's not far from where he works, so feasible he'd be there, right?'

'By woman, you're implying he's having an affair?' The words felt heavy leaving my mouth, like stones landing between us. 'She could have been a former patient, an ex, his cleaning lady.'

'Vic has a cleaning lady?'

'This isn't funny, Emma.'

'I know.' Her face hardened. 'She was about our age, dark-haired, attractive. They were arguing. It looked pretty heated, intimate.'

His ex? But she was in Helsinki, as far as I knew. His sister? She lived in Canada.

'I'd been trying to work out whether to say anything, but after what you've just told me . . .' She caught her lip between her bottom teeth.

'You've started, so you may as well finish,' I said, a chill creeping into my voice. I wondered whether this signalled the end of our friendship.

'What if he's related to the guy, the one who drowned that day?' Shock ran through me like a knife. 'Maybe *she* is too, the woman.' Emma was speaking quickly now, pushing the words at me as if she'd been saving them up. 'Maybe it's been his plan all along, to get close to you, mess with you, then take revenge for his father's death, and that's why he's so insistent on you going back to the place where it happened?'

Her gaze had gone inward, as if seeing it play out in her mind, while I sat as though turned to ice, hand still curled round my phone and keys. 'Who better to trust than someone in his position, or maybe she's the driving force . . . his sister, say, and he could be having second thoughts – it's obvious he genuinely cares about you, unless he's a brilliant actor – and he was telling her he couldn't go through with it.' She finally ran out of steam and refocused. 'It makes a lot of sense, Beth. That message you found on your car, *A LIFE FOR A LIFE*. Didn't that turn up just after you met him?'

'Wow.' I shook my head slowly, but my insides were churning, even though I'd suspected Vic to begin with. 'And . . . what? We met by chance, Emma. He didn't orchestrate our hospital appointment. How could he?'

133

Her expression faltered. 'Did your doctor refer you?'

'Not to Vic specifically,' I said. 'There was a long waiting list on the NHS and I wanted to be seen quickly, so she referred me to Oakdale.' I had to dismantle Emma's accusation before it became set in concrete. I knew her. She'd go in all guns blazing if I didn't talk her down; probably confront Vic when he came to pick me up. 'That's how I came to be there, to see someone, completely randomly.'

'Someone?' She pounced on the word. 'Not Vic specifically?'

My mind reeled back. The consultant I'd been booked in with had been called away to an emergency. I'd been asked if I'd like to rebook, or was I happy to see the ophthalmologist who'd been called in to cover his appointments: Vic Berenson. 'It was Vic,' I lied, my heart rapping a fast beat. 'And there's no way it could have been premeditated.'

'Luck?' She grabbed my wrist as I made to stand up. 'Maybe he'd have found another way into your life, if you hadn't wound up at the hospital, but your name came up and . . .' She clicked her fingers. 'Think about it, Beth.' I wrenched my arm free. 'At least ask him about the woman.'

'I will.' I got to my feet. 'But I know there'll be a simple explanation.'

'That he chose to keep from you?'

Looking down at Emma, I felt an urge to be cruel. 'What if it's you?'

'Sorry?' Confusion crowded her face.

'Maybe you made friends with me at college to get close to me and one day avenge the death of your father, drowned at sea, saving the life of a seven-year-old girl.' I made my voice dramatic to hide the tremble and instantly wanted to snatch the words back.

'Jesus, Beth.' Emma's voice was quiet. 'That's low.'

I affected a shrug. 'You told me you don't know what happened to your biological father, but maybe you do. Perhaps you knew exactly what happened to him and—'

'Beth, stop it.' Angry now, Emma stood and leaned over to grab her jacket off the seat opposite. 'I'm trying to help, believe it or not. I care about you and I think you're way off base about Matt, and your brother for that matter. And if you don't know I'd never do anything to hurt you, you don't know me at all.'

I badly wanted to cry now. Emma tried hard to pretend she hadn't existed before she was adopted – she'd said she didn't want to know why her mother hadn't wanted her, that searching for the truth would probably drive her mad. It's why she kept running, to put as much distance as possible between herself and the past, and I'd just made a mockery of it. 'So, that's what you wanted to tell me the other night?' I said, feeling wretched as I watched her angrily stuff her arms in her sleeves and pick up her pouch-like bag.

'No, actually, it wasn't.' She sounded sad, which was worse than if she'd shouted at me. 'I decided not to mention it. You seemed on edge – I know why now – and I thought you didn't need to hear it.'

'What then?'

She hesitated, one hand moving to her belly in an unconscious gesture – one I instantly recognised. 'I'm pregnant,' she said.

Chapter 18

'It wasn't how I'd imagined hearing the news that my oldest friend is having a baby.'

Marianne murmured in sympathy. 'It's a shame, but understandable after the conversation you'd had,' she said. 'You were hardly going to jump up and down and give each other a hug.'

'She didn't give me chance to say anything.' I felt the sting of shock all over again. *Pregnant.* Emma, who'd never wanted children. 'She just left.' Tears pricked. 'She doesn't want to speak to me.'

I'd tried to call her straight away, pushing outside the pub, but she'd already gone. She didn't pick up, texting me instead.

Talk to him, Beth. Think about what you really want. You don't need saving anymore. Cancel your trip. I love you xx

She'd never said that before. I knew she did, but it wasn't something we'd ever put into words. It scared me. When I tried her number again it went straight to voicemail.

Marianne touched my arm in a gesture of solidarity. 'I'm sure she'll come round in her own time,' she said. 'Let her have some space.'

I hadn't told her the whole story, just that we'd had words about Vic, giving the impression Emma didn't approve of our relationship. I'd had to say something. After bashing into Marianne the day before and running off without explanation, she'd been waiting for me outside Fernley House, wanting to know what was up. 'I only spoke to Emma briefly at your party,' she said, 'but I thought she was a bit of a troubled soul.'

'You didn't say.' I gave her a sideways look, secretly scoping the perimeter of the car park. It was becoming worryingly normal – checking whether I was being spied on; whether someone was watching my every move. I'd turned down Vic's offer to drive me to work, but he'd followed me anyway, parking at the end of the road until I waved him off. I hoped Marianne hadn't seen. I wasn't sure why I hadn't told her what was going on, or about running after Katya the previous day. Maybe I didn't want Marianne to question whether I was fit to be at work, or get Katya into trouble without knowing why she'd been there. 'Are you still coming to the pool tomorrow morning?' I said, keen to change the subject.

'Of course.' Marianne gave a quick smile but I had the impression she'd forgotten. Maybe she'd made other plans now her son was back home, but I didn't push it. I didn't want to give her an excuse to pull out. Marianne's presence at the swimming pool on my Saturdays there with Hayley was the only way I could get through them. I supposed I could ask Daisy and her mum to join us, but it was too last minute and they'd probably have other plans.

I wouldn't ask Vic. It had been our family thing and didn't feel right yet to include him.

'Maybe we'll try the outdoor pool if it's not too busy,' Marianne said as we walked into the building, which was blissfully cool after the sun's glare outside. The heatwave was showing no signs of ending. There'd been drought warnings on the radio this morning.

'You'd think we'd have enough water stored after all the rain earlier in the year,' Vic had commented over breakfast, in a determined attempt at making conversation. He'd clearly sensed something was off when he'd picked me up outside the pub, seeming surprised to see me standing there on my own.

I'd imagined saying jokingly, 'You'll never believe what Emma thinks . . .' Just to see him laugh at how ludicrous it sounded, but couldn't bring myself to do it. *What if he didn't laugh?*

In the end, when he'd said with gentle exasperation, 'You must have talked about something,' I told him Emma was pregnant.

'But that's great news.' He'd sounded puzzled. 'Isn't it?'

'She saw you with someone.' It came out then, without warning. 'A female.'

If he'd been thrown by the change of topic, he hadn't shown it. 'What sort of female?'

'You were arguing with a woman in the street.'

'Really?' He drew in his chin. 'That doesn't sound like me.'

I strived to lighten my tone. 'Emma said it looked heated.' Glancing at his profile, I saw him thinking, brows drawn down. I decided not to tell him Emma had said the woman was attractive.

'And this was, when?'

'Just before my birthday,' I said. 'She was shopping, on Broad Street.' I kept my eyes on his face. 'You don't remember?'

'Oh, hang on, of course I do!' He lifted his hands and brought them down hard on the steering wheel. 'This woman accused me of stealing her parking space,' he said. 'I'd completely forgotten about it. She said she'd been waiting for the previous driver to leave, and I pulled in from the other side of the road without even checking.' I'd listened for clues in his tone, but he sounded sincere, even slightly bewildered as he recounted the argument. 'I genuinely hadn't noticed,' he said. 'She was angry, but I wouldn't say we were arguing. I actually moved my car in the end.' He grabbed a look at my face. 'You thought I was having an affair?'

I'd tried to laugh it off. 'Not an affair. I thought . . . maybe it was your sister.'

'Fran?' He sounded astonished. 'She lives in Ontario.'

'I know, I know.' I'd leaned my head against the car window and closed my eyes, suddenly weary. 'I don't know what I thought.'

'One thing you don't have to worry about is whether I have eyes for anyone but you.' He'd been teasing, but serious too. 'I know Emma thinks she's looking out for you, but you know she'd prefer to see you back with Matt.'

His words had chased away any lingering doubts. Emma was trying to put Vic in a bad light because she really didn't approve of our relationship. She'd have been the same with anyone. It probably wasn't even personal.

'I'm sorry.' I'd rested a hand on his thigh, and once Pam had been dispatched with Baxter, who had to be coaxed from Hayley's room with a biscuit, we went to bed and made love. Afterwards, slipping towards sleep, listening to him breathing peacefully, I wondered why I mistrusted everyone so easily.

I had a group session, the final one before my trip to Cornwall, and I didn't have time to think about anything else. The dynamic in the room was different to my one-to-one client sessions. Ten women, aged between thirty and seventy with different anxiety disorders, required careful handling. Luckily, they'd got to know each other well over the past few months, and friendship bonds had formed. It was clear they looked forward to coming each week and were responding well to the sense of safety and inclusivity. My goal was to empower them to discover their inner artist and, more importantly, to see themselves as valuable members of society. It felt good to see it working. The course culminated each year with a trip to an art gallery and everyone appeared to be looking forward to it.

Every week, I set a task and talked to each of the women as they worked. Sometimes, they didn't want to talk. The emotional release of drawing or painting was enough. Today, after a discussion about the weather and a rundown of their progress since our last session, they were quickly absorbed in creating a superhero self-portrait, using whichever method they chose – charcoal, crayon, paint or a face collage on a mask. Soft music played in the background from the old CD player I'd used for years. It helped create the right atmosphere, and encouraged the flow of inspiration. Only once, with a previous group, had I been asked to turn it off. 'Gets on my tits, that classical shit,' the woman had said. 'Haven't you got any *Eminem?*'

As I went around the room, murmuring encouragement and offering advice, an idea floated into my head.

Checking I wasn't needed for a moment, I crossed to my desk, found a pen and a sheet of paper and wrote: *Meet me in the park opposite the fountain at 1.30 p.m. No tricks. We can talk.*

'I'm just popping to the loo, be back in a minute,' I said, hardly raising my voice, knowing they'd absorb what I'd said without really noticing.

I never normally left a class, even to go to the toilet, without letting someone know, but I'd be back in less than two minutes.

I rushed outside, folding the sheet of paper in half, and slid it beneath the wipers on my car. *Two could play at this game.* If someone was keeping tabs on me, they'd find it.

I hurried back inside, glancing at my watch. Eleven o'clock. Plenty of time for whoever was out there to get my message. It was a long shot but worth it. *Fear shuts down instinct and short-circuits the brain. Fear attracts what you fear the most.* I'd had enough of being scared. I needed to look my enemy in the eye.

The rest of the morning crawled by. The group was unusually subdued, which I put down to the heat. The windows were open, but the air coming in was soupy, stirred by a humming electric fan in the corner. I quietly sent Vic a text.

I'm going for lunch with Marianne. No need to come back, I'll see you at home at 2 xx

He'd said he might swing by the hospital this morning, and I didn't want him rushing back to follow me home. It was starting to feel a tiny bit claustrophobic.

For a while, the only other sounds were the insistent buzz of a bee against the backdrop of music, and an occasionally expelled sigh of frustration. Finally, there was a collective burst of laughter as the group shared their superhero selves, comparing notes, and we discussed how they felt about what they'd created.

By the time we'd cleared up and everyone had wished me a happy holiday and trickled out, it was gone one o'clock. I quickly wrote up my notes on the session, then grabbed my things. There was no time to see whether Marianne was about, or tell her where I was going. I pulled out my phone and fired off a brief message. *Going for a walk in the park. Need some air. See you 9.30 tomorrow? X*

I left the building, eyes on my car, and saw at once that the piece of paper had gone. Rushing over, I double-checked it hadn't somehow blown away and was lying on the ground, but the air was still, the gravelled area clear of litter.

I pressed a hand to my chest and felt my heart beating as fast as a frightened animal's. I felt an instinct to duck, as though in a sniper's eyeline as I half-ran to the edge of the park behind Fernley House, darting between two beech trees onto the stretch of grass that led to the fountain.

The park was busy with people with sleeves rolled up, faces tilted to the sun, and tourists taking selfies, keen to get the distant view of Oxford's spires into their shot. A group of pigeons meandered lazily around, scavenging for crumbs, and a drift of guitar music made me think of Matt.

Only one bench was free and I quickly sat down, claiming the space beside me by plonking my bag there. My eyes darted around. There was a toddler leaning into the fountain, holding his hands under the trickle of water. His mum was sitting on the side, scrolling through her phone, and I resisted the urge to get up and pull the boy away. At least he was comfortable around water. I didn't even like stepping in puddles.

I glanced at my watch: 1.25 p.m. Enough time for someone to

have watched me arrive, alone. I stupidly thought about setting my phone to record, but worried it might look as if I was trying to call someone.

Aware I was probably being watched, I made an effort to sit still but I was too hot, the sun beating down on my shoulders. I removed my overshirt and stuffed it in my bag then folded my hands in my lap.

The brightness was hurting my eyes. I pulled out my sunglasses and slipped them on, then took them off in case I didn't look like me. My nerves felt stretched. I couldn't regulate my breathing and my hands were shaking. I hadn't felt this frightened for a long time.

After my accident, when we'd returned from Cornwall, the world had seemed too big, the city of Oxford too vast. Nearly drowning had made me timid and I hadn't wanted to go further than the park at the end of our road, but my parents and grand-parents had worked hard on helping me overcome my fear. Now, it felt as though it had never gone away, as if London and art college had never happened, and I was back to being that timid girl again.

When someone sat a few inches away, it took a few seconds to register. I turned as the figure inched closer, my hand closing over my keys in my bag, feeling the hot plastic of the alarm.

'You're not going to pull a gun, are you?'

'Katya!' It sounded strangled as I turned to look at her. 'What are you doing here?'

She held up the piece of paper I'd left on my car, her smile enigmatic. 'I got your message,' she said. Her hair was piled in a precarious topknot, tendrils drifting down around her face. 'I suppose I owe you an explanation.'

I tried to rein in my scattered thoughts. 'You took the note?' *Katya? She* was the one who'd sent me the texts then hacked into my phone to delete them? It was Katya who'd left the parcel on my doorstep, been in my house and turned on the bath taps, scratched my painting, left the leaflet on my car? Was she somehow connected to the man who'd drowned? She was too young to be his daughter. *His granddaughter?*

'Katya, *why?*' I didn't do a good job of concealing my fright and confusion. 'Please, just talk to me.'

Her pale eyes were tensed against the glare of sunlight. 'I know I shouldn't have run away yesterday,' she said, reaching up to tighten the knot of her messy bun. She was wearing a pink vest top under a pair of white dungarees, and sparkly sandals that made her seem much younger. I thought about the scars on the insides of her thighs and knew I had to tread carefully. 'You weren't meant to see me.' Her shoulders drooped. 'I should have been at college.'

'Why were you there?' Maybe we could work backwards from her leaving the leaflet, to sending the texts on my birthday.

'I was watching out for you.' A sweet smile lit up her face and I remembered how quickly her mood could switch. My hand tightened around my keys. 'I know it sounds a bit weird, but I'm worried about you.'

It wasn't what I'd expected her to say. Determined to sound calm, I said, 'Did you put that leaflet on my car?'

Her brow creased. 'What leaflet?'

'About swimming lessons at the leisure centre.'

'Why would I do that?' She looked scared suddenly. 'You're frightened of water.'

I felt something sag inside. I should never have told her that. It had been months ago, not long after she came to me. I was trying to get her to talk about why she hadn't been sleeping and suggested she paint something that represented her worst fear, so we could change the narrative.

'What's yours?' she'd said, her face blurry with tiredness.

'Water,' I replied. 'Drowning.' I spoke from the heart, not thinking. 'That's why I paint the sea. At least, I used to. I've stopped now.'

'Because you're not scared anymore?'

I'd wanted to say yes, but couldn't. 'Tell me yours.'

'Not knowing who I am,' she'd said, tears spilling down her cheeks.

143

It had been a breakthrough and things became easier after that, my revelation forgotten. Or, so I'd thought.

'Why are you worried about me?' She gave me an anxious look. 'Katya?' I felt a prickle of damp heat in my armpits. 'Have you been in my house?'

Alarm leapt over her face. 'Of course not.' Her mouth trembled. 'Why are you saying that?'

'I thought . . .' *Oh God, this was going terribly.* 'It's OK.' Letting go of my keys, I scrambled a tissue out of my bag as she started to weep. 'Katya, tell me what's going on.' I rested a hand on her knee. Touching clients wasn't encouraged, but it was hard to watch someone cry and not offer some comfort, whatever else might be going on.

She quickly composed herself, dragging the tissue across her cheeks, which were pink and blotchy. 'What's wrong with looking out for people you care about?'

'Nothing, Katya, but it shouldn't distract you from going to college. You've such a promising future and—'

'I don't want you to go away.'

'Sorry?' The vehemence in her voice was startling.

'When people go away, they don't come back.'

I remembered Marianne saying Katya had reacted badly to the news that her birth mother had died. Was this about her seeing me as a mother figure after all, and nothing to do with what had happened in the past?

'That's not always true, Katya.'

She looked at me, eyes glassy with tears. 'What if you don't?'

Water, filling my lungs, choking, burning, pulling me down, sinking, sinking . . .

'Beth?' Her voice had risen an octave; a child's cry for reassurance.

I turned, took both her hands in mine. They were hot, like Hayley's. I gripped them tightly, past caring that I was crossing boundaries. 'I'm coming back, Katya.' I wasn't sure whether it was a warning, a promise, or reassurance to myself. 'You can count on it.'

Chapter 19

I arrived home to find Vic coming in from the back garden, his face wreathed with worry.

'I was starting to wonder where you were,' he said, pulling me into a bear hug and kissing my hair. 'I'd rather drive you around until we know you're safe.'

'I'm fine.' I ducked out of his embrace feeling hot and flustered. 'Honestly, Vic, you could have stayed at the hospital. I've got my alarm with me.'

'I couldn't concentrate.' He followed me into the kitchen. I was starving, but could hardly make something to eat when I'd supposedly had lunch with Marianne. I grabbed a yoghurt from the fridge. 'I thought you'd eaten,' he said.

'I'm still hungry, OK?' I couldn't tell him about my encounter with Katya, or my theory that she was possibly behind the threats. I needed to be sure, and I wasn't. She hadn't sounded like someone who wanted to harm me, but something was clearly wrong. She needed help and I had to go through the appropriate channels. I couldn't discuss it with Vic. 'I've got a headache,' I said, putting the yoghurt back. It wasn't a lie. I felt as if a giant hand was squeezing my skull.

'Again?' Vic's voice leapt into concern. 'I suppose it's not surprising, with everything that's going on. You know how stress gets to you.'

He was referring to the reason I'd turned up in his consulting room in the first place, when it turned out my symptoms weren't the brain tumour I'd feared. *Maybe he'd have found another way into your life, if you hadn't wound up at the hospital that day.*

'Shall I get you some ibuprofen?'

Banishing Emma's voice, I shook my head. 'I'll be fine,' I said, adding more gently, 'I'm definitely going to start a new painting today.'

'Why not leave it until after we've been away?' I turned to see him standing right behind me. 'You could take some photos while we're there,' he said, stroking his thumb down the side of my face. 'Get some fresh inspiration.'

'I need to do something, Vic.' I twisted away. 'It's the only way I can switch my brain off.'

He held up his hands and stepped back. 'I'll be outside if you need me.'

I noticed he'd changed into a pair of jeans and the checked shirt he wore for gardening. 'There can't be much more to do out there,' I said, injecting lightness into my tone.

'Not according to Pam.' His face flickered with a smile. 'She's keeping an eye on me over the hedge.'

Upstairs, I went into my painting room and sat on the wooden stool in front of my easel, going over and over my conversation with Katya, looking for clues, trying to decide on the best course of action.

On impulse, I texted Rosa.

Any news on what we talked about? There couldn't be or she'd have called, but maybe she needed prompting.

I jumped when my phone rang straight away and I recognised Jamie's number.

'What was that message about?'

My heart stalled. 'What do you mean?'

'I didn't know you'd exchanged numbers with Rosa.'

My mind scrambled. 'Why do you have her phone?'

'She left it in the van when I dropped her at the station this morning.'

A vision of her boarding a train popped up, then I realised he meant the police station. 'I only noticed when your text came through.'

'Should you be reading her messages?'

'Probably not,' he admitted. 'When I saw your name on the screen, I couldn't look away.'

A chill swept through me. 'Isn't her phone locked?'

'We know each other's passwords,' he said. 'We don't have secrets.' The words *At least, I thought we didn't* crackled between us, unspoken. I wondered whether he'd seen the photo of the footprint from my studio, but didn't like to ask.

'It's . . . about the robbery next door to Mum and Dad,' I said, remembering the break-in and stolen lawnmower. 'I was worried whoever it was might get into my studio.' A nerve twitched under my eye.

'Scared your paintings might get stolen?'

For once, I was glad to hear him mocking me. 'I know they're not priceless works of art, but I am quite fond of them.'

'Why keep them there, then?'

Good question. 'I won't be for much longer,' I said. There was no point mentioning the exhibition. He wouldn't be interested. I was surprised he was even speaking to me, after our recent exchanges. 'Not busy today?'

'Stop changing the subject.'

'I was hoping Rosa had looked into it, that's all.'

'I'm sure she'll be in touch when she has.' There was a note in his voice that I couldn't decipher.

'Please talk to me, Jamie.'

'I'm talking, aren't I?'

'Talk properly, I mean.'

'I'm not one of your patients, Beth.'

My patience snapped. 'You know what, Jamie? You need to get over yourself. And stop checking your girlfriend's phone. Some things should be kept private.'

A stunned silence met my outburst. 'You won't tell her, will you?' He sounded tense.

'I thought you didn't have secrets.'

He gave a hollow laugh. 'Yeah, well, I've never actually put it to the test until now.' There was a second's pause. 'And whatever you think, I don't have any deep, dark secrets I'm keeping from you.'

I closed my eyes, weariness falling through me. 'I've got to go.'

'Me too.' He hated me having the upper hand; had to have the last word. Too tired to take issue with his childish rejoinder, I let him cut the call and aimed a frustrated kick at my bag on the floor. It toppled and a book slid out; the one Katya had given me. I checked the time. Half an hour until I had to pick Hayley up. I glanced out of the window and saw Vic leaning on a spade. He'd begun digging a border by the fence, no doubt egged on by Pam who was hanging out washing and saying something to him over her shoulder.

Slightly soothed by the sight, I picked up the book. Maybe I would find some inspiration inside. I'd never gone this long without painting something. Usually, faced with a canvas, I only needed to start – a brush of colour, a shape, even a single line and an image would start to flow. Maybe being told to make the most of your final birthday would be a motivator for someone else – an opportunity to squeeze in as much as possible and live every day as though it was the last. I'd never subscribed to that. I would prefer to live each day as though I had plenty more.

Tightness gripped my chest and my vision blurred.

Determined not to give in to a wave of panic, I opened the book, fixing my eyes on the first seascape I came to; a striking image in oils of blurry waves and a stormy sky. The artist had used unusual shades, deep and dark with flashes of white, to create a sense of movement and atmosphere.

Not bothering to put a shirt over my clothes, I put the book down and opened my box of paints. I picked out a tube of raw umber and squeezed a worm of colour onto my palette, then added some ochre. Selecting a brush from my jar at random, I swirled it through the paints but the shade still wasn't quite right.

Putting my brush down, I returned to the book, but it had fallen open on a different page. There was a slip of paper tucked inside, acting as a bookmark. As I took in the image, my heart picked up pace. It was a painting called 'Gathering Storm' and the artist, Doris Bridges, had perfectly captured the absinthe-green of waves whipped up by the wind, the gunmetal sky and an arc of foamy spray. I immediately felt the icy grip of water, tasted salt in my mouth as it dragged me under, flooding my nostrils. Hardly breathing, I let my gaze fall to the paragraph underneath and felt a beat of shock. Two words had been crudely highlighted in pink. *Perran Cove.*

I could barely process what I was seeing, or what it meant. Katya must have done this, but how did she know? I'd never mentioned Cornwall to her, or the place where I'd nearly drowned. Had she been digging into my past? Or, had she asked Marianne, the only person at Fernley House who knew what happened there? But Marianne wouldn't reveal a confidence, and definitely not to a client, however persistent. It would have raised a massive red flag.

Katya often asked personal questions, most of which I deflected. Maybe she'd hoped I would open up and talk to her; was hurt that I hadn't and this was her way of telling me she knew about Perran Cove and the man who drowned.

I leapt with fright when my phone pinged. I slammed the book shut and shoved it on the shelf with a pile of others. Half-dreading looking at my phone, I was relieved to see Emma's name, but my stomach dropped when I read her message.

Have you talked to Vic yet?

Blunt and to the point. She clearly wasn't about to let this go. My fingers dithered over the screen. I could call her; tell her the woman she'd seen him with was no one important, and tell her about the art book, the highlighted text, the painting of Perran Cove. But would she turn it around and say that Vic was responsible? I hadn't shown him the book. I'd left it in my bag. In truth, I'd pushed it to the back of my mind and forgotten about it. I sensed movement, a presence behind me.

'What are you supposed to talk to me about?'

I screamed and dropped my phone. 'Jesus, Vic!' I spun round, heart pounding with fright. 'You scared me.'

He pulled back, hands up. 'I thought you'd heard me come upstairs.'

'You read the message?'

'I just glanced over your shoulder,' he said. 'I wasn't trying to be sneaky.'

'I didn't mean that. It was about the woman Emma told me she'd seen you with . . .'

'It's OK. I shouldn't have looked,' he said. 'I'm sorry.' He looked unusually dishevelled, a smear of dirt on his forehead, a tuft of hair sticking up at the front. 'I came to say it's almost time to pick Hayley up.'

My insides were a mass of nerves. 'Vic, I actually don't think we should go away.'

His face emptied out. 'Why?'

'Emma's worried it might affect me badly.' I made myself meet his eyes. 'What if she's right?'

'What do you think?'

Relieved he hadn't immediately tried to discredit Emma, I shrugged. 'I honestly don't know anymore.'

'Fine.' He wiped his face with the back of his hand. The room was stuffy and his skin had a sheen of perspiration. 'I'll ring up and cancel,' he said mildly. 'The last thing you need is more pressure. After what's been happening, returning to Perran Cove is the last thing you need.'

Now he'd shown he was willing to call off our trip – that he understood – I felt a perverse need to face the challenge after all; to go back to the place where my life had diverged, the place where it all began. Maybe there, I'd find some answers.

As Vic retreated to the landing, I made my mind up. 'Vic, wait.'

He turned, a quizzical frown on his face. 'What is it?'

'Don't cancel,' I said. 'We're going.'

Chapter 20

'Have fun and look after your mum,' Vic said to Hayley, parking outside the leisure centre the following morning.

'Mummy looks after me, silly!' She rolled her eyes, looking a lot like my mum. 'Can I get out now?'

'Just a minute, you.' I grabbed my bag from the footwell, returning Vic's smile.

He was clearly relieved I seemed more relaxed, after struggling to get through dinner the night before. I'd gone to bed early with a persistent headache in the end, only to lie awake fretting for half the night.

'Sure you don't want me to come in?' he said, wiggling his eyebrows. 'I've got my swimming gear in the boot.'

'You have?'

'I sometimes use the pool near the hospital.'

'Oh, that's right.' I spotted Marianne's ancient Volvo, back from the garage, parked a few rows away. 'We'll be fine,' I said. 'Weren't you going to the gym?'

'I might just go to the café and read the papers,' he said, glancing through the windscreen. The sky was ultramarine blue, the sun already hot. 'I don't fancy the treadmill this morning.'

I leaned over and kissed him. 'We'll be ready in a couple of hours.'

'Come *on*, Mummy.' Hayley had unclipped her seatbelt and was drumming her heels. 'You're always so slow.'

'And you are very impatient, young lady.'

Marianne was waiting for us by the pool area with her grand-daughter, Charlotte, a cherubic five-year-old with rosy cheeks and blonde ringlets.

'OK?' she said, touching my arm once Vic had headed up to the café on the second floor. 'You look pale.'

'You'd think I'd be used to this by now,' I murmured, while the girls compared swimming bags. The humid, chlorinated air seemed to clog my lungs, making it harder to breathe. 'It never gets any easier.'

'Shall we try the outdoor pool?'

Feeling the bite of failure, I shook my head. 'Sorry,' I said. 'Not today.' The outdoor pool was too deep, too busy. I couldn't risk it.

Marianne smiled her understanding. 'Another time.'

'Can we do paddles in the baby pool first?' Hayley asked.

'Of course,' I said, as I always did. Hayley knew that 'Mummy only goes in the baby pool' because Matt and I had presented it as a fact as soon as she was old enough to understand. I knew one day she'd ask why but, for now, she accepted it. 'I'll be watching,' I said, tapping my nose.

'I'm going to swim all the way up and down,' she announced, face bright with excitement, and I marvelled, not for the first time, that while my daughter truly loved being in the water, I'd happily never set foot near a swimming pool again. At first, just the feel of a swimming costume, cold and tight against my skin, would tip me back to that day at Perran Cove. I'd got around it by wearing a two-piece, not caring that it showcased my preg-nancy stretch marks or cellulite on my thighs – things I'd worried about revealing to Vic, who'd kissed every inch of me and told me I was beautiful.

153

In the changing cubicle, I fought back a feeling of claustrophobia and focused on stripping to my bikini, and helping Hayley undress.

Next door, Marianne was chatting to Charlotte and the sound soothed my nerves a little, quietening the questions roiling in my head. The last thing I wanted was Hayley picking up that anything was wrong, but she was happily oblivious as we emerged, her hair tucked into her Disney swimming cap. Apart from protecting her hair, it helped me keep her in sight, and to Marianne's delight, Charlotte had insisted on wearing an identical cap.

Marianne kept casting me looks of concern as we herded the girls to the pool. Glancing up, I saw Vic in the café above the viewing gallery, a mug and paper in front of him. He smiled and blew a kiss, and I banished the thought that he was probably wishing he was somewhere else. He loved me, and loved being with me. He'd been willing to cancel our trip to Perran Cove to prove it.

A movement caught my eye. Pam had arrived to join Vic, canary-like in a yellow sundress that showed off her suntanned arms. I watched him greet her, unable from a distance to read the tone of his smile. She often came to watch before she did her shopping – had even asked to come in the water once, which Hayley had loved. Mum had been with us that time and was a bit affronted by Pam's presence.

'Hasn't she got a family of her own to hang out with?'

'Actually, no,' I'd said. 'And Hayley likes her.'

Chastened, Mum had been extra nice to Pam, but it struck me now that she hadn't had much to say to her at my party the other night. I wondered whether Mum was jealous.

I returned Pam's cheery wave, then watched the girls high-step into the water holding hands, shrieking and giggling. My body fizzed with tension. I wouldn't relax until we were in the car, on our way home.

Understanding that it wasn't the best time to make conversation, Marianne shrugged off her enormous towel and placed it with a couple of smaller ones on the bench, next to mine and Hayley's. Her body was soft and white, the straps of her navy swimsuit cutting into the plump folds of her flesh, but she moved unselfconsciously after the girls.

'You coming?' She threw me a smile over her shoulder. I took my cue, wading after them, trying to pretend I was walking through a grassy meadow, not heading towards a deeper body of water.

I'd coped when Hayley was a toddler, able to splash with her in the shallows, and had trusted Matt with her in the bigger pool, even if I couldn't watch when he ducked her underwater. It was harder now she wanted to throw herself around, doing handstands and having breath-holding competitions, and she and Charlotte loved dunking each other. I was hyperaware of other children, watchful of her being pulled under or knocked into, but the odd time it happened, she'd been unfazed.

'Remember, you're projecting your own fears,' Matt had said in the past, hair plastered to his head, eyes pink-rimmed with chlorine. 'Hayley isn't frightened of the water – she's a good little swimmer.'

It was true, but that didn't stop my heart rate rising if she slipped out of sight for a second, though I did my best to hide my panic.

The pool was already getting busier, filling up with Saturday dads, toddlers with parents, teenagers, and plenty more headed up the steps to the outdoor pool.

I stared for a moment at the slice of sky visible through the open double doors, wishing I was outside, breathing fresh air. Preferably in the garden at home, painting, while Vic tended to the borders and Hayley played with Baxter on the lawn.

Tearing my eyes away, I glanced down at my feet, distorted by the clear water. My toenails were a vivid shade of fuchsia. I'd painted them the day before my birthday, which felt like a decade ago.

Hayley. With a jolt of adrenaline, I looked up, expecting to see her sturdy body next to Charlotte's, their feet kicking up the water, splashing each other, but there was someone else in front of me: a woman in a lurid green bathing suit, bending low, holding the chubby hands of a toddler stomping his feet, gurgling up at her with a look of wonder.

I shoved past, water splashing up my calves, nearly falling over two little girls on their tummies, wearing goggles that gave them an alien-like appearance, pushing a rubber duck between them.

'Hayley!' My voice was lost in the clamour of shouts, squeals and splashes that echoed around me. 'Marianne!' *Where was she?* I spun around, trying to catch a glimpse, in time to see a teenager slip on the tiles as he ran towards the main pool. He fell in sideways, creating a wave-like effect that sent his friends thrashing to the sides. Seconds later, his head bobbed up, face split with laughter.

Where was Hayley? I seemed to be rotating on the spot, eyes zooming in on people who weren't her. I looked frantically up at the café, but Vic was talking to Pam, not looking at the pool at all.

I made a whimpering sound as I scoured the area again for any sign of Marianne, moving closer to the gulley that joined the two pools. I pushed out a breath and pressed my lips into a smile for the mum with the toddler, who was giving me strange looks. As long as Marianne was with Hayley, she'd be fine, I told myself over and over. They went into the adjoining pool every week, at which point I got out and sat on the side to watch, pretending to enjoy myself.

I couldn't get out now. Not until I knew where they were.

As my eyes raked the water, I thought I saw a flash of pink, then a small arm shoot above the surface. *Hayley?* I flicked a glance at the lifeguard in his distinctive red and yellow top. He seemed to be keeping a lookout, but it was busy. He could easily miss someone in difficulty.

The lifeguard hadn't been patrolling the coves that day. If he had been – if he'd called the coastguard straight away – maybe the man wouldn't have drowned and I wouldn't be standing here, too terrified to move.

The arm appeared again, small and white in the midst of a circle of boys, the sound of their laughter distorted by the water.

My body lurched into action. I tripped through the shallows towards the gulley, the blood roaring in my ears. The water was higher, round my knees, my thighs. *'Hayley!'* People turned, their faces a blur as I thrashed past, a few startled shouts as I splashed water in their eyes. 'Where is she?'

Marianne was there, unfamiliar with her hair turned dark by the water and slicked to her scalp, her mouth a circle of shock. 'Beth!'

'Where is she?' I could hardly get the words out.

'What?'

I took a breath, dropped, and suddenly I was underwater, pressing air out through my nose, eyes stinging and burning as I held them wide open, looking for a small body at the bottom of the pool. All I could see were several sets of spindly legs treading water, and a young girl swimming towards me, hair trailing around her like fronds of sea grass.

I shot up like a scuba diver, gasping and rubbing my eyes, hair clinging to my cheeks like seaweed.

'Beth, what on earth's wrong?'

I felt the weight of Marianne's hand on my shoulder and shrugged away, heart drumming in my chest. 'Hayley,' I managed to choke out.

'Mummy, you're nearly swimming!'

I prised open my chlorine-rinsed eyes to see a blurred version of Hayley in front of me, head and shoulders poking out of the water, her eyelashes spiky and wet. I blinked, trying to rearrange my face. 'There you are!' It was an attempt to sound spirited, as though we were playing a game, but came out sounding mangled. 'I couldn't see you.' I was starting to shiver, my body juddering with a life of its own. I wanted to grab Hayley and run, but knew she'd be scared if I didn't act like myself.

'Mummy, you look funny.' She doggy-paddled closer and patted my cheeks with wet hands. 'Your hair's drippy.'

Charlotte joined her, bobbing like a seal, her eyes wide and curious.

'Go and play,' I said to Hayley, catching her hands and kissing each in turn. 'I just came to chat to Marianne.'

As they flipped away, agile as fish, I turned to meet Marianne's worried gaze. 'Don't,' I said through chattering teeth. 'I know they're safe with you, I just . . . I couldn't see her, that's all.'

'Look at where you are.' A smile broke over her face, which was damp and blotched with freckles close up. 'Beth, you're in the deep end.'

Sensation came flooding back. The deep end wasn't that deep in the junior pool, but the water felt like a belt around my waist. I waited for panic to rise, but felt nothing beyond a bone-deep relief that my daughter was safe. 'I couldn't see her,' I said again, eyes pinned to where she and Charlotte were swimming together, arms cutting through the water.

'This is good, Beth.' Marianne tipped onto her back and pushed away, towards the girls. 'Maybe you should book some lessons,' she called. 'You're stronger than you think.'

I stared after her, rubbing my upper arms, which were rippled with gooseflesh. Had Marianne sneaked Hayley out of sight as a test, even though she knew how terrified I'd be? *Terrified enough to come looking?*

I had to get out, even though it meant ripping my eyes away from Hayley for a few moments. The water felt weighty, but pushing through it wasn't hard after all. It was just a pool, I reminded myself. There weren't any giant waves waiting to enfold me; just ripples and eddies around my hips and legs.

I risked a glance up and caught Vic's eye in time to see him gesture that he was coming down. He must have seen what happened. There was no sign of Pam, but as I looked for Marianne and the girls, I thought I glimpsed Matt, heading through the swing doors to the exit. My heart bumped. It wouldn't be him, just someone with a similar gait. He didn't come here when it was my turn to bring Hayley, and anyway, he'd be preparing for their trip to France tomorrow.

I grabbed my towel and draped it around me before sitting on the bench, waiting for Vic to appear. Eyes back on Hayley, a peculiar feeling of calm settled over me. OK, so I hadn't exactly waded into a stormy ocean to save my daughter, but I'd rushed through water to find her, in spite of my crushing fear. As I let that sink in, another feeling rose and dug its claws in. A determination to face whatever was coming and beat it.

Marianne was right. I was stronger than I'd thought.

Swimming pools are strange places. Unnatural. That lifeguard wasn't really watching what was going on. You have to be alert all the time, but I suppose it gets boring. It was odd, seeing you rush to 'save' her. Mother's instinct, I suppose. I assumed your fear would override it. I was banking on it really. You surprised me. It means what's coming might be trickier to pull off. Tricky, but far from impossible.

Not long now.

Chapter 21

Vic was unusually terse on the way to my parents' house for lunch, barely responding to Hayley's stream of chatter. 'I wish we could go straight home,' he said, when I asked him what was wrong. 'I don't feel like being sociable right now, and I'm surprised you want to go there after that scene with your brother.'

'They'll worry if I don't.'

He sighed, and I wondered whether he was thinking: *Is this how it's always going to be?* Maybe he was hankering after the quiet life he'd had before he met me.

Once at my parents', he responded in monosyllables to Dad's questions about his work. Dad was fascinated by Vic's job, a bit in awe of it too. I knew for a fact he looked online for news of developments in eye surgery techniques and was always impressed when Vic talked about them.

Today, as we sat in a shady area of the patio to eat the picnic-style lunch Mum had prepared, his query about an advance in cataract treatment fell flat. It was obvious Vic was distracted, despite his polite responses. I found myself making up for it by being extra chatty about the art exhibition, but noticed Mum seemed on edge, hardly touching her plate of food. I guessed she was holding back from asking what my visit with Jamie had been about because Vic was there, and she didn't want to cause a scene.

She perked up when Hayley asked, 'Can I please have a go at your sewing machine, Grandma? You said I could, if I was a good girl?'

'Of course you can, sweetie.' Some of the tension drained from her face. 'Dessert first, though.'

After we'd eaten a summer fruit pudding, they disappeared inside. When I took our empty bowls into the kitchen, leaving Dad and Vic pondering the likelihood of heavy traffic on the way to Cornwall the following morning, I smiled to see Hayley on my mother's lap. Mum was gently guiding her hands as they stitched, just as she'd done with me years ago – though the machine she'd had back then had been older, clunkier, and I hadn't the patience to sit still for long.

'Look, I'm making an Elsa dress.' Hayley beamed at me. She was obsessed with *Frozen*. I admired the bunch of shiny material, my heart dropping as it sank in how much I was going miss her over the next few days.

When she'd got bored of sewing and headed back into the garden to play swing-ball with Dad – he was spectacularly bad at hitting the ball, which made her bubble over with laughter – Mum took me aside under the pretext of fetching more cold drinks.

'Why were you so angry with your brother?' she said, as though I was six years old. 'Why on earth would you think he wants you dead?'

'Oh, Mum, it was . . .' I tried to frame something believable. 'I got a prank message on my phone that wasn't very nice and thought it was from him,' I said. 'You know what he's like.'

'Yes, I do, and you really upset him.' Her cheeks had gone blotchy. 'He's extremely sensitive where you're concerned, and could do without you accusing him of things he hasn't done.'

This was new: Mum sticking up for Jamie. With a flash of insight, I saw how it must have been for her and Dad – to go from being ordinary, caring parents with two children who loved each other, to the fractured family we'd become after my accident, the focus shifting automatically to the daughter who'd almost died.

'I'm sorry,' I said, close to tears. 'Did he say anything?'

She shook her head, her hair swinging, grey showing at the roots. 'He stormed out after you'd gone, didn't even take the bike.' Her eyes were filled with reproach – an expression I'd never seen directed at me before; the sort of look she'd aim at Jamie whenever he'd prodded at me wanting a reaction, even if it was the wrong one.

'He'll be back,' I said, wanting to wipe the look off her face. 'Don't worry, Mum.'

She nodded, scooping some crumbs off the worktop into her hand, which she dropped into the bin. 'You know you don't have to go tomorrow, don't you?'

It took me a second to grasp the change of subject, decipher the anxious groove between her eyebrows.

'I want to go. I'll be fine.' It was hot in the kitchen. I went to the sink and turned the cold tap on, holding my wrists under the stream of water. 'I've told you, Mum, this is the year things change,' I said. 'I want to get over being scared of the sea. Or at least put it into perspective.'

Enjoy your birthday, Beth. It'll be your last.

'And you're sure you can't do that in, say, Brighton. Or Scarborough?' Her tone was unusually combative. 'It *has* to be Perran Cove?'

'I could probably cope with the sea just about anywhere else,' I said. 'From a distance at least.' I turned off the tap and dried my hands on a tea towel. My senses felt sharper, as if the cold water had entered my bloodstream. 'It's Perran Cove that still haunts me, gives me nightmares.'

'All the more reason not to go there.'

'Going back is the only way to stop them for good – I'm sure of that now.'

163

'But look how you were when we went to St Ives that time, when the counsellor suggested we all go together,' she persisted. 'We didn't get further than the harbour and had to come back.'

'That was a long time ago.' I suppressed a shiver. 'After that, I thought returning there might make things worse.'

'What if it does?'

'It can't do,' I said. *Why were we having this conversation now?* 'It can't possibly make anything worse,' I said with more conviction. 'It's the right thing to do.'

'Because Vic suggested it.'

The weighty feeling tightened in my stomach. 'Please, Mum. I don't need this, not today.'

She fired me a despairing look and emitted a sigh. 'Well, you know how I feel about it.'

'Everything all right?'

We turned to see Vic in the doorway, empty glasses in his hands. 'Came for a refill,' he said, looking between us. 'It's thirsty work, playing swing-ball. Your dad's having a lie-down on the grass.'

Mum inhaled, as if ready to speak, then seemed to think better of it. Her lips formed a smile that didn't crease her eyes. 'Coming up,' she said. 'We were just talking about your trip tomorrow, hoping there won't be too much traffic on the road.'

She busied herself with clean glasses and a bottle of sparkling elderflower juice.

I met Vic's gaze, and knew he'd heard every word.

Back home, when Hayley was up in her room and we'd wandered into the kitchen, he said, 'You know, Hayley was fine in the pool. I could see her the whole time.'

I paused, about to spoon coffee into mugs, and turned to look at him. 'Funny, because you were talking to Pam when I looked.'

'She was talking to me actually, but I was still looking out and nothing happened until you suddenly went charging through the water.'

So, this was what had been troubling him all afternoon. 'Imagine if Hayley or another child *had* been in trouble,' I said, irritated. 'At least I *did* something.'

I thought he might comment on that, even tell me he was proud of me, but instead he looked harassed. 'Hayley will pick up on your fears if you're not careful. You'd be better off not going to the pool at all.'

'We'll be better off if you don't come with us next time.' I switched the kettle off. 'I can't believe you're having a go at me about it.'

'I'm not having a go, Beth, I just . . .' He paused, massaging his forehead with his fingers. 'I know things have been weird lately, but there's no point looking for danger where there isn't any.'

I stared at him, suddenly cold. 'Do you even believe that someone's threatening me?' Before he could reply, I continued, 'I know none of it adds up to much, just a . . . a note on my car, a leaflet, that stupid inflatable someone put on the doorstep, but if you'd seen the message I got on my birthday, you'd be taking this a lot more seriously.'

'You think I'm not taking you seriously?' He sounded hacked off. 'I'm taking it *very* seriously, Beth, but it's hard to know what else I can do, except wait for this . . . this unknown person or persons – whoever they are – to come for you, or whatever it is they're planning. It's hard for me too.'

'Well, don't feel obliged to hang around,' I bit back. 'Leave whenever you like, I'll be fine. And if I'm not, at least you'll know you did your bit to help.' I picked up my keys and thrust them at him. 'You gave me an alarm that's probably next to useless.'

'Oh, Beth.' He reached for me then and I wept on his shoulder, soaking his shirt, but things were strained between us for the rest of the evening. I was glad in the end to escape his company and help Hayley pack for her trip, trying not to think about being without her, playing along with her excitement, and when Vic came up to bed, I pretended to be asleep.

Chapter 22

Hayley was overexcited the next morning, running circles in the garden, Baxter yapping at her heels, trying to grab his tennis ball from her fist.

Watching Matt walk up the path, I felt a nervous tightness in my stomach. 'You will keep an eye on her all the time, won't you?' I said, as he stepped into the hall.

His expression was sombre. 'No accusations for me this morning?' When I didn't respond, he said, 'Has anything else happened?'

It was on the tip of my tongue to ask whether he'd been at the swimming pool the previous day, but I couldn't bring myself to ask and risk him saying no. Or worse – threaten to keep Hayley with him for longer than a few days.

I shook my head, not meeting his eyes.

He seemed to be waiting for me to say something else – perhaps apologise, but I wasn't ready for that. With a frustrated sigh, he said, 'You know I'll look after her – you don't need to ask.' He glanced over my shoulder as if hoping Hayley was ready and waiting to go. 'No Vic?'

'Working,' I said briefly. In fact, he'd gone back to his place to grab a suitcase and some things to take to Cornwall, after inviting

166

Pam round for breakfast to keep us company – code for *keep an eye on Beth* – while he was gone.

'Sure you're OK?' Matt narrowed his eyes. 'You look tired.'

'Thanks a lot.' The truth was, I'd barely slept. Apart from dreading Hayley going to France, the upcoming trip to Cornwall was looming larger and larger in my mind.

'Vic keeping you awake at night?' Matt gave a sardonic smile. 'I take it he's staying over most of the time.'

'Not now, Matt.'

'Seriously, Beth, I'm worried.' His voice turned grave. 'What's going on here?'

'I'm going to miss my girl, that's all.' I already felt her absence like a breeze.

'Come with us then.' He lifted his chin, his gaze combative. 'Mum and Dad would love to see you.'

For a second, I pictured their farmhouse, rendered a dazzling white, shutters painted soft blue like the sky in spring. Chickens and ducks wandered freely in the courtyard, and the nearest body of water was miles away. 'I'd love to see them too,' I said, wistfully. I missed his family, the way I sank into my surroundings with them, absorbed into their easy camaraderie, but I couldn't carry on visiting, even if they'd made it clear I was always welcome. I could hardly take Vic; couldn't quite picture him squashed around the big table in their kitchen.

'We've got plans,' I said quickly.

'Of course.' Matt's eyes cooled. 'Perran Cove awaits.'

I could tell by the twist of his mouth he was angry and trying to disguise it.

'I'll be fine.'

'I hope that's true, Beth.' He tested the weight of Hayley's pink suitcase by the door 'Feels like she's packed everything.'

'She has, pretty much.'

Briefly united, we exchanged wary smiles.

'Done any painting?' he asked, unexpectedly.

167

'If you mean with the paints you gave me, no. Not yet.'

'I suppose Vic didn't approve of me buying them for you.' It wasn't a question, and I didn't respond. I didn't want to give him the satisfaction of knowing I hadn't told Vic.

'You have my number if you need anything,' I said instead, trying not to think how long it would take to drive back from Cornwall if anything happened. 'If Hayley wants to talk to me, any time, it doesn't matter if it's the middle of the night—'

'She can call whenever she wants to, Beth, but she'll be running around most of the time.' Matt rested his booted foot on the bottom stair. 'Casey and Ben will be there with the kids,' he said. 'You know she loves seeing them.'

Another reminder of what I was missing: watching our daughter play with her cousins, Matt joshing around with his sister and her husband – if he was still capable of joshing. Looking at him now – hair too long, stubble growing into a beard, his eyes shadowed – it was hard to picture the way he'd burst into song sometimes with both elbows raised, hands pressed to his chest, or make up dances, body-popping and shoulder-shrugging, making Hayley giggle.

'I'd like to say goodnight to her, at least.'

He nodded. 'Just call – she'll be there,' he said. 'Remember the time difference.'

'I will.'

'Daddeeee!' Hayley ran through and hurled herself at him.

'Hey, munchkin.' Face transformed, he hoisted her up, and she wrapped herself around him like a koala, nuzzling his cheek.

'Good morning, Matt.' Pam had followed, arms belted around her waist. She didn't look disapproving exactly, but her tone lacked its usual warmth.

'Hi, Pam.' There was a touch of sadness in Matt's response as he registered her lack of enthusiasm. He'd encouraged Hayley and Pam's relationship, knowing they both got a lot out of it. It must pain Matt that, in her eyes, he was less of a person for leaving

168

us. 'How's the garden?' he asked, as if desperate to connect. 'Not much rain lately.'

'A bit thirsty at the moment,' she replied, thawing slightly. She could never resist talking about her pride and joy. 'I'll be glad when this dry spell's over.'

'I think we're due a storm soon.' Matt tried to put Hayley down, but she brought her knees up, so her feet didn't touch the floor. 'Mummy nearly swimmed yesterday,' she announced. 'She was in the big pool with Marianne and Charlotte and me.' She'd been tickled by the whole thing, repeating it to Pam, who'd missed the excitement having 'popped to the ladies' room'.

'That's great,' Matt said flatly, and I knew instinctively that even though Hayley hadn't mentioned Vic, he was attributing my 'nearly swimming' to him – something else Matt had tried and failed to achieve. I couldn't tell him the truth – that I was as far from swimming as I'd ever been – without revealing I'd only been in the 'big' pool because I was terrified Hayley was drowning. 'Time we got going, Missy.'

Finally letting go, Hayley unwound herself and dropped to the floor her bottom lip stuck out. 'I want Mummy to come.' Before I could respond, she brightened and reached for her case. 'I can carry this by myself,' she said, tugging it so hard it tipped. 'I've got baby dinosaur and Mr Wobbles, and four books and *all* my best clothes and I've got to wear my sun-scream and a hat.'

Matt smilingly took the suitcase from her. 'Let me carry that, and give Mummy a kiss,' he said gently.

Hayley let go of the suitcase, pursed her lips and screwed her eyes shut. 'I want Baxter.' The dog, sitting by Pam, whined at the mention of his name.

'Baxter's fine. You go and have a nice time,' Pam said, a little too heartily. 'We'll be here when you come back.'

My heart felt as if it was being squeezed. Hayley was acting up because she was overwhelmed. Crouching, I held out my arms. 'Give a hug, ladybug.' She folded her arms. 'Blow a kiss, jellyfish?'

'Yuck!' She scowled and turned away.

'Hayley, that's not very nice.' Pam sounded shocked.

'Say goodbye nicely,' Matt said.

'It's fine.' I drew Hayley close and wrapped her unyielding body in a tight hug, understanding that she didn't want to say goodbye. I knew that once she was in the car with Matt, she'd be fine and would barely give me a second thought. It hurt, but perversely I was glad. She was happy with her dad, her grandparents, her cousins, my parents – all the people who loved her nearly as much as I did. *She could be happy without me.*

My throat tightened as she darted past Matt and out through the front door.

'Don't worry,' he said quietly as we followed. 'A break will be good for her.'

I knew he meant a break from me.

Unable to speak, I was careful to keep a smile on my face as I watched him strap her into the car, checking the seatbelt was safely plugged in.

'Love you,' I mouthed, blowing her a kiss.

Caving in, she grinned and blew kisses back, flapping both hands as Matt got in and started the engine before pulling away with a toot of the horn.

'I'll miss the little mite.' Pam was on the doorstep, watching Matt's car disappear. 'I think he will too,' she said, ruffling Baxter's silky ears. He was staring ahead with a doleful expression. 'And I'll miss you, Beth,' she said, as I tried not to cry. 'It won't be the same, the house empty.'

'I know, but it's only for a few days.' My voice was strained with the effort of holding back tears and, as if sensing I wanted to be alone, Pam bent to pick up Baxter.

'I'll leave you to it, love.' She tucked the dog under her arm like a parcel. 'I expect Vic's on his way back.' If she'd wondered why Vic had insisted on asking her round, she hadn't mentioned it, too happy to be included in our daily routine.

170

'Sure you don't mind keeping an eye on things while we're away?'

'Of course not – it's no trouble at all.' She paused in the kitchen, on her way to the back door. 'Where is it you're staying again?'

'Wayfarer's Cottage.' I felt a twinge of apprehension. 'Near Penzance.' I couldn't quite bring myself to say *Perran Cove*.

'Well, it sounds lovely,' Pam said firmly, as though convincing herself. 'I really hope it helps and you come back a whole new woman.'

'Me too.' My smile felt tight.

Coming back alive would be enough.

'Why don't you take the red dress? I don't think I've ever seen you in it.'

Vic was in the bedroom doorway, watching while I haphazardly threw some clothes into a holdall. 'We can go out for dinner while we're there.'

I glanced at the open wardrobe. I knew the dress he meant. It was Matt's favourite. I'd ordered it online, and wore it to dinner once with Jude and Lewis across the road, while Mum and Dad looked after Hayley. It was our first night out since Hayley was born, and neither of us could stop fretting about how she was doing without us. We'd gone home early, and once my parents had left, and we'd reassured ourselves our daughter was perfectly fine, he'd told me how beautiful I looked, before peeling the dress from me and lowering me onto the bed.

After he'd gone, I dreamt I was in the sea, the folds of the dress drifting around me like blood, Matt calling my name from the shore, too far away to reach me.

'I'm not really a dressing-up person,' I said, pushing the memory away, hoping Vic hadn't noticed the tremor in my hands as I zipped my bag shut. 'We should probably go.'

We hit slow traffic as soon as we reached the M4.

Vic hadn't said much, other than to ask if Hayley had got off OK and to say that someone at the hospital had mentioned a house for sale they thought we might be interested in. 'It's in Watlington, so only about fifteen miles away, and apparently the house has an annexe you could use as a studio.'

'Not sure my parents will like us moving all that way out.' I was only half-joking.

Vic was silent for a moment. 'Maybe it's time to cut the apron strings.'

'I like being close to them,' I said, but remembering the look on Mum's face in the kitchen the day before, I wondered whether he was right. Maybe if I'd never moved back to Oxford, Jamie would have had a better relationship with our parents – but if I hadn't moved back, I wouldn't have met Matt or had Hayley, and I doubted me living miles away would have stopped my parents from fretting; it might have made things worse.

When Vic didn't reply, I glanced through the car window, trying not to think about where we were going, how far we'd be from home. Pam had popped back round with a packed lunch for our journey and I took out a bottle of water and had a swig.

I laid a hand on Vic's knee. 'Can we forget about yesterday?' I said, the argument we'd had fresh in my mind. 'I don't want things to be awkward between us.'

He turned to me and smiled. 'It's forgotten,' he said, with an air of relief.

I smiled back, noting the sunglasses on top of his head. He was wearing leather sandals with rolled-up chinos and a light grey, short-sleeved shirt, clearly in holiday mode.

'You are sure about this?' he said. 'It's not too late to turn back.'

'I'm sure.' Smile fading, nausea swirled through me as the reality of our trip hit home. 'I can't believe we've another three hours of this.'

Everyone in the country seemed to be heading in the same direction. I'd read that Cornwall was the most popular holiday destination for Brits because the beaches and atmosphere made them feel like they were abroad. Right now, I wished we *were* going abroad. Or, that everyone else was.

I wondered how Hayley and Matt were; where they were. He'd messaged from the airport about an hour ago with a photo of him and Hayley, their smiles strikingly similar. The pang of loss I'd felt had made me feel untethered, as though I might start shouting.

'Look, why don't you call Rosa?' Vic's voice was a welcome intrusion. 'Just for an update.'

'That's a good idea,' I said, grateful for the suggestion. I hadn't told him I'd tried to phone her while he was putting our bags in the car, worried after his comments the day before that he might think I was being paranoid. My call had gone straight to voicemail and I daren't leave a message, certain now that Jamie was monitoring her phone. I didn't want to risk speaking to him. 'Maybe she'll have some news.'

Something about the way Vic's posture changed told me he hoped she wouldn't, that he didn't want anything to overshadow our trip, but he nodded anyway.

This time, Rosa answered right away. 'Hey,' she said. 'How are you?'

'OK, I think.' I hesitated, wondering how things were with her and Jamie, whether I'd made them worse now she was keeping things from him. 'You know Vic and I are on our way to Cornwall?'

'I do.' She'd lowered her voice. *Was Jamie listening?* 'I can liaise with the police there if you like and put them in the picture.'

'You could?' The feeling of relief was instant and overwhelming. 'I would really appreciate that, Rosa.'

'I'm not saying there's much they can do, but an officer could come and speak to you, put your mind at rest.' I gave her the address. 'If someone knows where you're going and they see the police turn up, it might be enough to frighten them away.' *Rosa thought I was in danger.* 'You should keep your phone with you all the time and make sure it's switched on.'

'I will.'

'Good,' Rosa said. 'And don't go anywhere on your own.'

'I . . . I won't.' Blood was pulsing hotly in my temples.

'It's just a precaution,' she said, as if suddenly realising the impact of her words. 'I know it's hard, but try not to worry.'

'I'll try.'

Vic mouthed, *What?*

I shook my head, half-wishing I'd made the call in private.

'I was going to ring you earlier,' Rosa went on, 'but I got called to a burglary in progress.'

I sat up straighter. 'The footprint?' Out of the corner of my eye I saw Vic frown and remembered too late that I hadn't told him about it. 'Did you find out who it belonged to?'

'No, sorry,' she said, regretfully. 'Only that it was around a size eleven, so probably male, a boot of some description.' I thought of Jamie's boots, kicked off in his study. 'The image was too faint,' Rosa continued. 'We'd need to go round and do a proper impression transfer, look for other evidence – fingerprints, hair fibres, that sort of thing.' She sounded as if she'd relish the opportunity, but she probably wasn't thinking along the same lines as I was. What if the boot *did* belong to Jamie? I didn't know his shoe size. Could I ask Rosa to check? But I didn't want to put her off, and she might check anyway.

'That won't be necessary,' I said. 'It probably has nothing to do with anything.' I remembered something she'd said. 'So, why were you going to call?'

There was a pause, and I felt a ripple of premonition. I knew what she was going to say.

'I've got a name for you.'

The car suddenly felt smaller, less full of air. 'Go on.'

'The man who saved you,' she said. 'His name is . . . was . . . Mike Barrett.'

Chapter 23

Mike Barrett. Such an ordinary name. Mike. *Michael?* 'How old was he?' Stupidly, it was the first thing that came into my head.

'Forty-two.'

So young. I lowered the window, taking tiny sips of air that smelt like petrol. 'Where did he live?'

'Not that far from where you're going, actually.'

Vic had put the handbrake on. I felt his eyes burning into me, knew they'd be full of questions, but all I could see was the name *Mike Barrett* as though it was written in front of me in flashing lights.

'He was local?'

'Not exactly.' Rosa sounded to be tapping a keyboard. 'From London, originally,' she said. 'He married a Cornish woman, a few years younger than him.'

Mike Barrett. A flesh and blood man with a family, just as I'd always suspected. He had a wife, who'd mourned him for twenty-six years.

'Children?' My voice was so low, Rosa didn't hear. She was saying something else and I had to ask her to repeat it.

'I'm trying to find her, to ask if she'll speak to you while you're down there.'

My throat was so tight with emotion now it was an effort to push any words out. 'This is more than I was expecting,' I managed. 'I . . . I don't know what to say.' A thousand questions flooded my mind. I didn't know where to start.

'You don't have to say anything.' Rosa sounded cautiously pleased. 'I'm glad I could help.'

'I need to find out where he's buried.' Beside me, Vic went still. 'Maybe his wife will tell me that, if she agrees to talk to me.'

'Beth, don't forget, if what's been happening at home *is* linked in some way, meeting her in person might not be a great idea.'

That's what we'd been told all those years ago. *Better not to stir things up; leave well alone; give them their privacy.* Maybe if we'd met when it happened there would have been some closure on both sides.

'I'm happy to talk to her on the phone,' I lied. Somehow, I'd have to persuade her to meet me. In therapy training, I'd learnt all about restorative justice; how face-to-face meetings between victims and offenders helped to facilitate forgiveness. Our situation was different, but I had a feeling we'd both benefit from looking each other in the eye. 'Will you let me know as soon as you find her?'

'As long as you promise not to rush into anything,' Rosa said sternly. 'Talk it through with someone first.'

'I will.'

If she guessed it wasn't a proper promise, she didn't comment. 'I'll contact the local police and someone will be in touch.'

'Thanks again, Rosa.' I swallowed. 'This means a lot to me.' In the background, someone called her name.

'Sorry, Beth, I have to go,' she said. 'Take care.'

I ended the call and dropped my phone in my lap. Nothing had changed. Traffic was still at a standstill, sun shimmering off the river of tarmac in front of us, the sky above intensely blue, but I felt as if a seismic change had happened.

'Are you going to tell me what that was all about?'

Vic's voice was an intrusion. My feelings had been scrambled and I needed to gather them together, arrange them logically.

Mike Barrett. The man who'd died so I could live. If I could talk to his wife, tell her how sorry I was, if I could see she'd found happiness again – even visit his grave and say thank you . . . maybe, finally, I'd be able to lay down my guilt.

'Beth?'

A gulping laugh escaped my throat. 'Rosa gave me the name of the man who drowned,' I said. 'He was called Mike Barrett.'

'Beth, that's . . . God, that's huge.' Vic was looking ahead, fingers drumming the steering wheel. For a second his profile looked carved and remote. 'How do you feel?' he said, his eyes returning to mine.

'I . . . I don't know.'

'What was all that about a footprint?' He released the hand-brake as the traffic started moving, picking up speed.

'Oh, that . . . I thought someone had been in my studio at Mum and Dad's,' I said. 'Rosa was going to check it out.'

'How come you didn't say anything?'

'I forgot.' *He was more concerned about that?* 'Vic, Rosa said she's trying to get hold of Mike's wife.' I sounded dazed. 'He was married.'

The car swerved suddenly. 'Sorry.' Vic took his foot off the accelerator. 'She must have moved on since then though, surely?'

'I hope so,' I said fervently. 'But don't you see?' I swivelled to look at him properly. 'I could talk to her, Vic. Say my piece, tell her I'm sorry for her loss.' I gripped his forearm, warm beneath my fingers. 'I've waited so long for this.'

He tossed me a glance. 'I know you have, Beth, and it's great but . . .'

My hand fell back to my lap. 'But, what?'

'What if everything that's happened is linked?' He sounded like Rosa now. 'What if he had children like we said, and one of them has traced you, been targeting you?'

I thought again of Jamie. 'I don't think it is that, Vic, but even if it is,' I rushed on as he started to speak, 'then there's even more reason to talk to his wife – his widow. Don't you think?'

'I don't know, Beth.' His expression was concentrated, but I had the feeling he wasn't seeing the road ahead. 'I think you need to tread carefully.' Another quick look. 'What else did Rosa say?'

I told him she'd offered to contact the local police.

'I'm not sure that's necessary.' I noticed a whitening of the skin on his knuckles. 'Not while you're with me.'

Despite warm air sweeping through the open window, a chill brushed over my skin. 'It's just a precaution,' I said, echoing Rosa's words.

'I suppose I just wanted us to enjoy a few days away on our own, without all this hanging over us. Get you used to being by the sea again.' Vic shook his head, as if clearing his thoughts. 'I'm sorry.' His lips pressed into a smile. 'I'm being selfish, but it really matters to me.'

'It matters to me too.' I made my voice conciliatory. 'And we will have a nice time, but this is a big deal to me, Vic.'

'I know it is, of course I do.' He pulled into the fast lane, overtaking a row of cars, a lorry, a coach, as if making up for lost time. 'But maybe we could put it aside until we get home. Try and beat one demon at a time?' He was trying to make light of it, saying *demon* in a dramatic voice, but my laughter sounded forced.

'Maybe,' I said.

His smiled widened. 'This is just the beginning.' His gaze flicked in my direction again. 'Things are going to be different, Beth, you'll see.'

I bit the soft inside of my cheek and allowed myself to breathe a little easier. Reminded myself that Vic had my best interests at heart.

He put the radio on, tuned into Classic FM. 'This OK?' he said, as the presenter announced a Bach symphony in G major.

I nodded, settling back as the powerful music filled the car. It was a fitting backdrop somehow, as I replayed my conversation with Rosa and let my eyes drift closed, pretending to sleep so I didn't have to talk anymore.

As we drew closer to our destination it felt oddly like travelling back in time, to Jamie and me in the back of the car playing number plate bingo, while Mum and Dad chatted in the front, occasionally singing along to Radio 1, all of us dipping into a big bag of pick'n'mix sweets. We'd been so looking forward to that holiday, the four of us, the atmosphere party-like. We'd had no idea our time would be cut dramatically short and our lives – my life – would change. Today, I had the sense of things coming to a head; that coming back to where it all began – and ended for Mike Barrett – was meant to be. Maybe I really would overcome my fear of the sea.

Maybe I'd even live to tell the tale.

Chapter 24

Our rented cottage was close to Porthen Beach, set well back from the winding, rocky cliff path that led to Perran Cove.

Despite my misgivings, I couldn't stop a gasp escaping at the view as I climbed out of the car, the scenery unfolding in a series of shades from my paint palette: Grecian blue sea, and cerulean sky streaked with titanium white; pink sea thrift and campion, and the blues and yellows of gorse and heather on either side of the cliff path.

'It's stunning,' Vic said, on the other side of the car, stretching his shoulders and flexing his arms as he looked around with a slow nod of approval. 'Like being in an Enid Blyton book.' He already looked less tired, despite five hours of driving. He'd refused to let me take a turn at the wheel, and neither of us had wanted to stop at the services, making do with bottles of water and the foil-wrapped sandwiches and fruit cake Pam had made.

Vic needed this holiday, I realised – maybe as much as I did. I just hoped I wasn't going to disappoint him. What would happen if my fear couldn't be conquered? He'd said it wouldn't matter, the important thing was to try, but I couldn't help thinking he might see me differently, see *us* differently, if I returned to Oxford the same person as the one who'd left. He'd had such a positive effect on my life so far. I knew it made him feel good, the idea that he was maybe as much of a saviour – a hero even – as Mike Barrett had been. If I couldn't face going down to the cove after all, couldn't bring myself to even paddle in the sea, how would that make him feel?

Think about what you really want. You don't need saving anymore.

It was starting to feel as if Emma was here with me too. I badly wanted to call her, tell her what Rosa had discovered, but Vic was coming around the car, a boyish light to his face.

'How do you feel?'

'A mess,' I said, looking down at my creased shorts and wrinkled top, the chipped varnish on my toenails. I pulled out my ponytail band and shook my hair free. 'Like I need a shower.'

'You know what I mean.'

'It's lovely,' I said truthfully, wavering slightly after sitting for so long. 'But I really need the loo and something to drink.'

Expectancy leapt in his eyes. 'You're not . . .' He gestured with his arm, encompassing the view. 'This isn't giving you flashbacks?'

I glanced at the curve of the Atlantic, benign and shimmering beneath the sky, red and white fishing boats dotted here and there, seagulls turning in the air. I couldn't quite locate the unwelcome tug of recognition I'd expected, or the panicky sensation I'd experienced in the past whenever I thought about returning to Perran Cove.

'Not at the moment,' I said. 'I think it's because we didn't stay here last time.' I pointed. 'We were quite a bit further down and I can't see the cove properly from here, so . . .' I looked around once more. 'In a way, we could be anywhere in Cornwall.'

Except, the smell was exactly the same; a cocktail of sunshine and sea and the slightly sulphurous scent of seaweed mingled with manure – probably from one of the many farms in the area. Strange to be recalling that, instead of what came after. Maybe Rosa's call had shifted my perspective. Or, perhaps my fear, fuelled by years of guilt, flashbacks and nightmares had simply burnt itself out.

As if reading my thoughts, Vic's face split into a grin. 'Shall we go for a paddle right now?' He was joking, but his words fanned a flame of panic.

'Give me a chance.' I cuffed his arm. 'I really do need the loo.'

We hauled our bags from the boot and made our way up a grassy slope to the granite stone cottage, the front door framed by two sash windows, a cluster of pots underneath blooming with pink and white flowers.

'It's pretty,' I said, as Vic released the key from a safe fixed to the wall and let us in. 'Nice and cosy.'

'You mean tiny,' he said good-naturedly, dropping his bag on the hardwood floor. 'No room to swing the proverbial cat.'

It was small and simple, a short, wooden staircase dividing the living room and kitchen, leading to a bedroom and bathroom on the second floor. It was decorated in typical seaside style, lots of red, blue and white, framed pictures of boats on the walls. There were two comfy armchairs, a sunken sofa covered with mismatching cushions, and a small TV in the corner. I wished Hayley was with us. She'd have already found a nook and made it her own. 'It's perfect,' I said, doing a slow spin. 'Nice wood-burning stove.'

'Not that we'll be needing it.' Vic crossed the living room in about three strides to unlock a pair of balcony doors, throwing them wide to let some air in. 'Remember there's no Wi-Fi.'

'That's fine,' I said. There wasn't a strong phone signal either, but we'd checked that there was a working landline at the cottage. 'What's that?' Seeing a folder on a low table by the wood burner, I went to have a look.

'House instructions,' Vic said, joining me. 'There's a list of tide times too.' He picked up a laminated printout and studied it. 'Looks like we've missed today's low tide.'

'What a shame,' I murmured.

He looked at me, one eyebrow raised. 'I'll make some coffee.' He crossed to the sink beneath the kitchen window, which offered more views of the sea and sky, and when he turned on the tap, I dashed upstairs to the bathroom.

'I still can't believe I'm here,' I said later, as the setting sun cast an otherworldly glow across the landscape, streaking the sky with pink and gold.

We were on the balcony decking, sharing a bottle of wine that the owner of the cottage had provided, after eating the steaks that Vic had brought in a cool box and cooked on the little stove, with mushrooms, and green beans from Pam's garden.

I'd spoken to Hayley on the landline, and she'd made it clear she had better things to do than talk me through everything she'd done since leaving the house that morning.

'We're sleeping in a big tent in the garden tonight, and Daddy's not allowed to come in, but he's going to keep watch like a captain,' she said, clearly in her element. 'And Granny Turner says we can make some bread in the morning, and that I'm a clever girl.'

'You are,' I'd said, blinking away tears, longing to feel the weight of her in my arms.

'Love you, Mummy; night, night, sleep tight.' She'd hung up in the middle of me trying to describe what the cottage looked like.

Matt had texted right away. *All good, don't worry. Hope you are too.* X

I'd looked at the kiss until Vic said, 'Everything OK?'

'Missing Hayley.'

He'd nodded and reached for my hand. 'Imagine how excited she's going to be when we tell her we're taking a trip to the seaside next half-term.'

I looked at him now, leaning back in the wicker patio chair, his long legs sprawled out, a half-smile on his lips. I couldn't remember the last time I'd seen him this relaxed.

I surreptitiously checked my phone for a message from Mum.

I'd texted earlier to let her know we'd arrived and sent a photo of the cottage, and a selfie with a view of the sea in the background, captioned: *Looks good from a distance!* It had taken a while to send because of the patchy reception and she'd no doubt been fretting since.

There was no message. I checked again, then looked at the signal bars on my phone. Enough for a text to have come through, or even a call. The ground seemed to shift slightly as it dawned on me that she hadn't replied because she was angry with me. I felt a curious sense of abandonment, as if something precious had been snatched away.

I started when Vic spoke. 'What is it?'

'Just Mum,' I said lightly. It was ridiculous to feel put out that my mother hadn't sent me a text, when in the past I'd complained about her messaging me all the time.

His indulgent smile hid a flash of irritation. 'Why don't you switch it off?' he said. 'Everyone's got the landline number.'

'Good idea.' I glanced at the screen once more, just as it pinged with a text. It was from Emma, sent three hours ago.

Tell me you're not in Cornwall.

I am, I typed quickly, in case I lost signal again. *It's surprisingly OK so far. Great view. I'll call tomorrow. I've got news xx*

I attached the same photos I'd sent Mum, of the cottage and me in the bedroom.

I've got news too, she replied. *Did you know Vic Berenson's not his real name?*

A cold feeling slid through my stomach. *What are you talking about?*

'Your mum again?' Vic asked drily, reaching for the bottle of wine while I waited for the message to send.

I nodded, not daring to catch his eye as he topped up our glasses.

'Maybe we can take these up to bed.'

It wasn't dark yet, barely 10 p.m. but the day had been long

184

and was catching up with us both. We'd been yawning in tandem for the past ten minutes.

'I'll be up in a minute.'

'Tell her you're in good hands,' he said as he got to his feet and stretched. With a final glance at the deepening sky, he picked up the wine and his glass and bent to kiss the top of my head. 'See you up there.'

'Won't be long.' I resisted the urge to cover my phone screen, hoping he hadn't looked. The wine I'd drunk curdled in my stomach. When he'd gone, I checked to see if Emma had replied.

Ask him, she'd written. *I don't trust him, Beth. Come home.*

I thought about calling her on the landline, but Vic would hear and would want to know what was happening.

What's his real name? I replied, hating that I was even asking. I'd looked him up myself. Of course he was Vic Berenson. I'd seen his name on the hospital websites, his LinkedIn profile. There'd been other links online too: a paper he'd written, a write-up of a talk he'd given. Of *course* he was who he said he was. Whatever Emma was doing, whether she thought she was helping me or not, she'd gone too far. Maybe pregnancy hormones were affecting her judgement. When I was pregnant with Hayley, I'd cried and slept a lot during the first few months, my mood all over the place for weeks after that as I came to terms with the changes happening inside me.

The message wouldn't send. I got up and walked around in the dying light, trying to find some signal, then stood for a moment, feeling the thud of my heart. I moved closer to the ribbon of cliff path and stared at the sea, which had dulled to a calm expanse of pinkish grey. I could hear it pushing into the cove; a shushing sound that belied its power. I remembered the rush of water filling my nostrils, the freezing grab of a wave folding me under. Bile rose to my throat. I turned back to the cottage, throwing my phone on one of the armchairs before closing the doors and locking them, pulling the nautical-striped curtains across the glass so no one could see in. *As if anyone would be casually passing this way.* All the same, I'd felt for a moment the feeling I'd had back home, as though I was being watched.

'You coming up, Beth?'

The sound of Vic's voice made me jump.

I stared at the ceiling, picturing him lying on the bed, waiting for me to join him, wondering what I was doing.

I rubbed the nape of my neck, wishing I could erase Emma's message from my mind. What if she was right, and Vic wasn't who he said he was?

What if coming here was the biggest mistake of my life?

Chapter 25

I dreamt I was in the sea again, the water choppy as I struggled to tread water like Dad had tried to teach me once, doing the motions in front of the television to make me and Jamie laugh. I fought to keep my face above the surface, but the weight of water made my body ache as I heaved against the pressure, and terror surged as I felt myself pinned down.

I woke with a jolt to find Vic half on top of me, his arm across my chest, pinioning me to the bed. Rolling gently from beneath him, I swung my legs from under the sheet and sat on the side of the bed for a moment, getting my bearings.

We were in Cornwall, only a few hundred yards from Perran Cove.

I rubbed my eyes and glanced over my shoulder. Vic's arm had flopped back down. He hadn't stirred, clearly worn out. *Did he have an ulterior motive for bringing me here?*

It was the thought that had kept me awake long after he'd fallen asleep, as I lay on my back, staring at the wooden beams above me.

I nearly said it, when I came upstairs. *The oddest thing just happened. Emma says Vic Berenson's not your real name.*

Then I imagined him passing it off as Emma trying to discredit him, and what if he was right? He'd be so disappointed I'd listened to her. We'd have it hanging between us, and even if she was right, there could be a simple explanation. Lots of people changed their names for reasons that weren't sinister. But if he had, why not mention it?

In the end, I'd decided I would call her today and ask for more details before tackling him about it. I'd barely acknowledged, even to myself, that I didn't ask him because I was worried it was true, and me knowing might make him angry. Now I knew he had a side that wasn't as calm and accepting as I'd thought, I wasn't keen to provoke it. At least, not while we were here.

He'd held out his arms as I came into the bedroom, which had been softly lit by a lamp shaped like a dolphin by the bed, and the idea that he might have anything but love for me had seemed outlandish. His kiss had been tender, his fingers gentle on my skin. He'd tasted of wine and his skin smelt warm and salty, but I was glad when he pulled away with another wide yawn.

'God, I'm shattered,' he'd said dropping back on the pillows. 'I'm sorry, Beth.'

'It's fine,' I said, guiltily relieved when he quickly slipped into sleep.

Looking now at the rise and fall of his shoulders, I couldn't believe he was anyone but Vic. If he had anything to hide, he wouldn't sleep so well, and Vic never had trouble sleeping. It was a running joke between us.

It was light outside, a strip of sunshine slanting through the single window, highlighting a painting of brightly coloured boats in a harbour on the whitewashed wall. Penzance, by the look of it.

I picked my phone off the bedside cupboard and peered at the time: 7.45 a.m.

Moving quietly on the ancient floorboards, I pulled some fresh clothes from my open bag and slipped into the bathroom next door to wash and dress. It was compact, like the rest of the

188

house. The plumbing was noisy, but there were no sounds of movement from Vic.

I pulled a brush through my tangled hair, half-expecting to hear Hayley's footsteps, pounding from her room to ours to demand breakfast because she was *so hungry*, and I felt a fierce longing to hear her voice.

In the shaving mirror on the windowsill, my eyes were glassy with tears, the shadows beneath them proof of my restless night. So much for a relaxing break. Apart from where we were – Perran Cove lurking like a monster – my mind was a hamster wheel of anxious thoughts. *You'll need a holiday to get over this one,* my grandmother had said when she came to see me in hospital after the accident, her attempt to make light of what had happened belied by a storm of tears. *Somewhere far from the sea.*

I didn't need a holiday. I wanted to be at home with my daughter, nesting on the sofa with a bowl of popcorn in front of a Disney film.

Downstairs, I padded to the kitchen to look for my phone charger, groaning when I spotted the dirty plates and pans from dinner last night in the sink. My charger was coiled by the toaster and I plugged my phone in and switched the kettle on.

Through the window, I watched a pair of seagulls glide past, carried on a breeze. Waiting for the kettle to boil, I unlocked the balcony doors and stepped outside, breathing in a lungful of fresh air. It felt cooler today, a stiff wind blowing off the Atlantic. The sky was duck-egg pale, the sun a hazy ball, and the rolling surface of the sea had a silvery sheen. A pair of surfers were battling the waves, and the sight of them made me shiver, remembering the man who'd brought me back to my parents.

The kettle was steaming in the brightness when I returned to the kitchen. I made two cups of coffee, grateful the owner had provided fresh milk, as well as bread and butter and a dozen eggs. Perhaps I'd make breakfast, surprise Vic in bed – put everything out of my mind for a while, and postpone going outside.

As I put the milk back in the fridge, I noticed a folded news-paper sticking out of the bin. *Weird.* I pulled it out. It was an ancient copy of *The Cornish Gazette*, the pages faded to yellow. I checked the date. July 30th 1992.

The teaspoon I was holding slipped through my fingers.

Next to the main headline about burglars cashing in on the hot weather was another, much smaller one: **Body washes up on beach**. Below it, my name leapt out, and the words got muddled as I read the paragraph, going back to the beginning to read it again.

A body believed to be that of the man who saved 7-year-old Beth Abbot from drowning on July 27th has been recovered from Porthen Beach. The man, thought to be in his late forties, may have been on holiday in the area. Efforts to locate his next of kin continue.

I was breathing fast as I read it a third time, trying to ration-alise the paper being here, at the cottage. It had clearly been left for me to find, but apart from the owner, only one person had access. My thoughts slammed back to Emma's message.

I don't trust him, Beth. Come home.

'Beth?' I leapt with fright at the sound of Vic's voice from upstairs. 'I don't suppose you're making coffee, are you?'

'I'll bring one up.' My voice sounded normal, but my hands were shaking as I shoved the paper back in the bin. My legs felt like rubber, making it hard to move. I looked at the landline on a table in the living room and thought about dialling 999, but what could I say?

Had Rosa been in touch with the local police yet?

I reached for my phone, relieved it had enough charge to come on. My heart lunged in my chest. I'd had two missed calls from Rosa and she'd left a message.

Angie Pascoe, 19 Meadowside, Newquay. She'll talk to you.

There was a phone number too, but I'd already opened Google Maps and tapped in the address. It was only fifty minutes away.

I read the rest of Rosa's message. *Call first. Don't go alone. Spoke to PC Andrew Fellowes in Penzance. He's going to ring you. Said to call if you're worried about anything. Stay safe. X*

My fingers felt too fat as I typed *Thank you so much for this. Worried Vic might be involved, I'll . . .* I deleted the last bit. I didn't know Vic was involved, couldn't begin to figure out how. Maybe, if I spoke to Angie, I'd know.

Don't go alone.

I couldn't go with Vic, not now. And I'd always known, deep down, if I ever got the chance, this was something I had to face on my own.

'That coffee's taking its time.'

I heard a creak of floorboards upstairs.

'Stay there, I'm bringing you breakfast in bed!' I grabbed the loaf of bread and crammed two slices in the toaster. 'Scrambled eggs OK?'

'Great!' He sounded sleepily delighted, hopefully misinterpreting the note of panic in my voice. I wasn't the best cook in the world and either cooked eggs for too long or not enough. 'I'll have mine well-done.'

I couldn't work out why he'd hidden the newspaper, or how he'd even got hold of it, but asking would only alert him to the fact I'd found it.

Maybe he'd planned to produce it over dinner tonight – or tomorrow, or our last night here. *But why?* It felt as if my head was about to explode.

I managed to produce an edible plate of food in record time, made a fresh cup of coffee and carried both upstairs, thinking about Angie Pascoe, trying to conjure an image to go with the name. Her surname suggested she'd either remarried or reverted to her maiden name at some point. The former, I hoped.

Vic was sitting up in bed, bare-chested, looking at his phone when I ducked into the bedroom, spilling some coffee on the rug. 'I feel spoiled,' he said, watching as I weaved towards him. 'We should come away more often.'

He was smiling and rumpled and looked about five years younger. Surely if he was plotting something dark, he'd look more troubled.

'I thought we could ease in slowly,' he said, taking the plate while I put down the cup of coffee. He ate a mouthful of eggs and nodded his approval. 'Perfect,' he said when he'd swallowed. 'There's so much to see and do,' he went on, as eager as a boy scout. 'I've been reading up about the smuggling haunts around here, but they all involve the sea, obviously.' He grimaced. 'Maybe we could head inland for a bit, explore the village, have a pub lunch. Then, if you feel up to it, we can head to Porthen Beach and look at the sea from there, first, before approaching Perran Cove.' He took another mouthful. 'I think we should go to the cove tomorrow morning; that's when the tide will be furthest out, according to the timetable. I've already set the alarm on my phone for four thirty.' Seeing my expression, he grinned. 'I know you're not a morning person, but it'll be worth it.' Registering that I was standing by the bed, empty-handed, he said, 'Aren't you having anything to eat?'

'Oh,' I said, vaguely thumbing the doorway. 'I was in the middle of making some more eggs—'

'Here, have mine.' Vic held out his plate, pushing aside the bedsheet, revealing his plain white boxers. With no Hayley in the next room there was no need for him to wear his T-shirt and pyjama bottoms, yet I found his nakedness, the sight of his muscular chest, unsettling. 'I'll go and make some more.'

'No, no, don't be silly.' I backed away, palms outstretched. 'I won't be long, eat yours while it's warm.'

Before he could stop me, I ran downstairs and dithered for a second by the door before rummaging in my bag for a pen and notebook. I tore out a sheet of paper and swiftly wrote, *Really sorry, Vic, but I can't face the sea today. I need shops and people. I'm going for a drive, and to have a look around. I'll be back later, don't worry xx*

Praying he hadn't taken his keys upstairs, I looked around and saw with a burst of relief they were on the table, next to the phone. After prising his car key off the keyring, I grabbed my phone and charger and slipped out of the cottage, closing the door quietly behind me. The bedroom was at the back, so hopefully Vic wouldn't hear the car engine, which sounded unnaturally loud when I turned on the ignition.

I glanced back at the cottage, remembering the feeling I'd had when I arrived home on my birthday, that someone was watching from the landing window.

Had it been Vic?

With a feeling of rising hysteria, I connected my phone to the in-car charger and almost leapt out of my skin when the radio burst into life with a clash of trumpets. I switched it off and drove fast down the bumpy lane, glancing in the rear-view mirror as if Vic might be charging after me, but all I could see was sky and the receding cliff path.

I estimated I had about five minutes at the most, before he noticed I wasn't there and ran down and read my note, which I'd left on the bottom stair.

It was exactly five minutes later, as I was heading to the A30, that my phone began to ring. Knowing it would make things worse if I didn't pick up, I answered, using the speaker system.

'Beth, where the hell are you?' Vic sounded so frantic, I wavered, slowing the car so the van behind me beeped.

'You saw my note?'

'Yes, but why did you run off? Why not tell me you wanted to go somewhere else?'

'I know you're not keen on shopping, and I thought you'd prefer to hang around there and see the sights, like you said.'

'I wanted us to see them together.' He sounded bewildered. 'That was the whole point.'

'I'm sorry I took your car.'

'I don't care about the car, Beth,' he said. 'And I don't mind what we do, but it would be nice to spend our first day here with each other, not doing different things.'

'We can go out for dinner later.'

'Where are you now?'

'I thought I'd go to St Ives,' I said. 'Have a look round the galleries.'

'I thought you wanted shops.'

'Well, it's the same thing.' I cringed. 'Art shops.'

There was a pause. 'What are you up to Beth?'

'I'm not up to anything.' He knew I was bad at lying and I needed to convince him. 'Honestly, Vic, the sight of all that sea . . . to be honest, I couldn't handle it.'

He exhaled a sigh. 'You're not supposed to go anywhere on your own.'

'I know, but I'll be fine.' I turned onto the Newquay road. It was early and traffic was still fairly light. I should be there in forty minutes. 'I've got my alarm and I'm charging my phone in the car.'

'Are you sure you don't want me to join you there?' he said. 'There's probably a local bus, or I can get a taxi over and meet you.'

'Why don't you scout the area there, find somewhere nice to eat?'

'Right.' The word was stripped of warmth. 'I guess I'll see you later then.'

My phone sat nav instructed me to take the first exit onto the A3075 just as Vic hung up. Had he heard? What if he guessed I'd seen the newspaper? I couldn't recall whether I'd put it back exactly as I'd found it. Remembering the headline made my stomach sway. *Body washed up on beach.* At that point, no one had known who the man was. And my own name, underneath in black and white like that. I'd had no idea it had even been reported. Had Angie Pascoe seen the paper that day? If so, she'd known my name, could have found me if she'd tried. The police would have told her anyway.

My mind swung back and forth, from Vic to Angie, and settled on Hayley as I glanced at the dashboard clock. She'd have been up for an hour or two, was probably in the farmhouse kitchen baking bread with Matt's mum.

When my phone signalled a text, I pulled into a lay-by to read it, in case it was from Matt.

What did he say? It was Emma. *Have you asked him?*

So what's his 'real' name then?

Ask him, Beth. He should be the one to tell you.

I threw my phone down and carried on driving, barely aware of my surroundings as I followed the phone's robotic directions, trying to imagine Angie's reaction when I rocked up on her doorstep. It had occurred to me that she might not be in – probably wouldn't be. She could be at work, or out for the day, and would be expecting a phone call, not to see me in person. I tried not to think beyond knocking on her door to what I would say if she *was* there.

Thirty-five minutes later I was in Newquay, pulling into Meadowside and parking outside number nineteen.

195

Chapter 26

It was an ordinary semi-detached house in sand-coloured brick, with a decorative wooden wheel attached to the wall beside a small covered porch.

The front garden was an immaculate triangle of grass, the path to the front door fringed with lavender, and blinds were drawn over the windows, presumably to stop the sun from fading the furniture inside.

My hands were gripping the steering wheel, my face prickled with sweat. Even with the window down, there wasn't much air coming in.

Children were playing in the street, riding their bikes up and down, reminding me again of Jamie and me during school holidays, before our trip to Cornwall, playing in the quiet alley at the side of the house with our friends.

I looked for signs of life and saw the downstairs window was open. Someone must be in. Was Angie thinking about me right now, wondering when I was going to call, planning what to say to me – speculating about what I was going to say to her? Would there be anger, after all this time?

Part of me wanted to stay in the car, to turn round and drive back to the cottage, but a bigger part – the part that had been waiting for an opportunity like this – propelled me out and up the neatly paved path to the front door.

As I raised my hand to knock, I paused. It felt significant, as if the moment should be marked with a fanfare. I heard shrieks and laughter from somewhere next door, and the splash of a paddling pool, which sounded ironic somehow.

Quelling a rush of nerves, I rapped on the door and stepped back. I looked at the open window. I couldn't see in, but sensed someone looking out, checking to see who was there. I arranged my face in a smile so I didn't look threatening, and seconds later, a blurred shape appeared behind the frosted glass. The door opened a couple of inches and a woman's face peered round, knotted into a frown. 'Hello?'

'Angie Pascoe?' My throat felt full of cotton wool.

'Who's asking?'

I swallowed. 'My name's Beth Turner . . . Abbot.'

The door swung wider, revealing a short, barrel-shaped woman about Mum's age, in cropped white linen trousers with navy flats, and a floaty top that matched her vivid blue eyes. She pushed her short, ash-blonde hair behind her ears, revealing big hooped earrings. 'You'd better come in,' she said, her Cornish accent strong. 'I thought you might pop over. Your friend said you was staying round 'ere.'

'Near Penzance.' I entered a cream-carpeted hallway painted primrose yellow, a smell of citrus air freshener making my nostrils itch. 'Thank you for seeing me.'

'This is a real surprise,' she said. ''Aven't thought about you in years.' She closed the door and looked me up and down with open interest. I must look a mess. I hadn't bothered with make-up, and my hair had been whipped around from driving with the windows down. I smoothed it back and tugged my top over my shorts, self-conscious under her scrutiny. 'You're the little girl who nearly drowned.'

'That's me!' It came out jaunty, as if I might do jazz hands. 'I didn't though, thanks to your husband, Mike.'

197

She made a noise, between a laugh and snort of derision. 'Only decent thing that bastard ever did, pardon my language.'

I froze, not sure I'd heard correctly.

She turned, indicating I follow. 'Let me get you a drink – you look hot.' As she headed down the hall, I noticed she had a slight limp. 'This weather's starting to get on my nerves,' she said. 'If I'm 'onest, and I never thought I'd say this, we could do with some rain. Mind you, there's a storm brewing. I can always tell because my arthritis plays up; it's in my hips, see?' She patted the left one. 'Tea, coffee, or something cold?'

I managed to unglue my feet from the floor. 'Water will be fine, thank you,' I said faintly, following her into a small, square kitchen that smelt faintly of last night's dinner – something spicy. In contrast to the hallway it was a messy jumble of colour, mostly due to the number of teapots in various shapes and sizes lining every surface.

'I collect them,' she said, seeing me blink at the huge array. 'Got a cabinet in the other room, full of them. My kids and grandkids buy me one every Christmas and birthday.' She shook her head, hooped earrings dancing, and her tanned face relaxed into a smile. 'I won't be able to move for them soon,' she said, taking a glass from a pine cabinet above the worktop. 'George reckons he might have to move out.'

It felt so surreal, standing there, listening to her everyday chatter, trying to work out why she'd spoken like that about Mike. A ginger cat came through the open back door and wound around my ankles, purring loudly.

'Tommy's come to say hello.' Angie beamed fondly as she handed me a glass of tap water, which I drank in a few gulps. 'Biscuit?'

At a loss for words, I nodded.

'Sit down.' She nodded to a table jammed against the wall, a chair at either end. I obeyed, and while she peeled the lid off a Tupperware box, I glanced around, looking for evidence of the other occupants of the house. 'You have children?'

'Three, all grown up now.' She offered me the box of biscuits, watching as I took one and ate it quickly. 'Have another.'

I shook my head and she replaced the lid before settling herself opposite me, wincing as she got comfortable. 'They're not his,' she said, without preamble. 'The kids. They're not Mike's, if that's what you were wondering.'

'Right.' I tried to work out what that meant. If they weren't his children, there was no history with me – no need for revenge for the loss of their beloved father. It sounded as if Angie hadn't lost any sleep over his loss, either.

'You said he . . . Mike . . .' For some reason, I stumbled over the name. 'You said saving me was the only decent thing he'd ever done.'

Her mouth puckered, creating grooves in her peach-coloured lip liner. 'He wasn't a good person,' she said starkly. 'I should never have married him; he was sixteen years older than me for a start. My mother tried to warn me. "Once a cheater, always a cheater," but I was in love, thought he'd be different with me.' She shrugged. 'I was wrong.'

'I'm sorry.'

'Don't be.' Her face hardened. 'He got what he deserved.'

Her words hit me like a slap. This wasn't going remotely how I'd imagined. There was no shrine here to a well-loved husband, no grieving widow and children. Angie sounded as if she'd hated Mike.

She was talking again. 'I thought at first he'd gone into the sea to impress *her*.' She spat the word like venom. 'His other woman, one of many I may add – he left a trail of broken hearts – but when I found the note and discovered he'd been planning to go, it must have seemed like divine intervention, you getting into trouble like that. A chance to die like a hero. Not that I was having any of that.'

She looked at me darkly, in the grip of an old emotion. 'I told the police not to release his name, said I didn't want any publicity,

199

any contact with the family.' *The family*. Me. 'I knew *she* wouldn't want it getting out, not that she was capable of much anyway, bloody mess she was – I think he'd woken up to that. It's why he wanted out, and me telling him I'd never divorce him didn't help, but why should I have made it easy for him?' Her gaze was faraway, somewhere tangled and dark. 'He'd had it easy for too long. Anyway, he took the coward's way out, because that's what he was, deep down. A coward.'

Her stream of words ran out and she refocused her gaze on me, as if trying to solve a riddle. 'I don't suppose this is what you were expecting to hear.'

My thoughts were running like mice. I couldn't seem to arrange them into any sort of order. 'Not exactly.' I gripped my half-empty glass. 'I've thought about him for so long, you see, about how he died saving my life, feeling so guilty and wondering how his family had coped, thinking you must hate me—'

'Hate you?' Her voice sharpened. 'You did us a favour.' Her hand came to rest on my knee. 'My life improved no end after he'd gone.'

I reeled back. 'That's . . . harsh.'

Angie sniffed and sat back, seeming to deflate a little. 'I wouldn't have met George if Mike hadn't died. He made me believe in love again.' Her face softened, the lines around her eyes smoothing out. 'Twenty-five years we've been married, and never argued once. He treats me like a princess.'

I clutched at her words, knowing them to be true. It was comforting to know she hadn't suffered, even if her reaction was a bit extreme. 'Are his parents still alive?'

She sat back, seeming startled by the question. 'They were getting on when they had him, were dead before I met him,' she said slowly. 'Partly why I fell for him, to be honest. He made out he was some lonely orphan who needed love, needed a big family . . . very charming he was. Until we were married, then he went off the whole idea and started having affairs. He liked the thought of being in love, not the reality.' Her eyes darkened. 'He could get nasty sometimes.'

The picture she was painting wasn't pleasant, but I had to say it. 'If it wasn't for him, I wouldn't be here. I . . . I thought I could visit his grave, at least.'

That gave Angie pause. 'Like I said, at least he did one good thing in his life before he died, and I'm glad for you.' She shook her head. 'But you shouldn't have spent all this time feeling bad about it, love. You don't owe him anything. You were only a child. It was his decision to swim out after you that day.'

Hearing the words so often repeated over the years by family, friends and counsellors sounded different coming from Angie. *His decision. You were only a child.* I could feel them seeping through me, wrapping around my heart. Would it have made a difference, knowing – as Angie had viciously put it – that Mike hadn't been a nice man; that he hadn't been mourned, there were no heartbroken children, that his parents had been long-dead? *Probably.* I didn't know whether to laugh or cry, thinking of all the times I'd imagined the lives ripped apart by his death. 'I'm who I am, because of that day,' I said. 'I became an art therapist so I could help other people, make my life worthwhile to justify Mike losing his.'

'There you go then.' Angie became brisk, matter-of-fact. 'Another good thing that came out of him dying.' She smiled properly, her eyes friendly. 'You know what, I'm glad you came. It's good to know things turned out well for you. I couldn't have cared less the day he was found, if I'm honest. I was so bloody angry with him.'

'You said there was a note,' I said. 'What sort of note?'

Her smile dimmed. 'He pushed it through the letterbox that morning. Not here, we lived in Truro then, big house with all the trimmings. He weren't short of money, even if it was inherited. Anyway . . .' She gave herself a little shake. 'I'd been out at work and when I got back it was there, on the mat. Said he'd had enough, he couldn't take any more, that I wouldn't be seeing him again.'

'Like . . . a suicide note?'

She raised one shoulder, let it fall. 'Either he was planning to do away with himself, or do a runner, get away from her. I don't know why he was there that day, unless he was planning to jump in the sea. There's a notorious spot nearby for jumpers.'

I was trying to get my head around what she was saying. 'You think maybe he didn't make it back to the beach deliberately?'

Both shoulders lifted this time. 'All I know is, Mike was a really strong swimmer. He competed at national level when he was younger. It was his favourite way to keep fit, or so he said. He used a friend's pool a lot, though it turned out he was sleeping with the wife.'

I ignored the last bit. 'You said he was seeing someone else when it happened.'

Angie's eyes frosted over. 'Linda Taylor,' she said, making a face as though the words tasted sour. 'An alcoholic. You could tell, even though she was pretty. Lot younger than him, that's how he liked them. She lived with her mum on the Gadsbrook Estate near Truro, probably still does, if she hasn't drunk herself to death. Worked nights in a fancy bar in the town – that's where she met Mike. God knows what he saw in her. I think he liked being in charge, or maybe he really loved her. Who knows?'

She stopped as a man appeared in the doorway. He was big, his fleshy face topped with thick grey hair, with eyes that twinkled behind round glasses. 'I didn't know you were expecting guests today.'

'This is George.' Angie got up and rubbed her hip with a wince. 'George, this is the young lady I told you about.'

I rose, returning his slightly bemused smile. 'I've got to go,' I said, desperate for some space to process all the new knowledge. 'Thank you so much for talking to me.' I turned to Angie. 'I can't tell you how much it's helped.' It was true. I felt lighter than I had half an hour ago – maybe than I had for years – even as my brain still seethed with questions. Had Mike really intended to take his own life and I'd unwittingly been his way out? It was an odd sort of consolation, if it was true.

'It was nice to meet you.' Angie's face worked briefly. 'You look after yourself now.' She opened her arms and I moved into them, not sure what to do with the rush of emotion in my chest. 'Don't give that man another thought.' She pressed a clumsy kiss on my cheek and I breathed in her flowery scent. 'Just get on with your life.'

I wanted so much to do exactly that, but as I left Angie and George on their doorstep and drove out of sight, my mind returned to the newspaper I'd found that morning; to Vic, and to everything that had happened since my birthday, and I knew it wasn't that simple.

Someone wanted me dead, and I still didn't know who, or why. All I knew was, it had nothing to do with Angie.

Maybe Linda Taylor would have some answers.

Chapter 27

I pulled the car over at the end of the road and googled the Gadsbrook Estate in Truro. Thirty minutes away.

I called Rosa. 'I'm sorry to ask for another favour, but can you check something for me, urgently?'

To her credit, she didn't ask questions, just took down the details. 'Give me five minutes,' she said.

While I waited, I checked my messages. Vic wanted me to let him know I was OK. *I'm missing you xx*

I wanted so much to call and tell him where I was, what I'd learnt, but no longer knew whether I could trust him and didn't want to dwell on what that meant for our relationship. *In a supply shop, looking at paints. Hope you've found a nice pub! XX*

When he didn't reply, I texted Matt.

How's Hayley?

He replied right away, with a photo of Hayley standing on a chair in his Mum's kitchen, wearing a daisy-patterned apron, her hands and face dusted in flour. Her hair was in lopsided plaits, and the thought of Matt painstakingly weaving her hair made my throat ache.

Having fun. You?

I replied with a smiley face, not trusting myself to write anything that might give away my mood, which was an unsettling mix of euphoria and fear, combined with a wild desire to howl at the sky.

Two minutes later, I had my reply from Rosa. *No Linda, but a Maggie Taylor at number 4 Kingfisher Road. Lived there 30 years.*

Maggie must be Linda Taylor's mother.

Thanks, Rosa. Talk soon. X

I'd just turned the corner at the end of the road when my phone began to ring. I pulled over, surprised to see Marianne's number.

'Have you seen Katya?'

'What?' It took a second for my brain to recalibrate. 'Why would I have seen Katya?'

'She didn't go home yesterday. She messaged her foster mum to say she was coming to find you.'

'Find me?' I was having trouble computing Marianne's words. 'She knows I'm away for a few days.'

'Exactly,' Marianne said. 'She's coming down there.'

'Why?'

'I don't know, Beth.' Her voice was sharp with worry. 'I thought *you* might know.'

I recalled my last conversation with Katya, remembered her tears, my promise that I'd be back, and felt a queasy flicker in my stomach. 'I've been worried about her lately,' I confessed. 'She's become too attached, I think.'

'And you're bringing this up now?' The usual warmth had been pared back. 'Don't you think you should have said something?'

'I was trying to decide how to deal with it, without getting her into trouble,' I said, going hot with shame. 'I thought I could get to the bottom of what was going on.'

'Well, clearly something is.' I knew it wasn't just concern for Katya. If it turned out she was suffering some sort of breakdown that we – *I* – hadn't flagged up, it would reflect badly on Marianne.

'I'm so sorry, I really am.' I tried to think through the chatter in my head. 'She can't know where I'm staying though, so I don't see how she can find me.'

'She's a bright girl; she'll have found a way.' Her tone was abrupt. 'The police aren't too worried because of the text she sent, but obviously Dee's concerned.'

'What can I do?'

'Just let us know if she turns up.'

'Of course.'

'I wish you'd talked to me, Beth.'

'Me too,' I said, miserably. 'Maybe I could call her, tell her to go home.'

'Her phone is switched off, and I don't think you telling her to go home is going to help.' Marianne grew more placatory. 'Do you know what it's about?'

I pinched the skin between my eyebrows. 'She was worried about me,' I admitted. 'She wasn't happy about me going away.'

'Did she say why?'

'No, but it could be a fear of abandonment, you know, because of her mother.'

'I thought that had all been dealt with in counselling.' Marianne's voice faded out, then came back. 'I have to go,' she said. 'Keep us posted, Beth.'

'I will.'

She hung up and I stared at my phone, feeling sick. Any euphoria from moments ago had dwindled to a sense of foreboding. I knew I should drive back to Penzance, forget about Maggie Taylor . . . but if I could speak to her about Linda, I had a feeling something crucial might slot into place – maybe even involving Katya.

If Maggie wasn't home, I would leave a message, asking her to call me.

Suddenly faint with hunger, I swung the car into the nearest petrol forecourt and bought a ham sandwich from the shop. I ate it one-handed as I drove, my mind swooping from Katya, to Angie, to Maggie Taylor, to Vic and back to Katya.

Could she really be in Cornwall – in Perran Cove? I had no

doubt she was capable of finding out where I was staying and Vic would call if she turned up – if he was there. She'd be safe at the cottage.

But, was I?

A now familiar headache pushed behind my eyes, not helped by the blazing sun bouncing through the windscreen. I wished I hadn't left my sunglasses at the cottage.

My nerves leapt when I arrived at the Gadsbrook Estate, which was a warren of cul-de-sacs, lined with boxy, identical houses. Kingfisher Road was narrow and winding, edged with cars on both sides, and a group of teenage boys with skateboards watched as I drove slowly down it, peering in vain for number four. In the end, I drew into the tiny car park behind a shop called Trewin's at the end of the street, with an overflowing litter bin outside, and made my way back on foot, feeling conspicuous. I was clutching my bag as if expecting someone to snatch it. I hoisted it onto my shoulder, walking with more purpose.

Number four was in a state of disrepair, paintwork flaking off the door and window frames, the garden parched and overgrown, the path cracked and weed-clogged. The elderly woman who answered my knock didn't look much better: stringy grey hair hanging limply around a gaunt, lined face, her hands and face dotted with liver spots.

'What?' Her irises were pale, the whites of her eyes a sickly yellow. She'd been drinking, the stench of alcohol seeping from her pores.

'Are you Linda Taylor's mum?'

'Piss off.'

As she started to close the door, I wedged my foot in the gap. 'Please, I just want to talk to her,' I said. 'Can you tell me where she is?'

The door swung wider. 'What's this about?'

'It's to do with Mike Barrett,' I said. 'A long time ago, he and Linda were—'

'Who *are* you?'

'It's a long story,' I began.

'I haven't got all day.' She glanced behind her, as if there was a stack of work waiting, one bony hand clutching the doorframe as if to hold herself up.

'I'd really like to speak to Linda.'

'You'd have to be a medium to do that,' she slurred. 'Linda died a long time ago.'

I stiffened. 'Linda's dead?'

'Overdose.' She sniffed, wiping the back of her hand across her nose. 'Booze and pills.'

I let that sink in for a second. 'Mike Barrett,' I said, more hesitant. 'Did you know your daughter was having a relationship with him?'

Maggie bared her teeth. One was missing at the front, the rest stained brown. 'Promised her the world,' she said with a half-hearted sneer. 'She got clean for him then he went and died. After that, she gave up.'

The pain in my temples intensified. 'I'm so sorry to hear that.'

'Lost cause, that one.' Her eyes had gone watery. Was this the tragedy I'd been expecting at Angie's? 'Started a long time ago,' she said, head drooping forward, as if the bulk of memories was too much. 'Like her mum she was, chip off the old block, always falling for the wrong man, probably looking for a father figure. Her dad was no effing good, took off when she was two. She should've . . .' She mumbled more words I couldn't catch, seeming to lose track of where she was, and started to close the door again. As she did, a crooked line of photos on the stained wall by the stairs leapt into focus. The nearest was of a boy, aged about ten, dark-haired with big, solemn eyes. Something about him seemed familiar. 'Is that your son?' I pointed and Maggie turned, swaying slightly. The billowing garment covering her from neck to toe was a nightdress, her bird-like frame visible through the cotton. 'My grandson,' she said in a maudlin tone. 'Jack's boy.'

'You have a son?' Perhaps he – Jack – could tell me more about Linda. 'Do you think I could have his number please, Maggie? I'd like to talk to him.'

She squinted at me, as if trying to remember who I was. 'Lives abroad,' she said, sparse eyebrows pulling together. 'Doesn't have nothing to do with me, haven't spoken to him in years.'

'Your grandson?'

'Just said, didn't I? They live in New Zealand, or America or somewhere. I can't remember.' Her face contorted. 'Piss off, you nosy bitch.'

The door slammed shut in my face, a flake of dull red paint floating to the ground.

I drove back to Penzance on autopilot, thoughts whirling like dried leaves. I thought about the differences between Angie and Linda, the two women in Mike's life; one he'd married and the other he'd . . . what? Promised the world to, according to Maggie.

And after he died, whether it was suicide or by accident, Angie had managed to move on and be happy, glad he'd gone for good, but Linda, in love with a man much older and – according to Angie – not short of money, who'd promised her a better future, had found life so bleak when he'd died, she'd chosen to end it.

And what about her brother, Jack? The son who fled to the other side of the world to escape his family? Had something gone wrong there? Was he back, wanting someone to pay for his sister's death? If Mike hadn't died, Linda might still be alive – they might have married, she could have had a child. All their lives would be different, just as mine and my family's would have been, if Mike had lived. We'd been damaged by what happened, but at least we were alive and well – thriving, even. Happy, in comparison to the Taylors. How hard would that be for someone whose life may have spiralled out of control and was looking for someone to blame? Like his sister, Jack may have inherited an alcohol addiction from their mother. I knew nothing about him, and yet . . .

Vic Berenson's not his real name.

It was ridiculous to think they could be the same person. And Vic had a sister, very much alive, in Canada. A sister I'd never met. What if he'd concocted a life that didn't exist, in order to infiltrate mine? He really would have to be a psychopath to do that and it didn't fit with everything I knew about Vic.

Psychopaths are convincing liars.

'Shut up, Emma,' I muttered.

I was nearly in Penzance, the miles having passed unnoticed, when I swung into a pub car park and picked up my phone.

'What's his real name?' I said, when Emma answered on the first ring.

'You still haven't asked him then?' Considering she must be at work and I rarely called, she didn't sound remotely surprised to hear from me.

'I'm asking you.' *Please, don't let it be Jack Taylor.*

'OK.' I heard her sharp intake of breath. 'It's Jonathan Ryder.'

For a second, I felt dizzy with relief. *Not Jack Taylor.* I exhaled a long breath. 'How did you find out?'

'I did some digging after our conversation the other day. Checking him out.' I let that go, for the moment. 'Turns out there's no birth record for a Vic Berenson anywhere in the UK, but there was a record in the National Archives from 1998 when he changed his name from Jonathan Ryder.' There was no triumph in her voice, just concern. 'He changed it when he was eighteen,' she said. 'You have to admit it's dodgy, Beth.'

'OK, it's odd, but he declared it, which he didn't have to do. It's not illegal to change your name by deed poll.' I couldn't remember how I knew that, but was certain it was true.

'But, why change it and not tell you?'

'Because he's been Vic Berenson for twenty-two years.' I rested my forehead on the steering wheel. My head felt like it was in a vice. I longed to feel fresh air on my face, to have a cold drink and to sleep for twelve hours straight.

'If he kept that from you, what else might he be hiding?'

I remembered the newspaper at the cottage. 'We'll talk when I get back.'

'Beth, wait—'

I rang off and shut my eyes. *Jonathan Ryder.* I couldn't associate the name with Vic. It was a sensible name, a nice name even. Why had he changed it, and why Vic Berenson? And what if he'd changed it more than once? He could have been Jack Taylor at some point.

I couldn't make it add up, or stop the questions rampaging around my head. I gave a strangled scream and jumped when a voice said, 'Excuse me, are you OK?'

I lifted my head. A young couple were peering through the car window with alarmed expressions. 'Are you ill?' said the female, her face a worried frown.

I summoned a smile that I hoped didn't look demonic. 'Thanks, I'm fine.' I rested a hand on the steering wheel. 'I've been driving all day and needed to stop for a rest.'

They nodded their understanding and moved away as my phone buzzed. It was a text from Tabitha at the art gallery.

Love the paintings, bring them in ASAP!! Got a couple of interested parties already. Think this is going to be your moment! T X

A burst of pleasure ignited and quickly died. It would be ironic if I finally became famous after my death, like so many great artists.

Not that I was great, and I didn't want to be famous.

I just wanted to live.

Chapter 28

I wasn't ready to go back to the cottage, and drove the few miles from Penzance to St Ives, where I parked the car and wandered through the narrow, cobbled streets, past whitewashed slate-roofed cottages, my thoughts zig-zagging. I looked unseeingly in the windows of shops, bakeries and galleries, Angie's face merging with Maggie Taylor's, their voices overlapping with Emma's in my head.

Avoiding the seafront – mindful of my last visit, when huge waves had leapt over the railings like crazy horses and I'd screamed with terror – I took refuge in a vegan café where I toyed with a salad and drank two cups of green tea, scrolling through photos of Hayley on my phone. I called Pam, who sounded thrilled to hear from me and assured me all was well next door. 'I've been watering the garden. Don't worry about a thing.'

Fat chance.

When my headache had eased a little, and the noise in my mind was quieter, I visited the Barbara Hepworth Museum and Sculpture Garden, and bought a Little Scientist jigsaw I knew that Hayley would love.

When I couldn't put it off any longer, I drove back to Perran Cove, spotting the police car as I wound up the path to the cottage.

It must be the officer Rosa had spoken to. Andrew Fellowes. I'd expected him to call, not drop round, but maybe this was better. If I was going to confront Vic – and I didn't see that I had a choice – it might be better to have a . . . the word *witness* sprang to mind and I pushed it down. It would be good to have someone else there.

My legs felt leaden as I got out of the car. As if in tune with my mood, the sun disappeared behind a bank of clouds and the breeze raised the hairs on my arms.

As I stepped through the door, the low voices from the living room stopped. A uniformed officer was sitting in the armchair, knees spread wide, a notepad in his hand. Vic was standing in front of him with his arms folded.

He spun round, a look of comical relief on his face. 'Here she is.' He came over, but I sidestepped his attempt at a hug so our arms clashed. 'This is PC Fellowes,' he said, after a moment's awkward silence. 'I've been talking him through everything.'

'Why did you change your name?'

The air seemed to thicken as the colour drained from Vic's face. 'How did you know about that?'

'It's true then?'

'Yes, but—'

'Is . . . everything OK?'

My gaze swivelled from Vic's sickly pallor to Andrew Fellowes. He was bulky and bearded with a heavy brow and dark, deep-set eyes that flicked between Vic and me. Reassured by his solid presence, I turned back to Vic.

'Tell me who you really are.'

'Beth, please—'

'It's not a trick question.'

He lifted his arms and ran his hands over his head. 'I'm exactly who you think I am.' He met my gaze with the slightly stunned look of a sleepwalker woken in the middle of a nightmare. 'I'm Vic Berenson.'

213

'Except . . .' I took a step back. 'You're not.'

'Would you like to explain, sir?' PC Fellowes had got to his feet, a look of watchful curiosity on his face. I noticed his hand stray to the radio on his shirt, as if he might need to call for backup.

Emboldened, I said, 'Yes, *Vic*. Would you like to explain?'

He looked cornered, turning once on the spot as if seeking an escape route, then seemed to make up his mind. 'Fine.' He smoothed a hand round his jaw. 'Vic Berenson wasn't the name I was born with,' he said. 'I changed it – *legally*,' he stressed, for the officer's sake, not looking at me. 'I did it because I wanted to break ties with my old life once I turned eighteen; become someone new.'

Watching a nerve jump under his eye, I knew with a chilling certainty I'd made a mistake.

'My childhood wasn't happy,' he went on, still directing his words to Andrew Fellowes, who was listening attentively. 'My parents died in a car crash when my sister and I were very young and we were raised by an aunt who was . . . let's just say, not the kindest person in the world, though I'm sure she did her best. I was badly bullied at school for being "brainy"—' he made quote marks '—and I decided I didn't want to be that person anymore, so I chose a new name. A combination of my father, Victor, and my mother's maiden name, Berenson, to honour my parents.' *Oh, Vic.* 'You can check it out if you want,' he said, again to the officer. 'There's no mystery – I just became . . . Vic. I don't even think about my old name. I just wanted to choose one that I felt suited me better.'

I had the feeling it would hurt him too much to look at me now – to acknowledge the extent of my betrayal.

'Well, that makes sense, and as you say, it's not illegal.' Andrew Fellowes turned to me, searching my face with friendly vigilance. 'Does that sound OK to you?'

I nodded, close to tears, knowing I'd flushed scarlet. 'I just wish you'd told me, Vic.'

'It didn't seem relevant.' He looked at the floor. His face was

214

set, hands loose by his sides. I knew with a sinking feeling that there was no coming back from this.

Buoyed up by something beyond my control, I stalked to the kitchen and yanked the newspaper out of the bin before storming back and thrusting it under his nose. 'Why did you bring this here?'

Startled out of whatever state he'd fallen into he took it from me, brow furrowed. 'What am I looking at?'

'The headline.'

His eyes flicked across the page. Seconds later, understanding spread over his face. 'Jesus, Beth.' The disgust in his voice made me reel. 'It was on the worktop when we got here,' he said. 'I saw it when I was making coffee, when you went upstairs to the bathroom. I assumed it had been left by whoever had been here before us and I threw it in the bin.'

'What's the headline?' I'd almost forgotten Andrew Fellowes was there.

'It's about me,' I said, my voice too high. 'And the man who saved my life in 1992.'

His eyebrows lowered. 'That seems like an odd coincidence.'

'It's not a coincidence,' I said. 'This is what's been happening, what Rosa, the officer who called you, was talking about.'

'It's nothing to do with me,' Vic said.

'Then how did it get here?'

'I've no idea.' His eyes narrowed. 'You actually think I'm responsible for this, as well as everything else?' Reading my face, he made a dull sound in his throat. 'Unbelievable.' He threw the paper onto the table and turned to PC Fellowes, who was watching our exchange with unnerving intensity. 'I promise, this isn't my doing,' he said, one hand patting the air in front of him. 'Everything I told you, before Beth came back, about the texts, about her being followed, or stalked, or whatever the hell's going on, it's not me, I'm not gaslighting her. I'm trying to help her, for God's sake. I love her.' His words, wrenched from deep inside him, had the unmistakable ring of truth.

The officer looked at Vic for a long moment, as though weighing up what he'd said, then turned to me. 'Do you feel safe here with Mr Berenson?'

'Of course I do.' But it was too little too late. Vic's humourless laugh felt like a recrimination.

'Obviously she doesn't, but it's fine, I'll go.'

'Vic, no. Don't be silly.' I put a restraining hand on his arm as he made to move away. 'We've only just got here.'

Andrew Fellowes cleared his throat. 'I'll leave you to it, shall I?' I had the impression from the look he gave Vic that he felt rather sorry for him.

'Is it possible to leave a car here, until we leave?' I said.

Vic gave another hollow laugh. 'I'm not going to murder you,' he said, with a bitterness I'd never heard from him before.

'Oh, Vic.' I felt wretched. 'Just as a precaution.'

'It isn't like in films,' the officer said, kindly. 'I'm afraid we don't have the resources for a stakeout.'

'No, of course not.' I felt my blush deepen. 'Of course you don't. I'm sorry.'

'I'll see myself out,' he said after a tricky pause. 'Call if you think of anything else we can help with.'

'Anything else?' I said under my breath, watching him head back to his police car, tucking his shirt more firmly into the waistband of his trousers. 'He hasn't done anything.'

'What were you expecting, Beth?' I felt Vic's breath on my neck. His voice was flat and empty. 'I'm going to pack.'

I spun round, regretting it when the pounding in my head increased. 'Vic, I'm so sorry.' I curled my fingers around his forearm. 'Please try and understand—'

'You've been investigating me.'

'Not me,' I protested. 'It was Emma, actually.'

He threw my arm off. 'I should have known.'

'She's worried, Vic – she put two and two together.'

'And made five.' He shook his head again, wearily this time as

216

he headed towards the stairs. 'I've never tried to hide anything from you.'

'I know that, now.'

'You should have known already.'

'I knew in my heart it wasn't you, but some of the things she said, they made me think.' My voice was rising towards tears. 'My head's all over the place, Vic. I didn't know what to think. I'm suspecting everyone . . . Jamie, Katya.' For some reason, I couldn't bring myself to mention Matt.

'Katya?' He turned, one foot on the stairs.

'Marianne called, said she's on her way here.' I grasped the change of topic like a lifeline. 'She's been acting oddly recently.'

'Isn't she one of your patients?'

'Yes . . . she's one of my clients, but—'

'Maybe you should have told the officer about that,' he said, as if he barely knew me.

Suddenly furious, I threw my bag down. 'How would you feel if it was you, Vic? How would you feel if *your* life had been threatened and you had no idea who was doing it, or why? Maybe your head would be fried too, trying to work it out.' I was crying now. 'I've got a daughter, Vic. I don't want her to be without me.'

'Maybe you should have mentioned your husband to the officer.' His voice shook with emotion. 'Matt has more reason than most to want you out of the way, now he knows you don't want him and he hasn't got access to his daughter twenty-four hours a day.'

'He can see her whenever he wants,' I sobbed, but I was deliberately missing the point and we both knew it.

For once, Vic didn't come to me, or attempt to reassure me, and I had the feeling again of something being withdrawn that I'd taken for granted. 'You're right – that I don't know what it's like to be in your shoes,' he said. 'But I've done my best to help you. I'm sorry that wasn't enough.' He took the stairs two at a time and I shot after him into the bedroom.

217

'Vic, please. Don't do this,' I cried, swiping tears from my cheeks.

He nodded at my open bag on the floor by the narrow wardrobe. 'I know you don't love me.' There was a catch in his voice. 'You haven't even unpacked,' he said. 'You decided not to bring your red dress, because you don't think I'm worth making an effort for.'

'That's not true.' But even as I said it, I wondered whether it was.

'You're not wearing the necklace I bought you, but I see you've kept the bracelet on.' I automatically looked at my wrist, circled by the bracelet Hayley had given me, picturing the ruby pendant coiled on the dressing table at home.

'It's not an everyday necklace, that's all.'

'I know you can't say you love me,' he went on, as though I hadn't spoken. 'I didn't want to push you, but now I know you don't feel it, either.' He pressed a fist to his chest and carried on before I could speak. 'I suppose I thought if I could get you here, get you into the sea and it went well, it might be enough to tip you over the edge.' He saw my expression and shook his head. 'Into loving me,' he said, lips compressing. 'Christ, Beth, what did you think I meant?'

He walked round to the window and stared out. He looked shadowy, distant, like an image I couldn't quite bring into focus. 'I booked us a table for tonight,' he said. 'I thought it would be nice to walk back in the dark and look at the stars.' His voice became self-mocking. 'How pathetic is that?'

I knelt on the bed and reached for him. 'It's not pathetic, Vic. It was a lovely thought.'

'Where were you really today?'

'I told you, I went to St Ives.' I felt sick. I wished my head would stop spinning. 'I bought a jigsaw for Hayley.'

'And you went to the Tate gallery, even though it's right by the sea?'

I sank down and pressed my knuckles to my mouth. 'I went to visit Angie,' I said. 'I wanted to talk to her about Mike.'

218

'What?' His face was a mask of disbelief. 'And you didn't trust me enough to tell me, I suppose.' I started to speak, but he held up his hands. 'You know what? I can't even talk to you right now.' He headed to the stairs.

'Where are you going?' I leapt up, steadying myself against the wardrobe.

'Into the village,' he said. 'I need some fresh air and a drink.' He paused and looked back, a greyish tinge to his face. 'Lock the door after me.' He sounded as if he hated himself for caring. 'I'll knock three times, so you'll know it's me when I come back.'

Seconds later, the door downstairs opened and slammed shut. I ran down and locked it, then sat on the stairs and wept into my hands.

Chapter 29

An hour later, I'd had a shower, taken a couple of paracetamols, eaten some toast and a banana and drunk a cup of coffee. I felt marginally better and called Hayley to say goodnight, letting her happy chatter dissolve some of my tension.

When she'd finished telling me how Grampy Turner had 'teached' her how to do fishing with a rod in the stream that ran by the farmhouse – the only water I could think of her being near without breaking out in a sweat – and about her bread, which had burnt, but 'Granny scraped off the black bits' she said, 'I wish I could give you a cuddle, Mummy.'

'I'm giving you a cuddle in my head,' I said, trying to keep the tears from my voice. 'Close your eyes and cuddle me back.'

'I can't!' She gave a shriek of laughter. 'Will you tell me a story when I come home?'

'I'll tell you six stories, I promise.'

'Sometimes, Daddy's sad,' she said out of the blue. 'I think it would be better if you'd comed with us to Granny's, like before, but you have to go to a holiday with Vic now don't you, Mummy?'

I closed my eyes, squeezing tears through my lashes. 'Daddy's happy because he's with you,' I said. 'I bet you're having a lovely time.'

'Are you sad, Mummy?'

I pulled a tissue out of my bag and pressed it to my face. 'Only because you're not here to tickle.'

She gave her throaty giggle. 'I'm going to tickle you on Friday.'

'I'll tickle you back.'

'I'll tickle you more and more and more.'

'I'll look forward to that.'

There was a clatter and then Matt's voice in my ear. 'Why are you sad?'

'I'm not.'

'Everyone sends their love.'

I wondered what Matt had told his family. Perhaps he'd painted himself as the good guy, worried that his daughter was living with her unstable mother and her lover. For all I knew, they were encouraging him to fight for custody.

'Your parents must hate me,' I said.

'Nobody hates you, Beth.'

'Somebody does.' His silence cut through me. 'Matt?'

'Has something happened?'

I couldn't work out his tone and felt too tired to try. 'Everything's fine.'

'Been in the big, bad sea yet?'

'No.'

More silence. Hard to believe we used to talk for hours, about everything and nothing.

'Vic had better be looking after you.'

As I pressed my lips together to stifle a sob, I saw my phone on the kitchen worktop light up with a call.

'Matt, I have to go,' I said quickly. 'Love you.'

I realised what I'd said as soon as I rang off. Obviously, it was a reflex, left over from when we were together. He'd know it didn't mean anything.

I dived for my mobile. 'Hello?'

'Is Katya there yet?' Marianne sounded breathless as though

221

she was running. 'There's CCTV footage of her getting on the train at King's Cross.'

A shockwave passed through me. 'She really is coming here?'

'She's not there then?'

'No, I'd have called.'

'We want to keep the police out of this, if possible,' Marianne said. 'Keep her there when she turns up and I'll come and get her, take her back.' She took a breath. 'What's your address?'

From nowhere, a memory jolted me. Marianne, outside Fernley House a few days ago telling me it was nearly the anniversary of her husband Mick's death. *Twenty-six years, but it doesn't get any easier.* Her husband's name was Mick. *Mike.* Both shortened versions of Michael.

My breathing stalled. Could they be the same person? Angie had said there were other women, that Mike left a string of broken hearts in his wake. Was Marianne one of those women? I'd told her bits and pieces about my past since we'd started working together. She could easily have put it together.

'Beth?' Was I imagining that she sounded nervous?

'How's Carl?' It was the first thing to pop out of my mouth.

'Pardon?' I imagined her eyebrows shooting up. 'What's he got to do with anything?'

Were Carl and Gemma Mike's children? What was it Marianne had said? *They've never had a good male role model in their lives.* They were the right age, too.

She said something else, but the signal was going and I couldn't make it out. I imagined asking how her husband had died, and was trying to frame the words when the signal cut out. I didn't answer when my phone rang again, relieved when it stopped abruptly.

I jumped when the landline shrilled, but Marianne didn't have the number.

'Just checking you're OK.' It was Vic.

'I'm fine, thank you.' I heard pub noises in the background and wished I was with him, sitting in the garden with a cold beer, or at a table in a cosy corner eating locally sourced food with a glass of wine.

'I'll be back soon,' he said.

'OK.' We sounded like acquaintances, not two people who frequently shared a bed and had explored each other's bodies. 'Vic . . .' I began.

'I'll see you later.'

When he'd gone the silence closed around me. I switched the TV on and turned it off again, unable to settle. Outside, the sky was fading to twilight. I pulled a cardigan over my vest top and pyjama shorts and went out onto the decking. The back of my neck prickled as my eyes strained through the gathering gloom. Something had snagged my vision: a figure crouching to avoid detection? There was nowhere to hide out here, just an expanse of gorse-covered grass as far as the cliff path. Beyond that, there was nothing but the rocky steps leading down to Perran Cove, where the sea would be swirling, dark and impenetrable.

'Hello?' My voice sounded small and insignificant. Would anyone hear if I screamed for help? I backed inside, locked the door and pulled the curtain across. Should I call PC Fellowes, ask if he could swing by? But I hadn't actually seen anyone. It was probably the night playing tricks, working on my overactive imagination.

Even so, I switched on all the lights and turned the TV on again. I sat on the sofa with the phone in one hand, the attack alarm in the other, and stayed there until I heard three knocks on the door.

'I thought you'd be in bed,' Vic said, when I let him in. Underneath a faint tang of beer, he smelt of the sea and I wondered whether he'd been for a walk on Porthen Beach without me. 'What's happened?'

He wasn't angry, but something had shifted, his concern tempered with caution, and with an overwhelming sense of sadness, I knew I couldn't confide in him anymore.

223

'Nothing,' I said, faking a lightness I was far from feeling. 'I was just on my way up.'

His gaze dropped away from mine. 'We'll head home in the morning.'

I nodded, unable to speak, but he was already halfway upstairs.

He fell asleep immediately, facing away from me. He was a still, quiet sleeper. There was none of Matt's tossing and muttering, or kicking off the duvet in the middle of the night, then wrenching it up again. I watched his outline for a while, trying to settle my mind, but when sleep wouldn't come, I got up and crept to the window. The sky was midnight-velvet, sprinkled with stars, and the moon had risen, tracing a silvery path across the sea. I thought about Mike out there in the ocean, battling the waves, but for once, no surge of guilt followed. If only the other thing wasn't still hanging over me.

Enjoy your birthday, Beth. It'll be your last.

I tensed as something caught my eye. For a second, I thought I saw the flicker of car headlights, further down the lane. I leaned closer to the glass. *Was that a car engine?* Maybe Andrew Fellowes had driven out to check up on us, something niggling at him about our encounter. Or had Katya finally arrived, dropped off by a taxi?

I craned my neck, waiting, but if there had been a car, it was gone. There was nothing out there but darkness and the endless, shushing sea.

It's almost time. It's come round too quickly. It's been more fun than I expected, watching you squirm, seeing you struggle to work it out, behaving like Miss Marple, suspecting everyone. I thought after your adventures yesterday, sneaking away like that, you might have worked it out, but I think I've given you too many red herrings. I noticed you didn't bother visiting his grave in the end. Turned your mind, didn't she? It's not far from here, actually. I went there myself, paid my respects. It never helps. Only reminds me of everything I lost because of you. Still. Not long now.

Soon, you'll be in your own, watery grave.

225

Chapter 30

I woke from a fitful sleep. Something had disturbed me. A gentle alarm on Vic's phone, waking us for our trip to Perran Cove.

He stuck his arm out and switched it off, falling straight back to sleep with a grunt.

Of course, he wouldn't want to go now.

Daylight had crept into the room. I slid out of bed, scooped up my clothes and slipped out of the bedroom.

Downstairs, I dressed quickly in my crumpled shorts and a T-shirt and checked my phone. My stomach lurched. There'd been a missed call, from an unknown number.

There was a message too. *Katya's back. The police were waiting when she got off the train at your end. She wanted me to tell you to be careful. She seems to think you're in danger. Marianne.*

Something loosened inside me. I hadn't realised just how worried I'd been about Katya. *If you speak to her again, tell her I'm OK and I'll talk to her when I get back.*

Marianne didn't reply, but it was early, and the message had come through hours ago. Remembering my theory, I wondered if it was even true that Katya had been coming to see me, or a way for Marianne to get the address of where I was staying. It wasn't as if I'd checked. Could she be on her way to Perran

Cove? I recalled Carl's shiny black car behind me as I drove to Fernley House the day after my birthday; how I'd been convinced the driver was following me, trying to scare me, but it was only Marianne. Marianne, with her love of true crime, her brilliant imagination that inspired creativity in her writing classes. She could probably dream up myriad ways to kill someone and get away with it. It seemed so unlikely she'd wish anyone harm, but it was always the last person you expected. At least, in films. But this wasn't a film, it was my life.

I poured myself a glass of cold milk and drank it quickly then looked around. The newspaper was still on the table, Vic's shoes tucked underneath, my cardigan thrown across the sofa, next to the phone handset. There was no evidence of anyone having a good time here. I knew we couldn't stay, not after I'd shown Vic that I didn't trust him. The damage was done. We'd go home, and then what? He'd move back to his place, I supposed, surprised that I was thinking like that, and not about trying to salvage what was left of our relationship.

I opened the curtains to see the end of a glorious sunrise, the sky marbled peach and rose pink, the sea like rippling silk. It would be a shame to go home without visiting Perran Cove. It had been the whole purpose of the visit. Then again, talking to Angie had been more valuable, and done more for my soul, than going back to the sea would. Even so . . . it would be good to know that I'd tried. And the water was calm today.

I quickly checked the forecast on my phone. Storm clouds tomorrow, but no rain today, just plenty of sunshine and a light sea breeze.

I picked up the laminate the cottage owner had left and studied the timetable of tides once again. Vic had been right; it was a very low tide right now. Maybe I could take some photos on my phone, run down and dip my toes in the sea, if I was feeling brave; be back before Vic woke up.

I briefly considered waking him, asking him to come with

me. Getting me down there had been his aim after all, but I had a feeling he'd want to set off back to Oxford right away, that indulging me now would be a step too far after yesterday. As it was, the journey home was going to feel uncomfortably long. Just the thought of it threatened to bring back my headache.

I ripped a sheet of paper from my notepad and wrote *Back soon, gone for a walk xx* so Vic wouldn't worry if he came down to find me gone.

I slipped my phone and keys into my pocket, pulled on my cardigan and grabbed an apple from the kitchen. My sneakers were by the door and I slid my feet in then paused for a moment, listening to the silence.

It was surely too early for anyone to be out there, waiting for me to emerge, so they could . . . what? I thought of the headlights I was sure I'd seen last night, but Katya was safe now.

She seems to think you're in danger.

Did Katya really know something? I thought about calling Dee to check Katya really was home, reassure her I was fine, but it might do more harm than good, and what if Marianne had lied? On impulse, I called the number PC Fellowes had given me instead.

'Good morning, Devon and Cornwall Police.' It was a different voice, female, slightly bored.

'Oh. Hi. It's Beth Turner,' I said. 'I'm staying at Wayfarer's Cottage.'

'How can I help?'

'I've a message for PC Fellowes.'

'PC Fellowes isn't due in until seven.'

'Oh. Right. Well . . . I wanted to him know, I'm going down to Perran Cove,' I said, as if it was perfectly normal to call the police station at five in the morning and relay this information. 'Now, I mean.'

'Right.' Her voice was neutral.

'He'll understand what it's about, if you could please let him know.'

'Can you be more specific?'

I moved away from the door as if Vic might be listening behind it. 'I'll call back in half an hour,' I said. That should give me enough time to get back up here. 'If I don't, I'm in trouble and you should send help.'

'Trouble?' The signal cut out as she started to say something else.

Heading away from the cottage, munching the apple, feeling the spring of heather beneath my feet, I tried not to give in to an urge to look behind me.

A woman in running gear with a swinging ponytail was jogging down the path, a glossy black Labrador lolloping at her side. She gave me a cheerful smile as she passed and raised a hand. 'Morning!'

I waved back and, reassured by the sight of normal life, carried on in the opposite direction, heading to where the path dipped, turning into steps that were roughly hewn into the rock face above the cove.

I paused and looked down, heart racing with sudden fear, and dropped my half-eaten apple. This was supposed to have happened with Vic at my side, but here I was alone, staring at the place of my nightmares.

The view shimmered and settled, not as I remembered at all. In my dreams, it was a place of crashing waves, a whirlpool of froth and ice sucking me down, flinging me about like debris, filling me up until I couldn't breathe. Only on waking could I superimpose the pale crescent of sand, the changing blues and greens of the water as it had looked when I went into it that day on my Lilo, while Mum and Dad lolled on towels, and Jamie ran out of the cave he'd been exploring and scrambled up the steps to buy ice-creams.

The urge to turn back and never look at this view again was strong, but I knew if I did, it would haunt me forever. Heart jumping, stomach sliding, I started down the shallow steps, gripping the iron rail that ran down the side – an addition that hadn't been there back when Jamie and I raced down, with no sense of fear, ignoring shouts of caution from Mum and Dad, excited to explore the rock pools, to look for treasure, and to get into the sea. We hadn't needed anyone else then, happy in each other's company.

'Race you,' Jamie had yelled from the bottom, eyes scrunched against the sun, skinny-limbed in his blue swimming shorts, already nut-brown from four days in the sun. I heard the echo of his voice as I reached the sand, feeling out of breath as I clung to a rock at the bottom, reluctant to let go.

The cove felt more secluded than it looked from above. Someone would have to peer right over to spot me there, and the water was closer than I'd thought, more than halfway up the small curve of beach. Maybe it was an illusion because I was physically closer. I knew from the timetable that the water wouldn't reach the steps for several hours.

'Come on, you can do this,' I urged, imagining I was one of my clients at Fernley House. 'One step at a time, and remember to breathe.' I took off my shoes and put them on the cluster of rocks behind me. Digging my toes into the cool, damp sand, I concentrated on moving my diaphragm up and down while keeping my eyes on the view.

It really was breathtaking; the sky a bowl of denim blue and blush pink reflected in the water. No wind disturbed the surface, which was a wrinkled expanse of silk, the sound no more than a gentle murmur as it lapped the champagne sand. It was too calm for surfing, though I knew round the rocky outcrop it could be a different story, white-capped waves blowing up onto Porthen Beach.

As I looked at the tranquil scene, a seal lifted its sleek head from the water and looked right at me, before bobbing under again. I laughed out loud with surprised delight, picturing Hayley's face when I told her. I imagined Matt beside me, scooping one arm around my shoulder, easing me forward. A swell of emotion moved through me.

I dug my phone out and snapped a picture. *Here I am,* I typed. There was barely any signal, but I sent it anyway, then worried it looked as if I was gloating. *Look at me! I did it without you, ha ha.*

I frowned at the screen. There was a message from Jamie, sent about ten minutes ago.

Where R U?

Jamie. I thought about him as I looked around me, inserting him into the scene; splashing through the water to push me around on my Lilo, both of us giggling as he tried to tip me into the shallows. *Hold your nose, Beth, it's easy. Put your head under. You can see the starfishes!*

I switched my phone to video and swept it round, noting the light on the water and sand, how black the rocks behind me looked, the cave he'd explored back then like a gaping mouth – seeing it all as I'd paint it once I was home.

I sent the video to Jamie, with a message. *Look familiar?*

It was an olive branch of sorts, but he'd probably think I was taunting him.

I remembered the screwed-up paper in his office, the footprint in my studio; how he'd always mocked my painting, my choice of career. How much he seemed to hate me, and what my counsellor had told me years ago, about him disguising his guilt – a guilt he'd denied ever feeling. My lungs grew tight and heavy. The memory of headlights the night before flew into my mind. Maybe I shouldn't have let Jamie know my exact location. What if he was here?

The video hadn't sent and, for once, I was grateful for the dodgy signal. I'd be back at the cottage soon. If Vic wasn't up, I'd wake him, and maybe we'd have breakfast together before leaving. I suddenly couldn't wait to get away.

My feet were wet. Surprised, I looked down and saw that the water had reached where I was standing. I took a stumbling step back. I'd checked the times of the tides, twice, and knew Vic hadn't got it wrong. How had the water moved so quickly?

It was OK. I could easily retreat. The steps were right behind me, no need to panic. I forced myself to stand still, to try to enjoy the satin caress of water around my toes. It was like being in the baby pool with Hayley – except it was the sea. The vast, unfathomable sea.

My pulse was racing. *Breathe, just breathe.*

There was no danger, I was safe. The sea was benign, as if showing me I needn't be scared. I took another photo, hands trembling slightly, this time of my feet. Further proof that I'd done it. I'd stood in the sea in Perran Cove and nothing terrible had happened.

Turning, I took a selfie with the sea and sky behind me, shocked by the wildness of the image looking back at me. I was pale, my hair a tangled mess, violet crescents beneath my eyes, which were wide and wary. I looked haunted.

I glanced around once more, committing the scene to memory, imaging it on canvas – a final painting for my exhibition in a few months' time.

Putting my phone in the pocket of my shorts, I reached for my shoes. One slipped into the water and I had to scrabble for it. As I straightened, holding out the sodden sneaker, I felt a familiar prickle at the back of my neck and whipped around. There was nothing now but the sea, lapping towards the cave on my right, just a metre of sand still visible at the mouth.

Glancing up, I searched for signs of life – dog-walkers, joggers on the path above – but saw only seagulls wheeling high, their mournful cries sending a shiver down my spine.

I reached for the iron rail, pulled one foot from the water and stopped.

A sound had reached me from somewhere: a child's cry. Every hair on my body lifted. *Hayley?* I knew it wasn't – couldn't be. A seagull dipped low, so close I felt a draught from its wings. I pressed a palm to my chest, feeling the rapid drum of my heart. It had been a seabird's cry, the sound amplified by the rocks rearing around me.

I began to climb, hand slipping on the rail, when the noise came again, faint but indisputable. Definitely a child. A cry for help.

Mummy!

My blood turned to ice.

It sounded to be coming from the cave, but how could that be? There'd been no one here when I arrived, no way of getting in that cave without being seen. A child couldn't have survived the night in there, not once the tide flooded in. Unless they'd clung to a rock . . . The thought made me breathless.

A wail, thin and eerie, sent adrenaline pumping through me. Dropping my shoes, I jumped, landing in ankle-deep water. I fished my phone out to call Vic, or the police. *No signal.* Should I go back to the cliff path and call for help? But there might not be any phone reception there either.

The water was still rising, but I could surely make it to the cave and back, just check there was no one inside.

I ran through the water, which splashed up the backs of my legs, and I was relieved when I reached the remaining sandy stretch in front of the cave.

I entered tentatively. 'Hello?' The acoustics bounced my voice back. *Hello, hello, hello.* 'Is there anyone in here?' *Here, here, here.*

I remembered following Jamie in during our treasure hunt, pretending to be pirates. It had the same smell as then, slightly sulphurous from the seaweed that had washed in. Shelves of black rock jutted from the walls and there was a boulder further down, covered in lichen, litter scattered around it. Dad would hate that. *Why can't people take their rubbish with them?*

Now I was there, staring into the blackness, it seemed unlikely the cave was inhabited. Whatever had made that noise, it wasn't a child.

About to back out, I heard another sound. Scrabbling, like

233

tiny claws on the slippery surfaces. *Rats?* I turned on my torch app and angled the beam around the damp walls of the cave. A movement, just out sight, made me drop my phone on the sand, which felt like damp concrete beneath my feet. Behind me, the water crept closer.

Frightened, I bent to retrieve my phone and heard the scraping sound again.

'Who's there?' I took a few steps back, trod on something sharp and gasped with pain. It was the jagged edge of a seashell, embedded in the sand. I lifted my foot to inspect it and a thin trickle of blood dripped from my sole. I needed to get out of here, now.

I turned, limping towards daylight and heard the voice again. *Mummy!*

It sounded ethereal, whispering around the cave like a voice from beyond the grave, but I didn't believe in ghosts.

Spinning round I called, 'Are you hurt?' My voice was louder, reverberating back. The wail started again and every hair on my body stood to attention. 'Hang on, I'm coming!'

I limped back the way I'd come, aiming my phone in front of me to light the way. I remembered the cave was long and winding, and how it had echoed with the roar of surf the last time I was here. It hadn't seemed scary back then, with voices and laughter trailing us from the beach; families like ours having fun. It had been an adventure.

Now, the walls felt as if they were closing in and fear sluiced in my stomach. My instincts screamed at me to get out, but I couldn't go without knowing who was in there. 'Are you hurt?' I called again. The sound of my own voice was my only reply.

I stopped as I came to a turning, knowing beyond that I'd be cut off from the light at the entrance behind me, where I knew the sea was waiting, inching closer. The torch beam was already fading as the phone charge drained. 'Please, tell me where you are.'

Are, are, are.

Something wasn't right. A sweep of goose bumps alerted me to another presence. I was worried I might faint, my legs giving way. *I shouldn't be here.*

As I turned to run, the remaining torchlight caught something in the blackness. Glittering eyes, watching me.

I screamed.

'You took your time.' A figure stepped forward. 'I thought you might not come in, but I guess no mother can resist a child's cry for help.'

A bulb of terror stuck in my throat, rendering me speechless.

'Thank God for my little recording, though it wasn't exactly convincing.' A laugh, devoid of humour, turned my insides to liquid. 'You're even more gullible than I thought.'

Horror circled my mind as the figure lunged, striking the side of my head with something hard. I felt a crack, my skull exploding with pain, and had only one thought before everything went black.

It really *was* the last person I'd expected.

Chapter 31

I opened my eyes, blinking into darkness, white-hot pain in my skull. I tried to lift my fingers to my temples, but my arms refused to cooperate.

Where was I? It was so, so cold. My teeth clattered. I was sitting in water, my shorts soaked through to my skin, something hard and jagged cutting into my back.

Reality crashed in. I was in the cave at Perran Cove. Sensing movement beside me, confusion ricocheted into panic.

'Sorry about that, but I had to make sure you couldn't get away.'

'My head . . .' Nausea clawed at my throat, making it hard to speak.

'Sorry, but I don't have any paracetamol on me.'

The voice, empty of warmth and emotion, made my skin shrivel. I tried to move, pain slicing across my shoulders. 'What have you done to me?'

'I've restrained you, just for now.' A humourless chuckle made my scalp prickle. 'Can't having you running off, now I've finally got you here.'

I realised with a pinch of terror that my hands were strapped behind my back, my shoulders straining out of their sockets. 'Why are you doing this?'

'I think you know why, *Beth*.' My name came out like a swear word. 'You're not that stupid.'

It hurt to move my eyes. 'I called the police,' I said, trying in vain to free my wrists. 'If I don't call back in half an hour—'

'They're supposed to send someone out, I know, but guess what?' A dramatic pause. 'That won't be happening.'

I closed my eyes. 'You spoke to them?'

'Let's just say, Andrew Fellowes is aware of your fragile state of mind, your paranoia that someone is out to get you.' The mocking tone was unbearable. 'I've assured him this has happened before, that it's nothing to be concerned about.'

'Until I turn up dead.'

'Ah well, the situation was worse than we thought.' Fake sympathy now, play-acting. 'It was all too much, which is why you came down here all alone to where it happened. You got into trouble, or took your own life, we'll never really know.'

'Someone could have seen you come down here.' My voice was a rasp I hardly recognised. 'You won't get away with it.'

'I was only trying to help.' Mock-surprise now, mixed with pretend sadness. 'I've been looking out for you. I was worried. I followed you here, saw you were in trouble. I did my best to save you but it was too late.'

A painful sob escaped. 'I have a daughter, Rosa.'

She dropped to her haunches in front of me, and the shock I'd felt when I recognised her smacked into me again. 'She'll get over it, just like I had to when my mother killed herself.'

I recoiled, her words landing like punches. 'Your mother was Linda Taylor?'

'Well done, Miss Marple.'

She returned to the rock she'd been sitting on and pulled her knees up, wrapping her arms around them. She was wearing a wetsuit, her hair slicked back from her face, her eyes black and bottomless in the white oval of her face. 'I thought you might figure it out when you spoke to my dear old granny.'

'She . . . she didn't mention Linda had a daughter.'

'Probably forgotten I existed, just like she forgot about Mum.' Her voice skimmed the surface of the words, but there was a seam of hatred running beneath. 'Old alkie,' she said. 'No wonder my mother couldn't cope, but we were good together, me and Mum. We didn't need that old bitch.' She smoothed her hair over one shoulder, wringing it out, then slid her feet into the water. It was rising quickly, covering my legs, which were stretched in front of me. I drew them up, wincing with pain. My chest constricted with panic and I wriggled against the bind around my wrists.

'You'll never get it off.' There was amusement in her voice. 'Good old cable ties.' She looked around as though we were in a restaurant. 'When the water's high enough for drowning, I'll take them off.' Her smile chilled me more than the water. 'It would look a bit suspicious otherwise.'

I tugged my wrists again, the pain excruciating. If the cable ties left cuts, it would raise suspicion when my body was found.

'They won't leave a mark,' she said, slicing through my lumpy thoughts as if she could read them. 'Why do you think I didn't use handcuffs?'

She dipped her fingers in the water and flicked it in my face.

I flinched away, crying out as agony seared through my head, becoming aware of a warm stickiness at my temple. 'My head's bleeding.'

'Plenty of rocks around,' she said, hunching her shoulders in a shrug. 'You fell and knocked yourself out.'

I let that sink in, fear pumping through me. 'How did you even know I'd come down here today on my own?'

'I actually didn't.' She spread her arms. 'I had a whole other plan, involving laying a trail to get you here, or Vic being with you, making it look like he was behind it all – maybe a murder, suicide event. I covered every possibility, believe me. I've been watching your every move, but you actually made it incredibly

238

easy by checking the tides, getting up early this morning and coming straight down.' She sounded almost disappointed.

'Have you been here the whole time?

She nodded. 'Staying in the old cottage at the end of the lane. It has a tunnel into here, would you believe? A lot of the cottages round here do – they were used by smugglers back in the day.' She sat back on the rock, head on one side as she studied me like I was a chemistry experiment. 'It's worked like a charm,' she said. 'You can't imagine how satisfying it is to finally achieve your life-long goal. The planning it's taken, you've no idea.'

'But how could you know we'd come to Perran Cove?'

'It's taken a lot of hard work,' she said, as if expecting a round of applause. 'I suggested it to your brother first, that it might be nice for the whole family to visit, but he was horrified.' She gave an unpleasant laugh. 'He thought it would be terrible for you, the poor sap.' She pressed her hands over her heart. 'But he's *my* sap,' she said, in a soppy voice. 'He doesn't hate you half as much as you think he does, but that worked in my favour.' She'd reverted to her normal tone. 'I worked on Vic after that. We get on well, you might have noticed.' Not waiting for an answer, she continued. 'I said I'd read this study about facing your worst fears, told him I reckoned if he could get you here while your dear ex-husband was away with your daughter, and get you in the water, you'd probably marry him you'd be so grateful.' She rested her hands on her knees and wagged her head. 'You do know he'd do anything for you, don't you?'

Not anymore.

'Anyway, the rest was easy,' she said. 'Fun really, like your face when you tried to show me the messages I'd sent and deleted from your phone while everyone was greeting the birthday girl.' She smacked her lips together. 'Hilarious, actually.'

She was literally insane. 'It was all you,' I said weakly. 'You ruined my painting, sent that inflatable, put the swimming leaflet on my car.'

239

She made a ticking motion. 'Top of the class, Beth. It was easy to pop in while no one was home, especially as I made a copy of your door key, although your nosy neighbour nearly caught me. I had to hide.'

'You left the bath taps running.'

'I did.' She was enjoying herself now, like a child showing off. 'Oh, and the art book your little shadow gave you – that was my idea.'

My head jerked painfully. 'Katya?'

'She's been working with me, without knowing why.' Rosa's teeth flashed white in a grin. 'It's obvious she's attached to you. I saw her trailing behind you after one of your sessions, like a love-sick puppy. I waited for her the next day and told her I thought you were being followed, asked her not to say anything, but to keep an eye on you for me, report back anything strange. I said she mustn't tell anyone in case it escalated.' She lowered her voice to a dramatic whisper. 'It was our little secret.'

'That's horrible,' I said, my words wobbling higher. 'Katya's vulnerable; you shouldn't have involved her.'

'Vulnerable's the best type.' Her delight was frightening. 'I said she should come to your party, even gave her an art book to give you as a gift—'

'That was you?'

'Of course.' She twirled her hand like a magician. 'She chickened out of coming, thought you might not like it, but I caught her the next morning hanging around outside your house. She was going to leave the gift on your doorstep, but I'd already left a parcel and didn't want her to see it, so I picked her up and told her she should stay away in case someone reported her.'

'You're sick.' I tried wrenching my wrists once more, realised the water had risen and was lapping around my waist. 'You've been playing with people's lives.'

'That was the point,' she said, as though it was obvious. 'I wanted to make you wonder about everyone in your little circle.'

'I suppose it was you . . . asking about my painting at . . . at the café.' My teeth had started to chatter, breaking my words up.

Rosa shook her head, pushing back a coil of damp hair that had fallen across her face. 'I asked someone to do it for me,' she said. 'I was outside, watching your reaction.' A smile split her face once more. 'You looked like a ghost when you came out.'

I could barely begin to process what she was saying, let alone take it in. 'Were you at the swimming pool the other day?'

She nodded. 'I was just watching. It was fun, seeing you try to hide how terrified you are. Did you know your husband – or should I say *ex* – was there too, keeping an eye on things. I don't think he trusts you, Beth.' She tutted and wagged a finger at me. 'But I have to say, I was impressed when you took off like a trained dolphin, because you thought Hayley was in trouble.' She cocked her head. 'It made me realise, you could be brave if you had to be, which makes this—' she brandished her arm around '—more of a challenge, but let's face it—' she gave an exaggerated wince '—this isn't the leisure centre, is it? There's no lifeguard coming to save you, just like there wasn't last time.'

My body juddered with cold and fright. She was nothing like the Rosa I thought I knew. But that Rosa wasn't real. 'Did you know . . . who I was when you met Jamie?'

'Obviously.' She snorted, not so cool anymore. 'Everything I've done has been with this moment in mind,' she said. 'I joined the police force so I could find you.'

'What?' I felt dizzy, as if I couldn't breathe; as if all the oxygen had been sucked out of the cave. 'That's crazy,' I whispered. 'Why would you do that?'

'Have you any idea how many Beth Abbots there are in the UK?' She threw up her hands. 'That's all I had to go on. A name in the local paper.'

'You put that newspaper in the cottage.'

'You really should take a Mensa test.' Her voice dripped with sarcasm. 'I got inside before you did,' she said. 'Being an officer

241

has so many advantages, the biggest one being that people trust you, but as it happened, you'd left a printout in your kitchen at home with the details of the cottage, including the code to the key box.' She mimed unlocking the door. 'You obviously found the copy of the tide table I left too.' She waited for the penny to drop. 'Yeah, that wasn't real,' she said, triumphant. 'I needed you to think you were safe to come down here, you see? Low tide is actually this evening.'

I made another, desperate attempt to release my hands, but felt the strength leaving my body. The water was icy as it stroked my chest, sloshing around my arms. I would probably die of hypothermia before I drowned. 'I'm truly sorry your mum died, Rosa, I really am.'

'Oh yeah, I know all about the guilt, the counselling. It's cute that you've suffered, but really, you all came through it pretty well,' she scoffed. 'You've no idea what it's like to really suffer, to lose the one person in the world you loved and relied on.'

I shrank from her words, frozen as much by the void in her gaze as the sea. 'How could I have known that would happen?' I said, pushing the words past my clattering teeth. 'I was only seven.'

'Mike was going to take us away from that crappy estate.' Her voice was low and intense now, pain spilling over. 'He'd bought a house, we were going to go travelling, he was going to send me to a private school. Mum stopped drinking because of him, she loved him, and she loved me better when she was with him and then he died.' She slid into the water in front of me, pushing her face close to mine. 'Because of you,' she hissed through her teeth, jabbing a finger at my collarbone. 'Because *you* were too stupid to learn to swim, his life – *our* lives – were over.' She grew still. 'I hated you from the moment I saw your name in the newspaper. When I found Mum dead, I vowed I'd find you one day and make you pay.'

In spite of my terror and the bone-numbing cold seeping through me as the water, disturbed by Rosa, splashed around

242

my chest, the urge to lash out was strong. 'He wasn't going to stay with you. He left Angie a note.' My breath was too shallow for my words to make much impact, but I saw her flinch. 'He'd had enough,' I said. 'He'd planned to kill himself – that's why he drowned.' I paused, panting. 'He *chose* to die.'

The relief of saying it, of finally feeling the truth of the words, gave me a burst of energy. 'You became a police officer, Rosa.' I wriggled again, trying to force my wrists apart, while the water slapped and danced against the rocks around us. 'You're a success, in spite of everything. Your mum would have been proud. You don't have to do this—'

The slap was a shock, snapping my head round, sending fresh ripples of agony reeling through me. 'It's not true about Mike,' she hissed, rattled for the first time. 'And don't talk about my mum. You know nothing.'

'I know you've used my brother, used us all.' Tears ran down my face. Water was around my throat like a soft pair of hands, waiting to strangle me. I braced my feet and tried to push myself upright, but Rosa gripped my shoulders, pressing me down, and I felt the strength in her arms. 'What do you think's going to happen when I'm dead?' I cried. 'My parents, Hayley, they'll be devastated.'

'Exactly.' Rosa let go of me and straightened. She flicked her hair back, calm again. 'And I'll be there, to step in. Be the daughter they no longer have, be Aunty Rosa to little Hayley. Jamie's not far off proposing, you know.'

I desperately wanted to stand up, even though I was terrified of toppling over and sinking under the water, but knew I mustn't risk Rosa lashing out again. 'You told me he was unhappy about your job.'

She gave a cruel laugh. 'Just another lie to make you suspicious.'

Poor, poor Jamie. I'd suspected him, when all along it was Rosa I should have been scared of.

'Please, Rosa, don't do this.' My voice cracked, my words

slowing as my energy suddenly drained. The cold was creeping into me, making me want to sleep.

As if sensing I was slipping away, Rosa pulled something from a belt around her waist. She leaned over and yanked me forward, pushing my face closer to the water as she freed me from the wrist ties. My arms bobbed forward, hanging uselessly in the water. I could taste salt on my lips, felt water rippling around my chin.

'Bye, Beth.' Rosa's voice was a distant echo all around me. 'I'd like to say it's been nice knowing you, but it wouldn't be true.'

I opened my mouth to say something, but I didn't know what.

'Have a nice death.'

I heard splashing and opened my eyes, lifting my head with an effort. Rosa was swimming away, her powerful arms slicing through the water, her feet kicking, creating a surge that sent spray into my mouth.

I coughed, tried to stand up and realised I already was, the water black and swollen all around me. Understanding flared bright in my mind. This wasn't a nightmare I could wake up from. It was real. I was going to drown and no one was coming to save me.

Chapter 32

Time seemed to shift and stretch. I held my arms out of the water, rubbing life back into them, shivering violently. I dipped my fingers in the water and skimmed the side of my head where Rosa had hit me. Pain rolled through my skull. My hair was matted, but at least the bleeding seemed to have stopped.

Not that it mattered. Whether I died of a head wound, hypothermia, or drowning, the outcome would be the same. I just hoped it would be over quickly.

Water dripped from the roof of the cave, rippling the sea around me. The boulder where Rosa had sat was now submerged. If the water rose any higher the entrance to the cave would be completely sealed off. How long before it closed over my head, filled my nostrils, dragged me out to sea?

Shoving my sodden hair off my face, I waded to the boulder, panting and whimpering with fear. I could cling to it if I had to, but for how long?

I tried to push further forward, but the weight of the sea pressed me back.

Maybe someone was out there now on the cliff path. It had to be six o'clock, maybe seven. I'd lost all track of time, had no idea where my phone was. Even if I had it, I couldn't call anyone.

With a shock of vertigo, I remembered my keys; shoving them in my pocket with my phone when I left the cottage. I sank my hand into the water to pull them out of my pocket, overcome with a brief, giddy burst of excitement.

Don't set it off by accident, Vic had said. *It can be heard for miles.* My fingers were numb and I nearly dropped the keys, but finally found the activation switch on the alarm and pressed it hard. *Nothing.* I shook it and tried again. Still nothing. The battery must be dead. Maybe it had been all along.

My cry of frustration echoed back, ending on an agonised sob. I slapped at the water then wrapped my arms around my chest. I couldn't feel my legs, and my sodden clothes were plastered to my skin. I tipped my head back and screamed until my throat was raw, the sound doubly shocking as it crashed against my ears. Tears coursed down my cheeks, mingling with the salt on my lips. No one was coming. And yet . . . I couldn't give up.

I thought of Hayley, fixing her face in my mind. I'd promised I would read her six stories when I got home. I'd promised Katya – Katya, who'd thought I was in danger, not realising the source – I'd come back.

The sea was pushing more strongly now, a breeze causing little swells that threatened to heave me off my feet.

Vic would see that I wasn't there; he'd come looking for me. I wished I hadn't said I was going for a walk, not wanting him to worry. *Would he worry anyway?*

Fear crawled over me, hollowing me out, threatening to erupt in hysteria.

I couldn't stay here, waiting. Waiting to die. The best chance I had of being seen was getting out of the cave and into the sea in the cove.

Pushing down the rising terror, I tried to remember everything I'd been told about swimming, about staying safe in the water; all the advice stored in my mind I'd been too frightened to put into practice.

Most people drown because they panic and tense up. Tense muscles use more oxygen. Stay calm. Tread water if you can. If not, get on your back and float.

With a great gasp, which was more like a screech of fear, I flipped round and launched onto my back, before I could think it through. The splash was terrifyingly loud in the tomb-like interior of the cave. *Starfish your arms and legs.* Dad's voice. *Gently move your arms to keep afloat.* I tried to regulate my ragged, squeaking breaths. If I tensed, if I panicked, I'd go under. My hand touched something and I swallowed a shriek. It was only a plastic bottle, one of the pieces of litter brought up by the water, bobbing past my head.

Keeping my limbs floppy, I moved my arms, inhaling several deep, slow breaths, emptying my brain of everything but the rise and fall of my stomach and Hayley's face, her smile, the sound of her pure, sweet laughter.

I was doing it. I was floating!

Water lapped around my ears, cradled my head, held my aching body in its chilly embrace as a gentle current swept me out of the cave. Suddenly, there was brightness all around and above me. Still breathing slowly – *in, out, in, out* – trying to slow my heartbeat in time with each breath, to not think how far below me the seabed was, I looked at the sky; a clear, true blue, like Hayley's eyes. *Matt's eyes.*

My body wanted to shiver, the water not yet warmed by the sun streaking across the horizon somewhere behind me. I tried to imagine I was in a heated pool, at a spa, in bed, underneath a puffy duvet with a hot water bottle, cuddled up with Hayley; anywhere but where I was.

I imagined the seal I'd seen earlier swimming up underneath me and whizzing me to safety, a school of dolphins transporting me on their backs.

As I breathed, I kept staring at the sky, blinking when water seeped into my eyes – or maybe they were tears, seeping out.

Memories reeled through my head: climbing the tree in the back garden with Jamie and hiding there, giggling, while Mum and Dad pretended they couldn't find us; Dad teaching us to ride our bikes – our best-ever present, we agreed; laughing behind our hands when we caught Mum and Dad slow-dancing in the kitchen one Sunday morning to a soppy song on the radio.

Other memories too. The first time I saw Matt in the pub, his tender expression the first time we kissed, the way he'd focused so carefully as we sliced the wedding cake his mum had baked for our wedding; the sound of our baby's heartbeat on the ultrasound machine; Mum's face when we broke the news that she was going to be a grandmother. Further back, to Emma laughing her outrageous laugh at college, head tipped back; dragging me to an awful party, doing a ridiculous jig until I joined in, helpless with giggles. Bella, my sweet-natured cat, who died the week after I went to college. The first painting I did that I was truly proud of, the one Mum hated.

Wasn't your life supposed to flash before you when you were dying?

I dragged myself back to the moment, began singing softly, anything that came into my head – nursery rhymes, snatches of songs I'd heard Matt play on the guitar, our song 'Paradise' and 'Let It Go', Hayley's favourite tune from *Frozen*, which seemed horribly apt.

My arms felt too hefty to move. My head tipped back too far, sending water up my nose. I coughed and felt like I was going to choke. I stopped singing as the urge to thrash and scream grew stronger. I must be far enough out now, visible to anyone looking in this direction. I tried to look at where I was, but my eyes were stinging, full of water.

The cold had numbed every part of me. I couldn't keep going, I couldn't—

Sounds reached my waterlogged ears. A shout. Seabirds over-head. And another sound, over the splashing of waves, like a motorbike. An engine, coming closer.

A powerful surge lifted me high and there was a commotion, a flash of orange – a lifeboat? Something bright was tossed into the water, there was a cry, then a splash that upturned me. I was under the foaming sea now, sinking lower, water in my throat and my chest; my eyes were burning.

It was happening all over again.

I felt resignation then, and a kind of grief came over me. As my lungs deflated, I began to rise, then suddenly there was another body in the water, a pair of strong hands beneath my armpits, lifting me up and up.

For a disoriented second, I thought the ghost of Mike was back to rescue me once more, but when we broke the surface it was my brother's face I saw; my brother, holding me above the water. I kept blinking and gasping, and I thought I was dreaming because it couldn't be Jamie and yet, somehow, it was.

'Hold on,' he said urgently. One arm around me, he reached for a rope that had been flung over the side of the boat. I was half aware of faces looking at me, flashes of orange waterproofs, large hands reaching out. 'Grab hold,' Jamie instructed, and I was being pulled effortlessly through the water and heaved over the side of the lifeboat and the crew were wrapping a silvery blanket around my shoulders. I collapsed in the bottom, suddenly weightless, crying and heaving while Jamie wrapped his arms around me from behind, pressing his face to my hair.

'I've got you, Beth, it's OK, you're going to be OK, you're safe now,' he was saying.

I hugged his arms, shivering and crying and retching, and never wanted to let go.

Chapter 33

Things became blurry after that. I was whisked to hospital by a waiting ambulance and kept under observation for the rest of the day, covered in thermal blankets, the most obvious worry being hypothermia. Unbelievably, when I'd drifted out of the cave, I'd only been in the water for fifteen minutes. It had felt so much longer – a lifetime longer.

I'd done everything right, I was told. Floating, keeping myself awake by singing, not panicking. Luckily, the water was a couple of degrees warmer than it would have been further out, where my body temperature would have dropped even further. As it was, with the time I'd spent in the cave – I'd been unconscious for a while before I came round – I couldn't have survived much longer. If there'd been a strong wind, I could have been thrown against rocks and it would have been much harder to stay afloat.

The main thing was, I hadn't panicked. I'd hung on for Hayley, I told Jamie, when I was capable of speaking. 'I couldn't leave her.'

He'd been at my bedside after talking to the police, and was filling me in on what had happened. 'I'd known something was off for ages, if I'm honest. When Rosa suggested we come down here for a holiday with the whole family.' He was perched on the chair by the bed, elbows on knees, hands locked under his chin.

His hair was still damp, curling around the collar of his polo shirt. He looked older under the stark hospital lighting, creases around his eyes and mouth, and his skin had a bleached appearance, in contrast to the bristle around his jaw. 'She said she was trying to help, that confronting fear was the best way to overcome it.'

He shook his head and briefly closed his eyes. 'She tried to hide how pissed off she was when I said it was a bad idea, but I could tell she didn't like it. Then, suddenly, you were going anyway with Vic, and I just . . .' He shrugged. 'I had a feeling she was behind it, that she'd talked him into it. I know how persuasive she can be, but I didn't know why.' He paused, face working. 'And there were silly things, like she wanted to have a look at your paintings at Mum and Dad's a few weeks ago, and we said she should ask you first, but I caught her in the boot room after she'd supposedly been to the loo, and I got the impression she'd been in there anyway.'

With one of Jamie's boots. I didn't tell him. It was bad enough he now knew the full extent to which she'd used him to get to me. From the moment she'd joined the Devon and Cornwall Police and used the national database to find out my married name and where I lived before transferring to Oxford. Once settled there, she'd engineered meeting my brother, flooding her flat on purpose and making sure he knew how 'grateful' she was when he fixed it, her sole aim to put me in the water at Perran Cove so I would drown.

It was terrifying how close she'd come to making it happen.

The police had spoken to her at the cottage where she'd been staying, but she'd stuck to her story, that she'd been concerned about my mental state, had received some worrying calls from me, asking for help, begging her not to tell anyone. She'd come down alone, not wanting to worry my family, was planning to talk to me that day. She had no idea I'd gone to Perran Cove at dawn that morning – how could she?

She was clever, convincing. There was no evidence linking her to anything; the texts had gone from my phone and everything else could be explained away, or put down to paranoia. There was no proof of anything, nothing she could be arrested for – my word against hers. So what if she'd used her job to look me up, had ended up dating my brother, policing in the city where I lived? It was nothing more than coincidence – a pretty big one, yes, but her police record was exemplary. She put in more hours than anyone. No one could doubt she was a good officer. No one could prove she meant me any harm, other than what I told them she'd tried to do. Even the marks on my wrists weren't proof of anything that could be linked to Rosa.

'*We* know,' Jamie said, voice rough with feeling. 'But she'll never be punished, never go to prison. Even if you'd died, she'd have got away with it; she made sure she would.'

It turned out that Vic had seen my note when he got up and came down to the cliff path, but even though he couldn't be sure I was down there, he'd called the police station and spoke to PC Fellowes. The officer had told him what Rosa had said about me being fragile, possibly suicidal.

Vic knew it wasn't true, guessed immediately that she was the one who'd sent me the texts on my birthday and must have deleted the messages. Once he'd convinced PC Fellowes, told them I could be in danger, they'd put out an alert to find me.

In the meantime, Jamie had notified the police too, after my selfie from Perran Cove landed on his phone at 5.30 a.m. and he realised where I was.

'I was already in Cornwall,' he said, 'on a hunch that something was wrong.' Rosa might have been too clever to leave a trail that would see her convicted, but she hadn't factored in that Jamie had been watching her, looking for clues, certain she was having an affair. He'd checked the search history on his computer and when he discovered she'd looked up the tide times at Perran Cove, something had clicked into place.

'I had no idea how or why she had it in for you, but it made sense of a few things, and explained why you'd accused me of wanting you dead.' His gaze slid from mine. 'She'd told me she was working a case and wouldn't be home for a couple of nights. I didn't question it because it had happened before, but I rang the station to check and they said she'd taken a few days' leave and wasn't due in until Friday.' He blew out his cheeks. 'I knew she'd come here, but I couldn't work it out.'

'Thank God you did.' When I told him her plan, he pressed his knuckles into his eyes and cried. 'I'm so sorry, Beth.'

'Jamie, don't.' I reached for him. 'You saved my life.'

He pulled his fingers from mine. 'I suppose it makes up for last time,' he said, with a trace of old bitterness. I realised with a plunge of sadness that I still wasn't forgiven.

'Anyway, Matt called me on my way here.' He wiped his face on his forearm. 'Apparently, your friend Emma got in touch last night, said she was worried about you, she thought you were in danger and didn't trust Vic, that he'd been using a different name.'

'It's a long story,' I said, my insides twisting. 'She was right about the danger, but not about Vic.'

Jamie nodded, apparently satisfied – or perhaps uncaring. 'Matt told her he'd exchanged messages with you yesterday and you sounded fine and she called him all the names under the sun.' I nearly smiled, imagining it. 'She said it was because you didn't want him thinking you were an unfit mother, but there was stuff going on that he didn't know about. He said he was getting a plane home with Hayley.'

Tears flooded my eyes. All I wanted was to see my daughter, hear her voice, feel her arms hugging my neck. I was going to grab this chance with both hands I'd decided, even before I got in the ambulance, so grateful to be back on dry land I wanted to sink down and embrace it. My life had been saved twice now. I wasn't going to waste a single second feeling guilty, or trying to justify my existence anymore. I was going to savour every moment, doing what I wanted and being with people I loved.

'It's just so sad,' I said, adjusting the heap of blankets weighing me down, wincing at the throb in my head where I'd needed a few stitches. 'Rosa thought my not being alive anymore was the only way she'd be happy.' A shiver travelled through me as I recalled her saying, *I'll be there, to step in, become the loving daughter your parents no longer have, be Aunty Rosa to little Hayley.* She'd wanted my family like some people craved fame and fortune. 'She was doing a job most people can't do,' I went on, my mind swimming with the enormity of it. 'She was already making a difference, had the respect of her colleagues, but it still wasn't enough.'

Jamie was shaking his head. 'She obviously never got over losing her mother,' he said. 'And I didn't even know she was dead.'

'That photo in the apartment.' I looked at him. 'They weren't her parents. She doesn't even have a brother.'

'I think it's her Uncle Jack and his wife and their son.' Betrayal was written all over Jamie's face. 'They live in New Zealand, if they actually exist.'

I thought of the picture I'd seen on the wall in Maggie Taylor's hallway. 'I think they do.' *My grandson* she'd said. I'd thought there was something familiar about the boy, and no wonder. He was Rosa's cousin, the grown-up version in the photo in her living room.

'Can you believe she lived around here back then, and we had no idea?' Jamie said. 'She even changed her accent.'

'To be honest, I think I'd believe anything right now.'

'Obviously, I'll be moving out once we're home.'

'Do Mum and Dad know?' I said, not sure I could bear it. 'About all this.' I indicated the hospital bed, the faded gown I'd been helped into, my ruined clothes in a bag in the corner, my stitches.

'Not yet.'

'I'd rather they didn't.'

Jamie's forehead contracted. 'We can't not tell them.'

'Maybe not everything.' Coming to terms with almost losing

me once had nearly undone our family. Knowing it had nearly happened again – that it wasn't an accident this time – might be too much. Rosa had said we were strong and it was true, we'd come through a lot, but I didn't want them to suffer any more than necessary.

'I suppose we can spare the details.' Jamie sounded more resigned than understanding, maybe at the idea of putting another barrier between himself and our parents, or, more likely, at having to do my bidding.

We fell silent for a while, lost in our own thoughts. Jamie went to fetch coffees and when he brought them back, I sat up, needing to get one last burning question off my chest.

'What do you think she'll do now?'

Jamie handed me a coffee and sat down. 'I can't imagine her staying around,' he said. 'I reckon she'll move on.'

I stared at the sludge-brown liquid in my cardboard cup. 'I don't want to be looking over my shoulder for the rest of my life, knowing she's out there somewhere, hating me.'

Jamie sat forward, his face stripped back to one I remembered from before, when he'd been the brother who loved me. 'Firstly, I don't think she'd dare try anything,' he said. 'She'd be the number-one suspect after this, and if letting you drown was her goal, she's failed. She'll never get that opportunity again.'

I heard it then; the protective impulse that had propelled him into the sea without a second thought, and while I hated Rosa for pointing the finger of suspicion in his direction, I hated myself more for believing it.

'How come you were in the lifeboat?'

'I wasn't,' he said. 'I called the coastguard, told them someone was in trouble and to send a boat out.'

'You saw me?'

He nodded his face contorting, as if seeing it again in his mind. 'I ran down and swam out, got there more or less at the same time as the lifeboat.'

255

'They should recruit you,' I said, tears hot in my eyes.

'Not much call for it in Oxford.'

We turned as the smiling nurse who'd been monitoring my 'vitals' came in. 'Visitors,' she announced.

I'd have spilled my coffee if Jamie hadn't grabbed the cup, but before I could get off the bed, Hayley had thrown herself on it, pressing her face to mine and squashing kisses all over my face.

'Mummy, we got on the aeroplane and Daddy said he wished it would go faster and then we came in a taxi car and Daddy kept telling the driver to go more quickly, but you're here waiting, so it doesn't matter.' She placed her palms on my cheeks and said in a solemn voice, 'Did you fall in the water, Mummy?'

I nodded, laughing and crying at the same time as I hugged her, rocking back and forth, trying not to let my tears spill over. 'I did fall in the water, but I'm OK and I'm so glad you're here.'

'Mummy, you have to learn to swim.' She stroked the crinkly blanket partly covering my shoulders. 'Daddy can teach you, can't you, Daddy?'

She looked round for confirmation, to where Matt was standing at the end of the bed. His eyes were bloodshot, his hair sticking out at odd angles, and he looked like he'd slept in his clothes. His jaw was set, his mouth a tight line, and when he spoke, I understood he was holding back tears.

'Matt, I'm so sorry,' I began, words piling up in my chest. 'I should never have—'

'Don't.' He shook his head once. 'It doesn't matter now.' He smiled at Hayley. 'Maybe we'll get Mummy some proper lessons,' he said, voice gruff with suppressed emotion. 'How does that sound?'

As his eyes met mine, I thought of the sky over Perran Cove, and knew it was the two of them – my twin bright lights – who'd saved my life, just as much as Jamie had.

I held out my hand to him. 'It sounds perfect.'

Chapter 34

Three months later

'All of them have sold.' Tabitha beamed as though it was her own collection. Then again, the gallery would get a healthy commission from my paintings. No wonder she looked like a Cheshire cat.

I peered at the stickers next to each, realising I'd be glad to see the back of them. 'Who knew seascapes were so popular?'

'When they're this good, they are.'

The exhibition had been a success, an event I'd remember for all the right reasons, unlike my birthday party.

'I'm sure we can sell the ones you didn't exhibit, unless you want to do it privately,' Tabitha said, when I'd signed the paperwork, and we'd finalised details for packing and delivery of the paintings.

'No, that would be great.'

'Do you have some news to share?' She glanced at my midriff.

My face warmed. I placed a palm on my stomach. 'How did you know? It's barely eight weeks,' I said. 'I haven't even told my parents.'

She smiled. 'You have that look about you, like my daughter. She's pregnant too.'

As I picked up my bag and walked away, I wondered whether

it was obvious to everyone, still amazed at how much my life had changed in such a short space of time.

Rosa had gone by the time we arrived back in Oxford and Jamie returned to their flat. She'd packed a few things and left a note, saying she'd resigned from the police and was going abroad for a new start and not to contact her – as if she imagined Jamie would beg her to come back.

He'd looked into it, to be sure she'd really disappeared, and discovered she'd bought a one-way ticket to New Zealand. 'Maybe she's decided to reconnect with her mother's family.'

Now, Jamie was gone too. He'd given up work, used his savings to buy a boat and was sailing single-handedly around the world. He was currently anchored off the coast of Singapore, according to his latest Facebook update. I doubted our relationship would ever recover properly. He couldn't forgive me for thinking he'd been behind the texts, or that he'd wanted me dead, my apologies weak offerings he couldn't, or wouldn't, accept. It was my biggest regret.

He'd told our parents everything in the end. I couldn't work out whether he'd done it because he couldn't bear to have secrets from them, or to position himself as a hero in their minds, but either way, I couldn't blame him. At the end of the day, he *was* a hero.

Since then, there'd been a shift in my relationship with my parents, once they'd got over their shock. They fretted about Jamie now, and I felt as though they blamed me. They never said so, but I read it in their reproachful looks whenever his name was mentioned, and despite trying hard to not feel responsible for their reactions, it wasn't easy after so many years.

They were delighted Matt and I had reconciled, that my wedding ring was back on my finger, and were still loving grand-parents to Hayley, but although they were relieved my ordeal was over – an ordeal they'd known nothing about, devastated to discover the person behind it was the woman they'd hoped would one day be their daughter-in-law – I knew my scene in the garage with Jamie had stayed with them, nudging their priorities in a different direction.

When Hayley told them that Mummy had fallen in the sea and was going to learn to swim, Dad had said simply, 'About time,' and hadn't mentioned it again.

I was sure they felt sorry for Vic, who'd slipped out of my life as quietly as he'd come into it, but maybe that was my guilty conscience.

He'd been at the cottage when I returned from the hospital to get my things, the bracelet from Matt and Hayley I'd left on the bedside table, while they waited outside with Jamie in his car.

'I'm glad you're OK,' he'd said, making no attempt to touch me, looking tired and defeated, his suitcase at his feet. 'She was the last person I would have suspected.'

'Me too.'

A wave of something passed between us, an acknowledgement maybe, of what we'd shared, but it was as if there was a force field around him, keeping me out.

'I'm so sorry, Vic. That I thought it was you.'

He looked at me squarely. 'At some point, you thought it was everyone.'

It was true. Even Marianne, who'd called as soon as I was back, to talk about Katya. She didn't say so, but I could tell she'd lost confidence in me, that she thought I'd handled the situation with Katya badly. She was probably right. Thankfully, Katya had seemed her usual self once she knew I was safe.

'I know it was a bit crazy, coming after you like that, but I honestly didn't know what else to do,' she said, when I met with her at Fernley House. She confided that Rosa had given her the creeps. 'She said you'd love that book about the artists, but you looked so scared when you saw it, I knew something wasn't right. She had this weird vibe, like, angry, but not so anyone would notice.'

'None of us noticed,' I said, not wanting to tell her the whole story, but knowing I owed some sort of explanation. 'She developed a bit of an obsession with me, but she's gone now. I'm

259

really grateful you were keeping an eye on me, Katya, but you frightened a lot of people, taking off like that.'

She'd promised not to do it again, seemed happier, more settled somehow. It turned out she had a boyfriend; someone new to occupy her mind.

I'd resigned from Fernley House, sensing Marianne's new wary watchfulness, especially after I turned down her suggestion of counselling. Maybe I needed a release from feeling responsible for others' well-being for a while. There'd been some interest from a London gallery after my exhibition was featured in the culture section on the local news. I was keen to start something new; spend more time at home.

Home. I stood for a moment outside the house, just as I had on my birthday. Then, I'd been dreading going inside, wondering which of my guests had wanted me dead. Now, there were only people who loved me behind the door, yet it no longer felt like home.

I looked at the 'For Sale' sign planted out the front. We'd decided to move away; put some distance between us and everything that had happened. A fresh start.

It would be good for all of us, especially Matt, who didn't need reminding that, for a while, he'd left a space in our home that I'd filled with someone new, whose clothes had nudged mine in the wardrobe, his shoes in the hallway – gone now to the charity shop. Vic hadn't wanted them back, but I'd insisted on returning the ruby pendant. I'd grown tearful when he asked after Hayley. I knew how much he would miss her. He was going to Canada, he said, to stay with his sister for a while, didn't know when he'd be back.

It seemed everyone was leaving, starting anew.

'Here she is,' Pam said, as I came inside to the smell of cooking. She was followed by Baxter and Bella, our newest addition – a golden Labrador named after my childhood pet. Hayley was close behind, eyes permanently shiny since her fifth birthday when Bella had joined us. She was only slightly more excited about having a baby brother or sister. I was just grateful she'd quickly adjusted to Vic's absence and Matt's return to our home.

'Mummy, come on,' she said, crouching to pet Bella's ears. 'Daddy's made sausages for dinner – they're better than your ones because they haven't got black bits on.'

Smiling, I said, 'I might not be able to cook, but at least I can nearly swim.'

My lessons were hit and miss. Sometimes, I thought I was making progress, other times, I struggled to get in the pool, clinging to the side as shivers racked my body. I had learnt how to tread water, though. I never wanted to almost-drown again.

'I'll leave you to it,' Pam said, beckoning to Baxter. 'We should be getting home.'

'You're welcome to stay.' Matt came through in his apron and kissed me, his gaze tender. 'The more people to appreciate my sausages the better.'

'Oh, well, if you're sure, I'd love to.' She hadn't talked about us moving, but I knew she was making the most of us still being next door, for now.

'Emma's on her way,' Matt said, returning to the kitchen. 'I'm expecting a lot of baby talk.'

Just as Matt had forgiven me, so had Emma. She was living back in London permanently, enjoying her job and looking forward to single motherhood; had talked about reconnecting with her adoptive parents.

As I headed into the kitchen after Matt, I paused to look in the living room, at the painting of Perran Cove above the fireplace. I'd lost my phone, but Matt still had the photo of the sunrise I'd sent him that morning. Not that I'd needed reminding; the view was etched in my brain, just like everything else about that day. I'd needed to get it out of my head and onto canvas and had hung the painting, not only to replace the picture Rosa had defaced, but also to remind me every day how lucky I was, and to make the most of the third chance I'd been given at life.

It was the last seascape I'd ever paint.

Epilogue

What a let-down. All that planning and you're still alive. I thought the cold would get you, if nothing else did. I watched for a while, from the cliff-top. Bit risky, but there was no one around. I got bored in the end. I was sure you were already dead.

I didn't know your brother had it in him. That was a shock. I really thought he was going to ask me to marry him. It shook me a bit, if I'm honest.

Good job I covered my tracks. I've had plenty of years of training.

No point dwelling. The thing is, I realised afterwards, when I'd talked my way out of it all – not sure PC Fellowes was convinced, but there's not much he can do about it – I had FUN. A lot of fun, actually.

I won't be back. I've made new plans.

Hearing how your brother saved your life made me think about Uncle Jack. How he could have done so much more for my mum. He was her big brother. He should have protected her, helped her. Instead, he went to New Zealand and left her to die.

I've applied to join the police force over there, in Auckland. That's where he lives with his perfect wife, Sarah. I've dug up some dirt on

262

dear old Uncle Jack. He's not the pillar of the community everyone thinks he is, and far from the perfect husband. Yet he's alive and my mum is dead. How is that fair?

I'm going to ruin his life.

Acknowledgements

It takes a lot of people to publish a book, and I'm lucky to have worked with the wonderful team at HQ, in particular my brilliant editor Belinda Toor whose skilful guidance made my story so much better. Thanks to Helena Newton for her meticulous copy-edits (hopefully, that hyphen can stay!), to Helen Williams for the proofread, Anna Sikorska for the amazing cover and the marketing team for all their hard work.

Huge thanks to my readers, bloggers and reviewers, to my writing (and real-life) friends Amanda Brittany, and Sherri Turner for being brilliant cheerleaders.

Last but not least, love and thanks to my family and friends for their continued interest in my writing; to my children, Amy, Martin and Liam, and to my husband Tim for his patience, belief and many cups of tea, especially during the 'frenzied' stage. I couldn't do it without you.